GENE WOLFE'S
BOOK OF DAYS

GENE WOLFE'S BOOK OF DAYS

GENE WOLFE

DOUBLEDAY & COMPANY, INC.
GARDEN CITY, NEW YORK
1981

All of the characters in this book are fictitious, and any resemblance to actual persons, living or dead, is purely coincidental.

Acknowledgments

"How the Whip Came Back" first appeared in *Orbit 6*, edited by Damon Knight

"Of Relays and Roses" first appeared in *World of If*, September–October 1970

"Paul's Treehouse" first appeared in *Orbit 5* edited by Damon Knight

"St. Brandon" first appeared as part of the novel *Peace*, and is here reprinted by permission of Harper & Row, Publishers, Inc.

"Beautyland" first appeared in *Saving Worlds*, edited by Roger Elwood and Virginia Kidd

"Car Sinister" first appeared in *The Magazine of Fantasy and Science Fiction*, January 1970

"The Blue Mouse" first appeared in *The Many Worlds of Science Fiction*, edited by Ben Bova

"How I Lost the Second World War and Helped Turn Back the German Invasion" first appeared in *Analog Science Fiction/Science Fact*, May 1973

"The Adopted Father" first appeared in *Isaac Asimov's Science Fiction Magazine*, 1980

"Forlesen" first appeared in *Orbit 14*, edited by Damon Knight

"An Article About Hunting" first appeared in *Saving Worlds*, edited by Roger Elwood and Virginia Kidd

"The Changeling" first appeared in *Orbit 3*, edited by Damon Knight

"Many Mansions" first appeared in *Orbit 19*, edited by Damon Knight

"Against the Lafayette Escadrille" first appeared as part of "Mathoms from the Time Closet" in *Again, Dangerous Visions*, edited by Harlan Ellison

"Three Million Square Miles" first appeared in *The Ruins of Earth*, edited by Thomas M. Disch

"The War Beneath the Tree" first appeared in *Omni*, December 1979

"La Befana" first appeared in *Galaxy*, January–February 1973

"Melting" first appeared in *Orbit 15*, edited by Damon Knight

ISBN: 0-385-15991-9
Library of Congress Catalog Card Number 80-1074
Copyright © 1968, 1969, 1970, 1971, 1972, 1973, 1974, 1975, 1977, 1980, 1981 by Gene Wolfe
All Rights Reserved
Printed in the United States of America
First Edition

CONTENTS

GENE WOLFE'S
BOOK OF DAYS

INTRODUCTION

Publishers tell me that no one reads introductions. I do not believe them, since I read the things myself, but I am willing to admit that there is probably some truth behind the myth—in other words, that you, who have read these few lines, are a member of a select minority.

I do not quite see how I can repay you. You already know, I hope, that the book you hold is a collection of short stories. The jacket will have told you that I wrote them. (And, yes, I wrote them. My name really is Gene Wolfe, and I am an actual person.) The front matter has perhaps told you about my other books, and even where these stories originally appeared. All that remains for me is to tell you a little something concerning the stories themselves.

To begin, they are largely what is called science fiction, though a good many are of that type of science fiction that is sometimes questioned, particularly by people who do not read much sf and therefore have a very definite idea of what it is and is not. Only "La Befana" and "Many Mansions" clearly take place off Earth. Several stories are not even futuristic. One at least is inarguably fantasy. Several are humorous, and I have been told often enough that I have a sense of humor that makes strong men faint and women reach for weapons; I should have known better than to include those, but now it is too late.

I will not bore you with a description of how I came to write these stories. Neither will I presume to instruct you about writing stories in general—there is a whole library of books on how to do that already, though few of them seem to be much good. But I would like to leave you with a handful of words on how to read stories, these stories at least.

I urge you not to read one after another, the way I eat potato chips. The simple act of closing this book and putting it away for another day will do a great deal for the story you have just read and even more for the next. If you are a purist, you might even go so far as to read each story on the designated day—"An Article About Hunting" at the opening of deer season, "The War Beneath the Tree" before Christmas.

Even if you are not a purist, I urge you to think for a moment about the day, before beginning each story. Think on very young men in leggings and pie-pan helmets before you start "Against the Lafayette Escadrille." Think about somewhat older men who carry a lunchbucket (or a briefcase with a sandwich in it) before "Forlesen."

Try to put aside your preconceptions. Don't be disappointed when you discover, as you will, that I am not Harlan Ellison or Isaac Asimov. Harlan and Isaac—as they would be the first to admit—are not me, either.

Lastly, let me urge you to treat this and all books with respect. We will all benefit if you do. You cannot judge this book now. You will not even be able to judge it rightly when you have read its last story. Ten (or twenty) years from now you will know it was a good book if you remember any of the tales you are about to read.

Meanwhile, its author begs you to preserve it as a physical object, so that at an appropriate time it can be shared by others. If you have bought it, those others may be friends you have not met or children you have thus far only dreamed of. If you have borrowed it from a library, they are your peers in the community, having the same rights in it as yourself. Let me tell you a story.

An acquaintance of mine who was a college student once discovered a secret door in the college library. It was a fire exit that was almost blocked by a huge bookcase full of fifty-year-old books in foreign languages—mostly Serbian, he said—and was unknown to the present staff. Outside, it was well screened by holly.

Because there was no handle on the outside, he could not use it to enter the library; but he could, and did, use it to leave in company with whatever books he fancied. And he fancied three or four nearly every day.

He lived in a small apartment he rented off-campus, and had no other home. As the semesters turned to years, this apartment grew crowded with stolen books. Books were piled on every table, in every corner, and even on his tiny dry bar. Books waited like burglars under his bed. Waterproof books on swimming, boating, tropical fish, and similar subjects stood in a row along the edge of the tub; the toilet tank groaned and leaked under the crushing load of a hundred or so humorous books, so that even as he sat thinking how he might free himself from his thousands of stolen volumes, he feared they might fall and crush him.

He considered simply returning the books to the library, but since they had never been checked out, they could hardly be returned, and it seemed to him that the head librarian—a woman with a singularly frigid gaze—suspected him already. He considered mailing them back anonymously, but the cost of postage would have been staggering. He considered setting fire to the building in which he lived, but he felt sure he would lose many valuable possessions now forgotten and buried under the books. Graduation loomed.

At last he hit on a scheme that seemed foolproof. Instead of accepting a lucrative offer from a major corporation, he would have a rubber stamp made reading: DISCARDED BY THE UNIVERSITY LIBRARY. During the months immediately following graduation, he would stamp all the books in violet ink. In October, he would sell his car and jogging shoes, borrow all the money he could, and open a small used-book store. The thought of having a rack of birthday cards somewhere near the door cheered him.

One fine day in May, as he was considering means of attracting shoplifters, he returned to his apartment and opened the door to see the sight he had most dreaded during all the grim years when he had been drowning in hoarded volumes. The head librarian sat waiting for him in his own chair (the only one clear of books) in his own living-dining-kitchenette. He would have fainted if he could, but he had never been quick. She had never been slow, and at this crucial moment she was icily calm. "I am sorry, sir," she said, "but this branch closes in five minutes."

It was noon Saturday, and he became a homeless wanderer on the face of the earth until 9:30 Monday morning.

This has been the story for "Date Due." The people who do not read introductions missed it.

HOW THE WHIP CAME BACK

Pretty Miss Bushnan's suite was all red acrylic and green-dyed leather. Real leather, very modern—red acrylic and green, real leather were the modern things this year. But it made her Louis XIV secretary, Sal, look terribly out of place.

Miss Bushnan had disliked the suite from the day she moved in—though she could hardly complain, when there was a chance that the entire city of Geneva and the sovereign Swiss nation might be offended. This evening she did her best to like red and green, and in the meantime turned her eyes from them to the cool relief of the fountain. It was a copy of a Cellini salt dish and lovely, no matter how silly a fountain indoors on the hundred and twenty-fifth floor might be. In a characteristic reversal of feeling she found herself wondering what sort of place she might have gotten if she had had to find one for herself, without reservations, at the height of the tourist season. Three flights up in some dingy suburban *pension*, no doubt.

So bless the generosity of the sovereign Swiss Republic. Bless the openhanded city of Geneva. Bless the hotel. And bless the United Nations Conference on Human Value, which brought glory to the Swiss Republic et cetera and inspired the free mountaineers to grant free hotel suites in the height of the season even to non-voting Conference observers such as she. Sal had brought her in a gibson a few minutes ago, and she picked it up from the edge of the fountain to sip, a little surprised to see that it was already three-quarters gone; *red and green*.

A brawny, naked triton half-reclined, water streaming from his hair and beard, dripping from his mouth, dribbling from his ears. His eyes, expressionless and smooth as eggs, wept for her. Balancing her empty glass carefully on the rim again, she leaned forward and stroked his smooth, wet stone flesh. Smiling she told him—mentally—how handsome he was, and he blushed pink lemonade at the compliment. She thought of herself taking off her clothes and climbing in with him, the cool water soothing her face, which now felt hot and flushed. Not, she told herself suddenly, that she would feel any real desire for the triton in the unlikely event of his being metamorphosed to flesh. If she wanted men in her bed she could find ten any evening, and afterward edit the whole adventure from Sal's memory bank. She wanted a man, but she wanted only one, she wanted Brad (whose real name, as the terrible, bitter woman who lived in the back of her skull, the woman the gibson had not quite drowned, reminded her, had proved at his trial to be Aaron). The triton vanished and Brad was there instead, laughing and dripping Atlantic water on the sand as he threw up his arms to catch the towel she flung him. Brad running through the surf . . .

Sal interrupted her revery, rolling in on silent casters. "A gentleman to see you, Miss Bushnan." Sal had real metal drawer-pulls on her false drawers, and they jingled softly when she stopped to deliver her message, like costume jewelry.

"Who?" Miss Bushnan straightened up, pushing a stray wisp of brown hair away from her face.

Sal said blankly, "I don't know." The gibson had made Miss Bushnan feel pleasantly muzzy, but even so the blankness came through as slightly suspicious.

"He didn't give you his name or a card?"

"He did, Miss Bushnan, but I can't read it. Even though, as I'm sure you're already aware, Miss Bushnan, there's an Italian language software package for me for only two hundred dollars. It includes reading, writing, speaking, and an elementary knowledge of great Italian art."

"The advertising package," Miss Bushnan said with wasted sarcasm, "is free. And compulsory with your lease."

"Yes," Sal said. "Isn't it wonderful?"

Miss Bushnan swung around in the green leather chair from which she had been watching the fountain. "He did give you a card. I see it in one of your pigeonholes. Take it out and look at it."

As if the Louis XIV secretary had concealed a silver snake, one of Sal's arms emerged. With steel fingers like nails it took the card and held it in front of a swirl of ornament hiding a scanner.

"Now," Miss Bushnan said patiently, "pretend that what you're reading isn't Italian. Let's say instead that it's English that's been garbled by a translator post-processor error. What's your best guess at the original meaning?"

"'His Holiness Pope Honorius V.'"

"Ah." Miss Bushnan sat up in her chair. "Please show the gentleman in."

With a faint hum of servomotors Sal rolled away. There was just time for a last fragment of daydream. Brad with quiet eyes alone with her on the beach at Cape Cod. Talking about the past, talking about the divorce, Brad really, *really* sorry . . .

The Pope wore a plain dark suit and a white satin tie embroidered in gold with the triple crown. He was an elderly man, never tall and now stooped. Miss Bushnan rose. She sat beside him every day at the council sessions, and had occasionally exchanged a few words with him during the refreshment breaks (he had a glass of red wine usually, she good English tea or the horrible Swiss coffee laced with brandy), but it had never so much as occurred to her that he might ever have anything to discuss with her in private.

"Your Holiness," she said as smoothly as the gibson would let her manage the unfamiliar words, "this is an unexpected pleasure."

Sal chimed in with, "May we offer you something?" and looking sidelong Miss Bushnan saw that she had put Scotch, a bottle of club soda, and two glasses of ice on her fold-out writing shelf.

The Pope waved her away, and when he had settled in his chair said pointedly, "I deeply appreciate your hospitality, but I wonder if it would be possible to speak with you privately."

Miss Bushnan said, "Of course," and waited until Sal had coasted off in the direction of the kitchen. "My secretary bothers you, Your Holiness?"

Taking a cigar from the recesses of his coat, the Pope nodded. "I'm afraid she does. I have never had much sympathy with furniture that talks—you don't mind if I smoke?" He had only the barest trace of Italian accent.

"If it makes you more comfortable I should prefer it."

He smiled in appreciation of the little speech, and struck an old-fashioned kitchen match on the imitation marble of the fountain. It left no mark, and when he tossed in the matchstick a moment later, it bobbed only twice in the crystal water before being whisked away. "I suppose I'm out of date," the Pope continued. "But back in my youth when people speculated about the possibility of those things we always thought of them as being shaped more or less like us. Something like a suit of armor."

"I can't imagine why," Miss Bushnan said. "You might as well shape a radio like a human mouth—or a TV screen like a keyhole."

The Pope chuckled. "I didn't say I was going to defend the idea. I only remarked that that was what we expected."

"I'm sure they must have considered it, but—"

"But too much extra work would have had to go into just making it look human," the Pope continued for her, "and besides, a furniture cabinet is much cheaper than articulated metal and doesn't make the robot look dead when it's turned off."

She must have looked flustered because he continued, smiling, "You Americans are not the only manufacturers, you see. It happens that a friend of mine is president of Olivetti. A skeptic like all of them today, but . . ."

The sentence trailed away in a shrug and a puff of smoke from the black cigar. Miss Bushnan recalled the time she had asked the French delegate about him. The French delegate was handsome in that very clean and spare fashion some Frenchmen have, and she liked him better than the paunchy businessman who represented her own country.

"You do not know who the man who sits by you is, mademoiselle?" he asked quizzically. "But that is most interesting. You see, I know who he is, but I do not know who *you* are. Except that I see you each day and you are much more pretty than the lady from Russia or the lady from Nigeria, and perhaps in your way as chic as that bad girl who reports on us for *Le Figaro*—but I hope not quite so full of tricks. Now I will trade you information."

So she had had to tell him, feeling more like a fool each second as the milling crush of secretaries of delegates, and secretaries of secretaries, and unidentifiable people from the Swiss embassies of all the participating nations, swirled around them. When she had finished he said, "Ah, it is kind of you to work for charity, and especially for one that does not pay you, but is it necessary? This is no longer the twentieth century after all, and the governments take care of most of us quite well."

"That's what most people think; I suppose that's why so few give much any more. But we try to bring a little human warmth to the people we help, and I find I meet the class of people I want to meet in connection with it. I mean my co-workers, of course. It's really rather exclusive."

He said, "How very great-hearted you are," with a little twist to the corner of his mouth that made her feel like a child talking to a grownup. "But you asked the identity of the old gentleman. He is Pope."

"Who?" Then she had realized what the word meant and added, "I thought there weren't any more."

"Oh no." The French delegate winked. "It is still there. Much, much smaller, but still there . . . But we are so crowded here, and I think you are tired of standing. Let me buy you a liqueur and I will tell you all about it."

He had taken her to a place at the top of some building overlooking the lake, and it had been very pleasant listening to the waiters pointing him out in whispers to the tourists, even though the tourists were mostly Germans and no one anyone knew. They were given a table next to the window of course, and while they sipped and smoked and looked at the lake he told her, with many digressions, about a great-aunt who had been what he called "a believer" and two ex-wives who had not. (History at Radcliffe had somehow left her with the impression that the whole thing had stopped with John XXIII, just as the Holy Roman Empire had managed to vanish out of sheer good manners when it was no longer wanted. On the teaching machines you filled in a table of Holy Roman Emperors and Popes and Sultans and such things by touching multiple-choice buttons. Then when you had it all done the screen glowed with rosy light for a minute—which was called reinforcement—and told you your grade. After which, unless you were lucky, there was another table to be filled—but Popes had disappeared and you put the Kings of Sweden in that column instead.)

She remembered having asked the French delegate, "There are only a hundred thousand left? In the whole world?"

"That is my guess, of real believers. Of course many more who continue to use the name and perhaps have their children wetted if they think of it. It may be that that is too low—say a quarter million. But it has been growing less for a long time. Eventually—who knows? It may turn about and grow more. It would not be the first time that happened."

She had said, "It seems to me the whole thing should have been squashed a long time ago." . . .

The Pope straightened his shoulders a little and flicked ashes into the fountain. "At any rate, they make me uncomfortable," he said. "I always have the feeling they don't like me. I hope you don't mind."

She smiled and said something about the convenience factor, and having Sal shipped in a crate from New York.

"I suppose it's a good thing my predecessor got the government to take responsibility for the Vatican," the Pope said. "We couldn't possibly staff it now, so we'd be using those things. Doubtless ours would have stained glass in them."

Miss Bushnan laughed politely. Actually she felt like coughing. The Pope's cigar was the acrid, cheap kind smoked in the poorer sort of Italian cafés. Briefly she wondered if he himself had not been born into the lowest class. His hands were gnarled and twisted like an old gardener's, as though he'd been weeding all his life.

He was about to say something else, but Sal, reentering on silent wheels, interrupted him. "Phone, Miss Bushnan," Sal said at her elbow.

She swiveled in her chair again and touched the "On" and "Record" buttons on the communications console, motioning as she did for the Pope to keep his seat. The screen lit up, and she said, "Good evening," to the office robot who had placed the call.

The robot answered with an announcement: "Her Excellency the Delegate Plenipotentiary of the Union of Soviet Socialist Republics, Comrade Natasha Nikolayeva." The image flickered and a striking blonde, about forty and somewhat overblown and overdressed, but with a remarkably good complexion and enormous eyes, replaced the robot. The Russian delegate had been an actress at one time and was currently the wife of a general; gossip said that she owed her position at the conference to favors granted the Party Secretary.

"Good evening," Miss Bushnan said again, and added, "Comrade Nikolayeva."

The Russian delegate gave her a dazzling smile. "I called, darling, to ask if you like my little speech today. I was not too long? You did not find it difficult, wearing the headphones for translation?"

"I thought it was very moving," Miss Bushnan said carefully. Actually, she had been appalled by the Russian delegate's references to Hitler's gas chambers and her cant phrases about restoring economic value to human life. It came to saying that if people had no value alive they should be made into soap, but she had no intention of telling the Russian delegate that.

"I convinced you?"

Brad made into soap. It should have been funny, but it wasn't. One of Brad's fingers slowly exposed as she scrubbed herself with the bar. The Russian delegate was still looking at her, waiting for her to reply.

"It isn't necessary that you convince me, is it?" She smiled, trying to turn the question aside. "I'm merely an observer, after all."

"It is necessary to me," the Russian delegate said, "in my *soul*." She pressed a hand flashing with diamonds against one upholstered breast. "I myself feel it so deeply."

"I'm sure you do. It was a wonderful speech. Very dramatic."

"You understand, then." The Russian delegate's mood changed in an instant. "That is wonderful, darling. Listen, you know I am staying at our embassy here—would you have dinner with us? It will be Tuesday, and nearly everyone will be there."

Miss Bushnan hesitated for a moment, looking briefly at the Pope, seated out of range of the Russian's vision, for guidance. He was expressionless.

"Darling, I will tell you a secret. I have sworn not to, but what is an oath when it is for you? The French delegate asked me to invite you. I would have in any case, of course, but he came to me. He is so shy; but if you come I have promised him I will seat you beside him. Do not say I told you."

"I'd be delighted to come."

"That too is wonderful then." The Russian delegate's smile said: *We are women together and I love you, little one.*

"Tuesday? The day after the final vote?"

"Yes, Tuesday. I will be looking forward so much."

When the screen went dark Miss Bushnan said to the Pope, "Something's up."

The Pope only looked at her, as though trying to weigh what might be behind her attractive but not arresting face and brown eyes.

After a moment Miss Bushnan continued, "The French delegate might buy me a dinner, but he wouldn't ask for me as a dinner partner at an official function, and that Russian woman has been ignoring you and me ever since the conference opened. What's going on?"

"Yes," the Pope said slowly, "something has happened, as you say. I see you hadn't heard."

"No."

"I was more fortunate. The Portuguese delegate confides in me sometimes."

"Will you tell me?"

"That is why I came. The delegates caucused this afternoon after the public session. They decided to ask for our votes at the final meeting."

"Us?" Miss Bushnan was nonplused. "The observers?"

"Yes. The votes will have no legal validity, of course. They cannot be counted. But they want total unanimity—they want to get us down on the record."

"I see," said Miss Bushnan.

"Church and charity. People surrendered their faith in us to put it in the governments, but they're losing that now, and the delegates sense it. Perhaps the faith won't return to us, but there's a chance it might."

"And so I'm to be wined and dined."

The Pope nodded. "And courted too, I should imagine. The French are very enthused about this; their penal system has been at loose ends ever since they lost their African colonies over fifty years ago."

Miss Bushnan had been staring at her lap, smoothing her skirt absently where it lay across her knees; she looked up suddenly, meeting his eyes. "And you? What are they going to offer you?"

"Not the lost sees of eastern Europe, you may be sure. Mostly flattery, I suspect."

"And if we oppose them—"

"If we oppose them we will be raising standards about which all the millions who detest the idea, and all the millions more who will come to detest it when they see it in operation, can rally."

"My husband—my former husband, technically—is in prison, Your Holiness. Did you know that?"

"No, of course not. If I had—"

"We plan to be remarried when he is released, and I know from visiting him what the alternative to the motion is. I know what we've got now. It's not as though they're going to be snatched from some Arcadia."

Unexpectedly Sal was at her elbow again. "Phone, Miss Bushnan."

The American delegate's puffy face filled the screen. "Miss—ah—Bushnan?"

She nodded.

"This is—ah—a pleasure I have had to postpone too long."

In order to save him time she said, "I've heard about the decision to ask the observers to vote."

"Good, good." The American delegate drummed his fingers on his desk and seemed to be trying to avoid her eyes. "Miss Bushnan, are you aware of the—ah—financial crisis now confronting our nation?"

"I'm not an economist—"

"But you are an informed laywoman. You know the situation. Miss Bushnan, there are close to a quarter of a million men and women in state and federal prisons today, and to maintain each of them there costs—costs us, Miss Bushnan, the taxpayers—five thousand dollars a year *each*. That's a total of a billion dollars a year."

"I believe you brought out those figures during your speech at the third session."

"Perhaps I did. But we are all interested in restoring the preeminent place the United States once held in world affairs, aren't we? Miss Bushnan, to do that we have had to take quite a few pages from the So-

viet book. And it's been good for us. We've learned humility, if you
like."

She nodded.

"We used to believe in job security for everybody, and a wage based
on classification and seniority. That was what we called Free Enter-
prise, and we were proud of it. Well, the Communists showed us
differently: incentives, and discipline for underachievers. They forced
us to the wall with those until we learned our lesson, and now—well,
you can say whatever you like, but by God things are better."

"So I understand," Miss Bushnan said. Here it came.

"Now they've got a new trick," the American delegate continued.
"They used, you know, to have these gangs of—ah—laborers out in
Siberia. Then one day some smart commissar thought to himself: By
God, if the peasants can grow more vegetables on private plots, couldn't
the prisoners be used more effectively that way too?"

"If I recall your speech correctly," Miss Bushnan said, "you pointed
out that if half the federal and state prisoners could be leased out to private owners at five thousand a year, the revenue would take care of the
remaining half."

"Lessees, not owners," the American delegate said. "Lessees with op-
tion to renew. It will lift a billion dollar millstone from about our nation's neck."

"But," Miss Bushnan continued innocently, "surely we could do the
same thing without entering into the international agreement being
discussed here."

"No, no." The American delegate waved a hand in protest. "We
should enter the world community with this. After all, Miss Bushnan,
international trade is one of the few, and one of the strongest, cohesive
forces. We need by all means to establish a supranational market structure."

The Pope, sitting outside the range of the American delegate's view,
said softly, "Ask him if they're still going to call them slaves."

Miss Bushnan inquired obediently, "Are you still going to call them
slaves? I mean in the final agreement."

"Oh, yes." The American delegate leaned closer to the scanner and
lowered his voice. "In English language usage. I don't mind telling
you, however, that we—I mean the British and Canadians as well as
our own country—have had a hard time getting that one past the Soviets. It comes from the root-word 'slav,' you know, and they don't like
that. But it's a *selling* word. People like the idea of having slaves; robots
have gotten us used to it and tranquilizers and anti-aggressants have

made it practical; what's more, it's a link with the past at a time when too many such links are phasing out. People feel manipulated today, Miss Bushnan. They want to be master of someone themselves."

"I see. And it will get them out of prison. Place them in decent surroundings."

"Oh, it certainly will. And—ah—you asked about the necessity of an international agreement and an international market a moment ago. You must remember that our nation needs hard currencies very badly today; and we have the curse—or, ah—the blessing, blessing if you think of it in a positive fashion, of having the highest crime rate among major nations. The United States will be an exporter in this market, Miss Bushnan."

"I see," Miss Bushnan said again.

"You may have heard some of these rumors about the Soviets pressing a certain number of—ah—country people into the market to satisfy the demand. These are slanders, of course, and in any event that sort of thing would be unthinkable in the United States. I understand you're a wealthy woman, Miss Bushnan; your father is in the government, I suppose?"

"He was," Miss Bushnan said. "He's dead now. The Department of Agriculture."

"Then with a family background of public service you understand that in a democracy we have to listen to the voice of the people; and the people want this. The—ah—most recent polls have shown seventy-nine percent favoring. I won't try to hide the fact that it would be an embarrassment to our country if you voted in opposition, and it would not benefit the organization you represent—in fact it would do it a great deal of harm."

"Are you threatening us?"

"No, of course not. But I'm asking you to consider what would happen to your organization if you lost your tax-exempt status. I believe a vote in opposition to the motion might—ah—make Washington feel that you were engaged in political activity. That would mean loss of the exemption, naturally."

"But a vote in favor of the motion wouldn't be political activity?"

"Washington would expect your organization to support this humanitarian cause as a matter of course. I doubt very much that the matter would come up. You must understand, Miss Bushnan, that when—ah— a measure as revolutionary as this is under consideration humanity must be practically unanimous. Even a token opposition could be disastrous."

Paraphrasing the Pope, Miss Bushnan said, "It would raise a standard about which all the millions who detest the idea could rally."

"Millions is surely an exaggeration; thousands perhaps. But in principle you are correct, and that must not be allowed to happen. Miss Bushnan, Washington has sent me a dossier on you. Did you know that?"

"How could I?"

"Your former husband is confined in the federal penitentiary at Ossining, New York. In the letters you have exchanged both of you have stated an intention to remarry upon his release. Were those letters sincere, Miss Bushnan?"

"I don't see what my personal life has to do with this."

"I merely wish to use your own case as an example—one which will strike home, so to speak. It will be at least five years before your former husband will be released under the present system; but if the motion passes it will be possible for you to lease—ah—" The American delegate paused, looking at some paper on his desk.

"Brad," Miss Bushnan said.

"Yes, Brad. You could lease Brad from the government for those five years. You would have him, he would have you, and your government would be twenty-five thousand dollars to the better as the direct result of your happiness. What's the matter with that, eh? In fact, in your case I think I could promise that your husband would be one of the first prisoners to be made available for the plan, and that he would be, so to speak, reserved. There would be no danger of someone else leasing him, if that's worrying you. Of course you would be expected to supervise him."

Miss Bushnan nodded slowly. "I understand."

"May I ask then if you intend to support the measure?"

"I hesitate to tell you. I know you're going to misunderstand me."

"Oh?" The American delegate leaned forward until his face filled the small screen. "In what way?"

"You think that this is going to help Brad and me, and that because of that I'm going to consent to your selling the Americans you don't want, selling them to die in somebody's mines. You are wrong. This is going to ruin whatever may be left between Brad and me, and I know it. I know how Brad is going to feel when his wife is also his keeper. It will strip away whatever manhood he has left, and before the five years are out he'll hate me—just as he will if I don't buy him when he knows I could. But you are going to do this thing whether the organization I represent favors it or not, and to save this organization—for the good it does now and the good it will do among the slaves when you have them—I am going to vote for the motion."

"You will support the motion?" His eyes seemed to bore into her.

"I will support the motion. Yes."

"Fine."

The American delegate's hand was moving toward the "Off" switch of his console, but Miss Bushnan called, "Wait. What about the other observer? The Pope?"

"He can be taken care of, I feel sure. His church is almost entirely dependent today on the goodwill of the Italian government."

"He hasn't agreed yet?"

"Don't worry," the American delegate said, "the Italians will be contacting him." His hand touched the switch and his image vanished.

"So you gave in," the Pope said.

"And you wouldn't?" Miss Bushnan asked. "Even if you knew you'd be running your church from an empty store the day after you voted no?"

"I might abstain," the Pope admitted slowly, "but I could never bring myself to give a favorable vote."

"How about lying to them, if that were the only way you could get to vote?"

The Pope looked at her in surprise, then his eyes smiled.

Miss Bushnan continued, "Could you tell them you were going to vote yes when you were really going to vote against them, Your Holiness?"

"I don't suppose I could. It would be a matter of my position, if you understand me, as well as my conscience."

"Fortunately," Miss Bushnan said, "I don't feel that way. Hasn't it occurred to you that this business of asking for our votes must be predicated on the idea that they'll be favorable? It hasn't been announced, has it?"

The Pope nodded. "I see what you mean. If the decision had been made public they couldn't change it; but as it is, if they don't like what they hear from us—"

"But they'll have every news agency in the world there when the vote is actually taken."

"You are a clever girl." The Pope shook his head. "It is a lesson to me to think of how very much I have underestimated you, sitting in the gallery there beside me all these days, and even this evening when I came here. But that is good; God wants me to learn humility, and He has chosen a child to teach it, as He so often does. I hope you understand that after the council I will be giving you all the support I can. I'll publish an encyclical—"

"If you feel you can't lie to them," Miss Bushnan interposed practically, "we'll need some excuse for your being absent from the vote."

"I have one," the Pope said. "I don't"—he paused—"suppose you've heard of Mary Catherine Bryan?"

"I don't think so. Who is she?"

"She is—or at least she was—a nun. She was the last nun, actually, for the past three years. Ever since Sister Carmela Rose died. I received a call this morning telling me Mary Catherine passed away last night, and her rites are to be this coming Tuesday. The government still lets us use St. Peter's sometimes for that sort of thing."

"So you won't be here." Miss Bushnan smiled. "But a nun sounds so interesting. Tell me about her."

"There isn't a great deal to tell. She was a woman of my mother's generation, and for the last four years she lived in an apartment on the Via del Fori. Alone, after Sister Carmela Rose died. They never got along too well, actually, being from different orders, but Mary Catherine cried for weeks, I remember, after Sister Carmela Rose was gone."

"Did she wear those wonderful flowing robes you see in pictures?"

"Oh, no," the Pope said. "You see, nuns no longer have to—" He stopped in the middle of the sentence, and the animation left his face, making him at once a very old man. "I'm sorry," he said after a moment, "I had forgotten. I should have said that for the last seventy years or so of their existence nuns no longer wore those things. They abandoned them, actually, just a few years before we priests dropped our Roman collars. You have to understand that from time to time I have tried to persuade someone to . . ."

"Yes?"

"Well, the old phrase was 'take the veil.' It would have kept the tradition alive and would have been so nice for Mary Catherine and Sister Carmela Rose. I always told the girls all the things they wouldn't have to give up, and they always said they'd think about it, but none of them ever came back."

"I'm sorry your friend is dead," Miss Bushnan said simply. To her surprise she found she really was.

"It's the end of something that had lived almost as long as the Church itself—oh, I suppose it will be revived in fifty or a hundred years when the spirit of the world turns another corner, but a revival is never really the same thing. As though we tried to put the Kyrie back into the mass now."

Miss Bushnan, who did not know what he was talking about, said, "I suppose so, but—"

"But what has it to do with the matter at hand? Not a great deal, I'm afraid. But while they are voting that is where I shall be. And afterward perhaps we can do something." He stood up, adjusting his clothing, and from somewhere in the back of the apartment Sal came rolling out with his hat positioned on her writing shelf. It was red, Miss Bushnan noticed, but the feather in the band was black instead of green. As he put it on he said, "We started among slaves, more or less, you know. Practically all the early Christians who weren't Jews were either slaves or freedmen. I'll be going now to say the funeral mass of the last nun. Perhaps I'll also live to administer the vows of the first."

Sal announced, "Saint Macrina, the sister of Saint Basil, founded the first formal order of nuns in three fifty-eight." The Pope smiled and said, "Quite right, my dear," and Miss Bushnan said vaguely, "I bought her the World's Great Religions package about a year ago. I suppose that's how she knew who you were." She was thinking about Brad again, and if the Pope made any reply she failed to hear it. Brad a slave . . .

Then the door shut and Sal muttered, "I just don't trust that old man, he makes me feel creepy," and Miss Bushnan knew he was gone.

She told Sal, "He's harmless, and anyway he's going to Rome now," and only then, with the tension draining away, did she feel how great it had been. "Harmless," she said again. "Bring me another drink, please, Sal."

Tuesday would be the day. The whole world would be watching, and everyone at the conference would be in red and green, but she would wear something blue and stand out. Something blue and her pearls. In her mind Brad would somehow be waiting behind her, naked to the waist, with his wrists in bronze manacles. "I'll have them made at Tiffany's," she said, speaking too softly for Sal, busy with the shaker in the kitchen, to hear. "Tiffany's, but no gems or turquoise or that sort of junk."

Just the heavy, solid bronze with perhaps a touch here and there of silver. Sal would make him keep them polished.

She could hear herself telling their friends, "Sal makes him keep them shined. I tell him if he doesn't I'm going to send him back—just kidding, of course."

VALENTINE'S DAY

OF RELAYS AND ROSES

"Good luck," everyone had said. "Good luck, good luck." He did not believe in luck and never had. He believed in hard work and the theory of probability, necessarily in that order. "Good luck—good luck, Ed."

Outside the corridors had been a bedlam. Here in the chamber everything was hushed, sedate. The Senator in the center, who chewed tobacco and called square dances when he was electioneering in his home state, believed in dignity and decorum for these hearings. Even the television technicians were quiet, going about their wire stringing like so many laboring spiders in the eaves of an old barn. The audience was funereal.

They're frightened to death of being thrown out. This is the big day of the hearings. The day I go on the stand . . .

He sat down between the company's attorneys.

One of them touched his hand lightly and said, "We'll make it, Ed."

Without thinking he said, *"Wish me luck."*

Both of them said, "Good luck—" solemnly.

The hush deepened. A red light on one of the TV cameras came on and the Senator in the center rapped his gavel for order.

"These hearings are now in session," he said.

He had a dry, colorless voice—like an old law clerk's.

"As I do at the beginning of every session, I wish to remind you that these proceedings do not constitute a trial. This is merely the Senate's means of informing itself. Although anyone appearing here may have legal counsel if he so desires, any quibbling will be disposed of in short order by my colleagues and myself.

"Most of you are doubtless aware of the subject of these hearings. We are inquiring into a practice initiated by one of this nation's largest manufacturers of digital computers—a firm which also happens to be fast becoming one of our largest vendors of computer services. Many of the witnesses who have appeared before this committee believed that the economic life of our country is gravely endangered by this company's business practices. It is no secret that many people in the news media agree with them."

The Senator on the right interrupted to say, "A great many people consider the practice immoral," and the Senator in the center nodded sagely.

"During our last session we heard from a representative of the American bar and from the presidents of the chambers of commerce of the cities of Las Vegas and Reno. Today—"

He paused to whisper to the chief counsel of the committee.

The chief counsel said, "Call Madame Felice Dubois."

A slender woman who seemed literally to shimmer with chic stood up and glided toward the witness box.

The counsel asked her, "You are Felice Dubois, a leading couturiere, with salons in Washington, New York, Los Angeles, London, and Paris—is that correct?"

She nodded almost imperceptibly. "It is."

"Do you wish to make a statement to the committee?"

The woman's laugh was a quick succession of notes struck on platinum bells.

"I should really like to make several. I would need them to tell you all that has been done."

"One statement will be sufficient," the Senator in the center said.

"Let me make an obvious one then—about wedding gowns. Our art has given these great study recently—long-skirted, short- or miniskirted, even the bare midriff and see-through. Most of all we have given thought to the succession of gowns proper in so-called serial marriages. Our economy has come to depend on people's marrying more than once. Our industry has promoted certain colors—white first, of course. For second marriages, some shade of blue—then peach or pink, then pastel green and so on. We are not quite in agreement for the fifth—but it is of little importance. By then we're willing to compete. But we've invested a great deal of money in promotion and—"

"And what has been the effect of the business practice under investigation here?"

"Disaster! Only two years ago, you comprehend, a third of all marriages ended in divorce, the cultured classes averaging higher, of course. Of those who were divorced—"

The Senator rapped with his gavel. "We heard the statistics yesterday at some length, madam." Evidently the testimony at this point was not going exactly as he had anticipated. "What has been the effect on other areas of your business?"

Madame Dubois was subdued now.

"A good deal of money spent by women in our industry has been removed from circulation. The divorcee, as a class, you know—was much interested in *haute couture*—"

"I believe that will be sufficient," the Senator in the center said. "Unless my colleagues have some questions for you, you may step down."

The woman waited for a moment, then left the box, making her way gracefully back to her seat. In a whisper picked up by one of the PA microphones the Senator in the center asked the chief counsel, "It's that psychologist fellow next, isn't it?"

"Call Dr. Claude Honnicker."

He was a tall, spare man in a dark suit. He wore ordinary, black-rimmed glasses but by some trick of mannerism he wore them as if they were pince-nez.

The chief counsel identified him as a specialist in industrial psychology who operated a placement agency exclusively for upper echelon executives and scientists. He was given the same invitation to speak which had been tendered Madame Dubois.

"If you don't mind," he replied in a precise voice, "I should prefer to be questioned directly. A general statement might be subject to misinterpretation."

"Very well then. In your experience is there a diminished supply of the men in whose services you deal?"

"Unquestionably. As compared to a similar period a year ago it is down seventeen per cent. As compared to two years past, twenty-two per cent. That is a very serious decrease and I have reason to believe that this—uh—this matrimonial service is largely responsible."

"And will you explain—or can you explain—how something we have all been led to believe is no more than a computerized—in your own phrase, matrimonial service—could lead to this shortage?"

"I shall try. In my opinion our own country and every other advanced country in the world is heavily dependent upon a certain type of man. This man may be an executive, a scientist, a general or a coal miner—but he is the man who works harder than there is any immediate need for him to work and harder than any of the incentives offered him by society justify. He does this because work offers him an outlet for the tensions a hostile environment has built up in him and society exploits him to its benefit."

"You make him sound like an alcoholic," the Senator on the right said.

"Frankly"—Dr. Honnicker shifted in his seat—"such men fairly frequently become alcoholics. Particularly the sales managers, advertising men and other extroverted types. The introverts—scientists, for example —may tend toward paranoia eventually."

"Then you believe that the computer service we have been discussing actually benefits these people?"

"To the detriment of society as a whole—yes. The question is: How much can society stand? There are indications that it cannot take much more."

"In other words a great number of our most productive people have stopped producing."

Dr. Honnicker nodded. "In a certain sense—that is literally true."

The Senator on the left asked, "In your opinion has this affected labor—I mean the officers of American unions—to the same degree that it has managerial executives?"

"I cannot answer that from certain knowledge but I doubt it. Important union leaders tend to be older than the hardest hit group. The problem has struck most directly at the sort of men who have postponed marriage for reasons of career. This is the rising generation upon whom we depend. I might add that in my experience men who have already made a reasonably successful match have not tended to subscribe."

There was a long silence.

Then the Senator in the center said, "I think that will be all."

The chief counsel announced, "Call Mr. Edward Teal Smithe."

He had been waiting for it. He put hands flat on the table in front of him to raise himself to a standing position.

"Take the stand please."

He slipped into the aisle and walked up to the witness box. It was as though he were walking through the pews in church again—the feeling came back across all the years. He had felt then that he was somehow ridiculous and that the people were snickering as he passed. Wanting to turn back and see, he did not. The witness chair was of hard oak, like a school chair.

"You are the vice president in charge of your company's operations? Did I understand your title correctly?"

The first part, the formalities, had flitted past while he had been in a sort of waking dream. Mentally he shook himself, tried to believe that this was no more frightening than a board meeting.

"Yes. Operations as differentiated, for example, from sales or research."

"It is your department that offers the public the service to which we have been alluding?"

"Yes."

"But I believe you have stated to the press that you yourself did not originate the concept of such a service."

Tom Larkin had come into his office. Tom was tall and intense and wore a shop coat, often, when he lunched with the Old Man —an unheard-of thing. He had thrown himself into one of the free-form chairs and announced, "I've got something." Tom was in the Caribbean somewhere now, damn him.

Ed had not said, *Executive's Itch?* as Tom himself might have under reversed circumstances. He had not felt up to it.

He had merely grunted, "Oh?"

"Something that will make this company ten fortunes."

"We need it. We just lost a government contract."

"I'm aware of that. What's the greatest strength of our Mark XX digital?"

Ed had sighed. "Data storage capacity. With the ability to read an alteration in a single molecule as a binary digit the Mark XX can put more information in a hockey puck than most other machines can in a memory bank as big as Long Island. You worked it out. You don't need lessons from me."

The Senator in the center asked, "Aren't you going to reply, Mr. Smithe?"

"I wasn't aware that your statement required answer. No, I did not originate the concept. You were also correct in stating that I have so declared in the past."

"Would you explain to this committee just how your service operates, please?"

"From the viewpoint of the customer? A person wishes to make an ideal matrimonial liaison with another. Computers have been used for this in the past, usually on college campuses or by semi-serious entrepreneurs with inadequate machines and facilities."

"Your program is different?"

"Our company has evolved a computer capable of absorbing a truly vast number of facts and a program which permits us to enter almost anything as datum with the assurance that irrelevancies will be canceled out and that we will be notified of any discrepancies. We put this at our client's disposal."

"And from this hodgepodge the machine can select a suitable wife for a man or a husband for a woman? Unerringly? I find that incredible."

"So did I at one time. As for our percentage of error—we seem to have attracted attention by not erring."

He had read his morning paper, as he always did, in the coffee shop of the residential hotel in which he lived. The story was on the front page, unmissable. Being a thorough man he read it from beginning to end before he finished breakfast and also the editorial it had inspired. Then he had taken a taxi to the plant and, without stopping to hang up his hat in his own suite had gone to Tom's office.

Tom had said, "You've seen it. Wild, isn't it?"

"It's absurd and fantastic. According to this you told some young man that he would find his beloved—that's what it says—in an obscure village in Ethiopia. He sold everything he had, bought a ticket on a jet and he and the girl are now married and ecstatically happy."

"The story was wrong. He didn't sell anything. If we could give him all that free computer time under the tryout program I saw no reason not to give him a plane ride, too—it was far less expensive. Round trip for him to Ethiopia, one way for the girl back. It increased his confidence."

"Mr. Smithe," the Senator on the right said, "don't you feel that you are treating your computer as an oracle?"

"No, I don't. Laymen often do so, I admit. We've done everything in our power to counter that impression. Do you remember the man who went to Ethiopia? It was the first case that was played up by the news media and it did a lot to confuse things."

The Senator in the center said, "I remember the case well. It seemed almost miraculous."

"The man in question was an intelligent young Negro. He had volunteered for the service while we were still trying to get it out of the egg, so to speak. We gave him extensive psychological tests, fed the results to the computer and then gave the new tests it recommended. A fantastic number of hours of machine time were required then, but

Tom Larkin, who is our vice president for research and the real instigator of the service, had faith in it."

"And what, in the opinion of the computer, did the tests show?"

"Well, for one thing, the young man was intensely interested in Coptic Christianity. The Mark XX felt someone of his own faith would make the best partner for him. It also found that since he had spent his early childhood in a rural area and reacted unfavorably to urban life when his family moved to the city, a girl from a semi-rural, rather isolated locale would suit him best. In this country there are very few Coptic Christians in isolated areas. In Ethiopia Coptic Christianity is the state religion and there are a great many. This is simplified, naturally—but you see the approach. Thousands of other correlations like this were made before the specific girl was selected."

"The newspapers make your Mark XX sound like a pythoness but now you're making it sound as if it's only someone's wise old tin grandmother, Mr. Smithe."

"It's neither. It is a machine for manipulating data. Senator, may I say something that's been on my mind for a long time?"

"Please do. That's what we're here for."

"As I've said, all of us in the computer industry have fought the public desire to make something supernatural of our machines. But there is one way in which the public's misconception is useful. It often makes people do the logical thing when the logical thing is something that would be called silly if it were suggested from another source. If a town stood on the slope of a dormant volcano and the volcano started to rumble and smoke, a lot of the people might not want to leave. Because, after all, the volcano had never erupted before—at least as far as their knowledge went. But if a computer told them it was prudent to move they probably would. It may be that the man in the street is right to be a bit awed. If awe impels a man to follow a logical course of action, then awe has its uses. I've noticed that the common man is often most right when he seems most wrong."

"That was quite a speech, Mr. Smithe," the Senator said dryly. "My impression is today that the man in the street believes his country's going to the dogs, and I understand from some of the testimony we heard yesterday that the company you represent has offered your marriage-broking service—I think I can call it that—to more than a hundred thousand Americans without fee. Do you have any comment on the last?"

From the first word he had known a sick and sinking feeling. There had been a ring in the Senator's voice that suggested he stood tried and condemned—of what? Something sneaky and perhaps un-American? "You see, Senator," he began, "when Mr. Larkin persuaded our president to put the service on the market—"

The service hadn't been much of a success. Oh, it succeeded in satisfying customers—it became better and better and processing required less time with every new client. But there hadn't been enough clients. Not nearly enough.

They had all been called into the Old Man's conference room that day and there wasn't a one of them—himself from Operations, Larkin from Research, representatives from Sales, Advertising, and Manufacturing—who hadn't known what was coming.

The president, the Old Man, never tore into anyone; that was part of his charm and his effectiveness. He always spoke logically and fairly and when he could give the man on the carpet the benefit of the doubt he gave it. But he always had the facts.

"Mr. Larkin," he had said slowly, "I know you remember the meeting at which it was decided to put this experiment of yours on a commercial basis. I had almost said, 'it was voted,' but you will also recall, I think, that only you and I voted in favor. So we did it anyway."

Tom had said he would never forget that.

"But we are losing money on it. The sales curve for—what do you call it?"

"Program Roses."

"For Program Roses has been nearly flat and recently, in fact, has started slanting downward. Roses is in the red and I'll tell you frankly that if the rest of our business were not experiencing a goodish upturn we wouldn't have been able to carry it this long. Can you give me any reason why Program Roses should not be terminated?"

The Senator interrupted. "From all you've said, Mr. Smithe, it seems to me your company should have sent Mr. Larkin to testify before this committee instead of yourself."

"We wanted to," Ed said, "but he couldn't be reached."

"Couldn't be reached?"

"You see, he himself eventually subscribed. He and his bride are taking a six-month honeymoon in a sloop. Tom's always been quite a sailor in his spare time, and as it turned out the girl Roses picked for him is, too."

"Did you say six months?" The Senator sounded incredulous.

"With pay. Our president didn't want to let him have more than three but Tom threatened to quit."

"It would seem"—the Senator was smiling coldly—"that you have been victimized by your own cleverness."

"We don't think so. You see—"

Tom had waited until the Old Man was finished before he exploded his bombshell. Until he was finished and there been a long, pregnant pause. Then he hadn't addressed the president directly; he appeared to speak to Sales: "I don't want Roses discontinued—it's the best thing we've got. I want to give it away."

No one had spoken. Ed remembered that he himself had known a sick realization that Tom had cracked up at last.

"Roses," Tom had announced, "has already brought us three million in new contracts and accounts. You don't charge people to read your advertising, do you? They might be willing to pay—some who are interested enough—but you make more money when it's free."

Sales had said slowly, "He's right. He and I have combed through the new accounts one by one, and in ninety per cent of the cases we've found that the decision to swing the business to us was either made or strongly influenced by someone who'd be a client for Roses."

The Senator in the center cleared his throat. "You mean to sit there and tell us that Roses is just a sales gimmick for the rest of your business?"

"A gimmick," Ed Smithe said, "is when you give away a plastic bathtub toy with a box of breakfast cereal. And that brings us to something else Tom made us realize. Roses not only made these key people familiar with our machines and impressed with them, it also made the Mark XX a permanent part of their lives. The competition has found that it can talk a long time and not erase that."

"And so you have actually offered the service free."

"To people who we feel will be in a position to specify computers or computer services as part of their careers—yes."

There was a stir in the chamber. The Senator said heavily, "You seem to be destroying the fabric of society as a sort of side effect."

"Not really." Ed drew a deep breath. "Senator, who's the better farmer, the man who hitches up his tractor and runs it until it breaks or the man who oils and services it and lets it cool off if the engine overheats? And who gets more plowing done in the long run? These men and women who have lived half their lives in loneliness are often thrown off balance temporarily when they finally find someone with whom they can relate, I admit. Sometimes they just want to quit—to be with their new partner every hour. But eventually they come back—and when they do they're working *for* something, not just to get away from something. Right now we're in the trough the service has been building rapidly and a majority of our clients are still in the honeymoon stage. But the earlier ones are coming back stronger than ever and I can prove it."

He did. The charts and slides helped but the facts really spoke for themselves. Numbers of theses written, numbers of patents granted, earnings of firms whose executive ranks were heavy with early clients. He was no salesman but he could feel the whole chamber swinging over; it thrilled him.

When he finished he was wrung out. His shirt was sticking to his chest and his legs felt weak. But at least he had convinced them.

The Senator on the left said, "You give the service to—"

"People in private industry, government, or nonprofit institutions who in our judgment may eventually be in a position to give us business. Others are charged a minimal fee. I'm happy to say we've gotten that down quite a bit."

The Senator in the center smiled suddenly. It was the charming, slightly lopsided smile he had used on a thousand campaign posters.

"If I'm not being impertinent, Mr. Smithe," he asked, "could you tell us your own marital status?"

"I have been a widower for almost twenty years."

"You haven't used the Roses service yourself?"

In a voice that was barely audible he said, "To tell the truth, Senator, I've had to postpone my trip to England because of these hearings. You see, our president wanted to make certain I'd be here to testify. Marcia—that's her name; she's a librarian in Liverpool—Marcia and I have written and talked by long-distance telephone but we've not yet been able to meet."

"I hope you will be able to soon," the Senator in the center said. "You may step down, Mr. Smithe."

He began the long walk back to his seat, glad he hadn't been forced to tell them that it was Marcia who had requested Roses from the company's British subsidiary. That she had found him. It would have sounded too silly.

ARBOR DAY

PAUL'S TREEHOUSE

It was the day after the governor called out the National Guard, but Morris did not think of it that way; it was the morning after the second night Paul had spent in the tree, and Morris brushed his teeth with Scotch after he looked into Paul's bedroom and saw the unrumpled bed. And it was hot; though not in the house, which was airconditioned.

Sheila was still asleep, lying straight out like a man on the single bed across from his own. He left her undisturbed, filling his glass with Scotch again and carrying it out to the patio at the side of the house. The sun was barely up, yet the metal furniture there was already slightly warm. It would be a hot day, a scorcher. He heard the snip-snack of Russell's shears on the other side of the hedge and braced himself for the inevitable remark.

"It's going to be a hot one, isn't it?" Sticking his head over the top of the hedge. Morris nodded, hoping that if he did not speak Russell would stay where he was. The hope was fruitless. He could hear Russell unlatching the gate, although he purposely did not look.

"Hotter than the hinges of hell," Russell said, sitting down. "Do the gardening early, that's what I told myself, do it early while it's cool, and look at me. I'm sweating already. Did you hear what they did last night? Beat a cop to death with golf clubs and polo mallets out of a store window."

Morris said nothing, looking up at Paul's treehouse. It was on the other side of the yard, but so high up it could be seen above the roofline of the house.

"Beat him to death right out on the street."

"I suppose some of them deserve it," Morris said moodily.

"Sure they do, but it's *them* doing it. That's what gets to me. . . . Drinking pretty early, aren't you?" Russell was tall and gangling, with a long neck and a prominent Adam's apple; Morris, short and fat-bellied, envied him his straight lines.

"I guess I am," he said. "Like one?"

"Since it's Saturday . . ."

It was cool in the house, much cooler than the patio, but the air was stale. He splashed the cheaper "guest" whisky into a glass and added a squirt of charged water.

"Is that your boy Paul's?" When he came out again Russell was staring up at the treehouse just as he himself had been doing a moment before. Morris nodded.

"He built it on his own, didn't he? I remember watching him climb up there with boards or something, with his little radio playing to keep him company." He took the drink. "You don't mind if I walk around and have a look at it, do you?"

Reluctantly Morris followed him, stepping over the beds of flame-toned, scentless florabundas Sheila loved.

The tree at the other side of the house gave too much shade for roses. There was nothing under it except a little sparse grass and a few stones Paul had dropped.

Russell whistled. "That's way up there, isn't it? Fifty feet if it's an inch. Why'd you let him build it so high?"

"Sheila doesn't believe in thwarting the boy's natural inclinations." It sounded silly when Morris said it, and he covered by taking another sip of the whisky.

Russell shook his head. "If he ever falls out of there he'll kill himself."

"Paul's a good climber," Morris said.

"He'd have to be to build that thing." Russell continued to stare, craning his body backward. Morris wished that he would return to the patio.

"It took him almost two weeks," Morris said.

"He swiped the lumber off the housing project, didn't he?"

"I bought him some of it." For an instant Morris had seen Paul's small, brown head in one of the windows. He wondered if Russell had noticed it.

"But he swiped most of it. Two-by-fours and four-by-fours; it looks solid."

"I suppose it is." Before he could catch himself he added, "He's got buckets of rocks up there."

"Rocks?" Russell looked down, startled.

"Rocks about the size of tennis balls. Paul built a sort of elevator and hauled them up. He must have eight or ten buckets full."

"What's he want those for?"

"I don't know."

"Well, ask him." Russell looked angry at having his curiosity balked. "He's your kid." Morris swallowed the last of his second drink, saying nothing.

"How does he get up there?" Russell was looking at the tree again. "It doesn't look as if you *could* climb it."

"He cut off some of the branches after he got the place built. He has a rope with knots in it he lets down."

"Where is it?" Russell looked around, expecting to see the rope tangled in the tree's branches somewhere.

It was bound to come out now. "He pulls it up after him when he goes in there," Morris said. The Scotch was lying like a pool of mercury in his empty stomach.

"You mean he's up there now?"

Neither of them had heard Sheila come out. "He's been up there since Thursday." She sounded unconcerned.

Morris turned to face her and saw that she was wearing a quilted pink housecoat. Her hair was still in curlers. He said, "You didn't have to get up so early."

"I wanted to." She yawned. "I set the clock-radio for six. It's going to be hot in town and I want to be right there when the stores open."

"I wouldn't go today," Russell said.

"I'm not going down *there*—I'm going to the good stores." Sheila yawned again. Without makeup, Morris thought, she looked too old to have a son as young as Paul. He did himself, he knew, but Sheila usually looked younger to him; especially when he had had something to drink. "Did you hear about the National Guard, though," she added when she had finished the yawn.

Russell shook his head.

"You know how somebody said they were shooting at everything and doing more damage than the rioters? Well, they're going to protest that. I heard it on the radio. They're going to hold a march of their own today."

Russell was no longer listening. He leaned back to look at Paul's treehouse again.

"Ever since Thursday," Sheila said. "Isn't that a scream?"

Morris surprised himself by saying, "I don't think so, and I'm going to make him come down today." Sheila looked at him coolly.

"How does he live up there?" Russell asked.

"Oh, he's got a blanket and things," Sheila said.

Morris said slowly, "While I was at the office Thursday he took blankets out of the linen closet and a lot of canned food and fruit juice out of the pantry and carried it all up there."

"It's good for him," Sheila said. "He's got his radio and scout knife and what not too. He wants to get away and be on his own. So let him. He'll come down when he's hungry, that's what I tell Morris, and meanwhile we know where he is."

"I'm going to make him come down today," Morris repeated, but neither of them heard him.

When they went away—Sheila to start breakfast, Russell, presumably, to finish clipping his side of the hedge—Morris remained where he was, staring up at the treehouse. After two or three minutes he walked over to the trunk and laid a hand on the rough bark. He had been studying the tree for three days now and knew that even before Paul had lopped some of its limbs it had not been an easy tree to climb. Walking only a trifle unsteadily, he went to the garage and got the step-ladder.

From the top of the ladder he could reach the lowest limb by stretching himself uncomfortably and balancing on the balls of his feet with his body leaning against the trunk. Suddenly conscious of how soft his palms had become in the last fifteen years, how heavy his body was, he closed his hands around the limb and tried to pull himself up. Struggling to grip the tree with his legs, he kicked the ladder, which fell over.

From somewhere below Russell said, "Don't break your neck, Morris," and he heard the sound of faint music. He twisted his head until he could see Russell, with a transistor radio clipped to his belt, righting the ladder.

Morris said, "Thanks," gratefully and stood panting at the top for a moment before coming down.

"I wouldn't do that if I were you," Russell said.

"Listen," Morris was still gulping for breath, "would you go up there and get him?" It was a humiliating admission but he made it: "You ought to be able to climb better than I can."

"Sorry," Russell touched his chest, "doctor's orders."

"Oh. I didn't know."

"Nothing serious, I'm just supposed to stay away from places where I might take a bad fall. I get dizzy sometimes."

"I see."

"Sure. Did you hear about the fake police? It came over our radio a minute ago."

Morris shook his head, still panting and steadying himself against the ladder.

"They're stripping the uniforms off dead cops and putting them on themselves. They've caused a lot of trouble that way."

Morris nodded. "I'll bet."

Russell kicked the tree. "He's your kid. Why don't you just tell him to come down?"

"I tried that yesterday. He won't."

"Well, try again today. Make it strong."

"Paul!" Morris made his voice as authoritative as he could. "Paul, look down here!" There was no movement in the treehouse.

"Make it strong. Tell him he's got to come down."

"Paul, come out of there this minute!"

The two men waited. There was no sound except for the tuneless music of the radio and the whisper of a breeze among the saw-edged leaves.

"I guess he's not going to come," Morris said.

"Are you sure he's up there?"

Morris thought of the glimpse of Paul's head he had seen earlier. "He's up there. He just won't answer." He thought of the times he had taken the pictures his mother had given him, pictures showing his own childhood, from their drawer and studied them to try and discover some similarity between himself and Paul. "He doesn't want to argue," he finished weakly.

"Say." Russell was looking at the tree again. "Why don't we chop it?" He dropped his voice to a whisper.

Morris was horrified. "He'd be killed."

The radio's metallic jingling stopped. *"We interrupt this program for a bulletin."* Both men froze.

"Word has reached our newsroom that the demonstration organized by Citizens For Peace has been disrupted by about five hundred storm troopers of the American Nazi Party. It appears that members of a motorcycle club have also entered the disturbance; it is not known on which side."

Russell switched the radio off. Morris sighed, "Every time they have one of those bulletins I think it's going to be the big one."

His neighbor nodded sympathetically. "But listen, we don't have to cut the tree clear down. Anyway, it must be nearly three feet thick and it would take us a couple of days, probably. All we have to do is chop at it a little. He'll think we're going to cut it with him in it, and climb down. You have an ax?"

Morris shook his head.

"I do. I'll go over and get it."

Morris waited under the tree until he had left, then called Paul's name softly several times. There was no reply. Raising his voice, he said, "We don't want to hurt you, Paul." He tried to think of a bribe. Paul already had a bicycle. "I'll build you a swimming pool, Paul. In the back yard where your mother has her flowers. I'll have men come in with a bulldozer and dig them out and make us a swimming pool there." There was no answer. He wanted to tell Paul that they weren't really going to chop down the tree, but something prevented him. Then he could hear Russell opening the gate on the other side of the house.

The ax was old, dull and rusted, and the head was loose on the handle so that after every few strokes it was necessary to drive it back on by butting it against the trunk of the tree; each blow hurt Morris's already scraped hands. By the time he had made a small notch—most of his swings missed the point of aim and fell uselessly on either side of it —his arms and wrists were aching. Paul had not come down or even looked out one of the windows.

"I'm going to try climbing again." He laid down the ax, looking at Russell. "Do you have a longer ladder than this one?"

Russell nodded. "You'll have to come over and help me carry it."

Russell's wife stopped them as they crossed Russell's patio and made them come inside for lemonade. "My goodness, Morris, you look as if you're about to have heat prostration. Is it that warm out?" Russell's house was airconditioned too.

They sat in the family room, with lemonade in copper mugs meant for Moscow Mules. The television flickered with scenes, but Russell's wife had twisted the sound down until Morris could hear only a faint hum. The screen showed a sprawling building billowing smoke. Firemen and soldiers milled about it. Then the camera raced down suburban streets and he saw two houses very like his own and Russell's; he almost felt he could see through the walls, see the two of them sitting and watching their own houses—which were gone now as police fired up at the windows of a tall tenement. Russell, winking and gesturing for silence, was pouring gin into his mug to mix with the lemonade now that his wife had gone back to the kitchen.

He felt sick when he stood up, and wondered dully if Sheila were not looking for him, angry because his breakfast was getting cold. He steadied himself on the doorway as he followed Russell out, conscious that his face was flushed. The heat outside was savage now.

They moved cans of paint and broken storm windows aside to un-cover Russell's extension ladder. It was as old as the ax, dirtied with white and yellow splashes, and heavy as metal when they got it on their shoulders to carry outside.

"This'll get you up the first twenty feet," Russell said. "Think you can climb from there?"

Morris nodded, knowing he could not.

They hooked the two sections together and leaned them against the tree, Russell talking learnedly of the proper distance between the bottom of the ladder and the base of the object to be climbed. Russell had been an engineer at one time; Morris had never been quite sure of the reason he no longer was.

The ladder shook. It seemed strange to find himself surrounded by leaves instead of looking up at them, having to look down to see Russell on the ground. At the very top of the ladder a large limb had been broken off some years before and he could look straight out over the roof of his own home and all the neighboring houses. "I see smoke," he called down. "Over that way. Something big's burning."

"Can you get up to the boy?" Russell called back.

Morris tried to leave the ladder, lifting one leg gingerly over the stub of the broken limb. Giddiness seized him. He climbed down again.

"What's the matter?"

"If I had a rope," Morris gestured with his hands, "I could put it around my waist and around the trunk of the tree. You know, like the men who climb telephone poles." Sirens sounded in the distance.

"I've got some." Russell snapped his fingers. "Wait a minute."

Morris waited. The noise of the sirens died away, leaving only the talk of the leaves, but Russell did not return. Morris was about to go into the house when the truck pulled up at the curb. It was a stake-bed truck, and the men were riding on it, almost covering it. They were white and brown and black; most of them wore khaki shirts and khaki trousers with broad black leather belts, but they had no insignia and their weapons were clubs and bottles and iron bars. The first of them were crossing his lawn almost before the truck had come to a full stop, and a tall man with a baseball bat began smashing his picture window.

"What do you want?" Morris said. "What is it?"

The leader took him by the front of his shirt and shook him as the others circled around. A stone, and then another, struck the ground and he realized that Paul was throwing them from his treehouse, trying to defend him; but the range was too great. Someone hit him from behind with a chain.

ST. BRANDON*

We had fish and roast beef, and I think I remember green beans cooked with mushrooms. After the pie I was sent away again, but Doherty had unsaddled Lady, and he said it was too dark for me to ride anymore. I suppose I whined at that, as small boys will, because after showing me the puppies a second time he began to tell me a story he said he had from his grandmother, "the old Kate."

"It was when there was kings in Ireland. There was a man then named Finn M'Cool that was the strongest man in Ireland; he worked for the High King at Tara, and he had a dog and a cat. The dog's name was Strongheart and the cat's was Pussy."

I laughed at that, causing Doherty to shake his head over the unseemly merriment of the young generation. He was sitting cross-legged on top of an empty apple barrel. "Why and from where do you think the name come, for all of that?" he said. "Did you ever know a cat in your life that hadn't a sister of the name?

"Well, upon a day it happened that Finn M'Cool was bringing in the cows, and the High King at Tara said to him, 'Finn, there's a job of work I have for you,' and Finn answered him, 'It's done already, Your Majesty, and what is it?' 'It's the king of the rats, that's aboard St. Brandon's boat gnawing at the hull of it and doing every kind of mischief.' 'I've heard of that boat and it's stone,' says Finn, 'he'll not get far gnawing that.' ' 'Tis wicker,' says the king, 'like any proper boat, and if you'll not be moving those lazy feet of yours soon Brandon'll never be reaching the Earthly Paradise at all.' 'Well, and why should he, now,' says Finn, 'and where is it, anyhow?' 'That's not for you to ask,' says the High King at Tara, 'and it's to the west of us, as you'd know if you weren't a fool, for the other's England.'

"So Finn walked every mile of it to Bantry Bay where Brandon's boat was, and the boat was that large that he could see it for five days before he could smell the sea, for it was so long it looked like Ireland

* from PEACE

might be leavin' it, and the mast so tall there was no top to it at all, it just went up forever, and they say while Brandon's boat was docked there an albatross hit the top of it in a storm and broke her neck, though that was all right, for the fall would have killed her anyway, for she fell three days before she hit the deck, and the deck so high above the water she fell three more after Brandon kicked her overboard.

"But when he could get sight of the water around her, Finn said, 'That's the good man's boat as I breathe, and she's about to sail, too, for there's a rat as big as a cow gnawing the anchor cable, do you see.' And the dog agreed with him, for dogs is always an agreeable sort of animal, and that one would have had this tale if you hadn't laughed at the cat. Then the dog drew his sword (and a big one it was, too, and the blade as bright as the road home) and lit his pipe and pushed his hat back on his head and said, 'And would you like that rat dead now, Finn?' And Finn said, 'I would,' and they fought until the moon come up, and then the dog brought Finn the rat's head on the end of a piece of stick about this long, and never told that it was because the cat had come up from behind and tripped him, for the dog's the most honest animal there is or ever was except when it comes to sharing credit, but Finn had seen it. Finn winked at the cat then, but she was cleaning her knife and wouldn't look. The next day they went out to be seeing the boat again, and sure there was two old men on the deck, each of them with a beard as white as a swan's wing and leaning on a stick taller than he was, alike as two peas. Then Finn scratched his head and said to the cat, 'As sure as it rains in Ireland, I've looked at one and the other until I'm that dizzy, and the devil take me if there's a hair of difference between them; how can you tell which is Brandon?' And the cat said, 'Faith, I've never met him, but the other one is the king of the rats.' 'Which?' says Finn, to make sure. 'The one on the right,' says the cat. 'The ugly one.' 'Then that's settled,' says Finn, 'and you're the girl for me.' And he picked up the cat and threw her aboard and went back to the High King at Tara and told him the thing was done.

"But the cat lit on deck on her feet as cats do, but when she stood up the king of the rats was gone. Then Brandon said, 'Welcome aboard. Now we've captain, cat, and rat, all three, and can sail.' So the cat signed the ship's papers, and when she did she noticed the king of the rats was down for quartermaster. 'What's this,' she said, 'and is that one drawing rations?' 'And don't you know,' says Brandon, 'that the wicked do His will as well as the just? Only they don't like it. How do you think I could have weighed anchor, a sick man like me, without the rat gnawed the rope? But don't worry, I'm putting you down for CAT, and

the cat's above everyone but the captain.' 'When do we sail?' says the
cat. 'That we've done already,' says Brandon, 'for the cable parted yesterday and our boat's so long the bow's in Boston Bay already, but
there's an Irish wind ahead and astern of us—that blows every way at
once, but mostly up and down—and whether our end will ever make it
is more than I could say.' 'Then we'd best go for'rd,' says the cat.

"And they did, and took a lantern (like this one) with them, and it
was a good thing they did, for when they got to the Earthly Paradise it
was as black as the inside of a cow. 'What's this?' says the cat, holding
up the lantern though she could see in the dark as well as any. 'If this
is the Earthly Paradise, where's the cream? Devil a thing do I see but a
big pine tree with a sign on it.' The king of the rats, that had joined
them on the way for'rd, says, 'And what does it say?' thinking the cat
couldn't read and wanting to embarrass her. 'No hiring today,' says the
cat. 'Well, no cream either,' says the rat, and Brandon said, 'It's two
o'clock in the morning in the Earthly Paradise. You don't expect the
cows milked at two o'clock, do you?'

"Then the cat jumped off the boat and sat on a stone and thought
about what time the cows *would* be milked, and at last she said, 'How
long until five?' and the rat laughed, but Brandon said, 'Twenty thousand years.' 'Then I'm going back to Ireland where it's light,' says the
cat. 'You are that,' says Brandon, 'but not for some time,' and *he*
jumped off the boat and set up a cross on the beach. Then the boat
sank and the king of the rats swam ashore. ''Twas stone all along,' said
he. 'That it was,' says Brandon, 'in places.' 'Shall I kill the cat now?'
says the king of the rats, and the cat says, 'Here, now, what's this?' 'It's
death to you,' says the rat, 'for all you cats are fey heathen creatures, as
all the world knows, and it's the duty of a Christian rat to take you off
the board as may be, particularly as it was for that purpose I was sent
by the High King at Tara.' Then the two began to fight, all up and
down the beach, and just then an angel—or somebody—come out of the
woods and asked Brandon what was going on. ''Tis a good brawl, isn't
it,' says the saint. 'Yes, but who are they?' 'Well, the one is wickedness,'
says Brandon, 'and the other a fairy cat; and I brought the both of them
out from Ireland with me, and now I'm watchin' to see which wins.'
Then the angel says, 'Watch away, but it appears to me they're tearin'
one another to pieces, and the pieces runnin' off into the woods.'"

EARTH DAY

BEAUTYLAND

The first time I saw Dives he was down on the sidewalk coughing his lungs out; an old lady had his mask up on the tip of her umbrella, and a kid, a tall, pimply kid with bushy hair and thick glasses, had been tripping him every time he tried to grab it from her. I went over to them and said, "You better give that back or he'll die," and the old woman was going to, but the kid grabbed it from her and threw it down in the gutter; I couldn't give it to him to put back on with that stuff on it, but I kicked the kid and managed to flag a T-E-E aircab, and once I had him in there he was all right. I took off my own mask and told the driver to cruise; like all of them the windows showed the city the way it's supposed to look after it's rebuilt, so that if you believed it you'd give your ass to be born a hundred years from now.

Dives (I'm going to call him that because his mother didn't) thanked me and tried to give me some money. I didn't take it—there was quite a bit of it, and I figured if he let go of that much that easy the thing to do was get close to him, not piss it away for a few lousy Cs.

The first thing I noticed about him was that his nose had been broken a lot, like an old fighter's; and there were a bunch of little scars on his face. I found out afterward that they were from surgery to erase bigger scars, and one of his eyes was solid state. After a while he said, "Where are we going?" and I said anywhere he wanted to, that I figured he might be a little shaky yet and I'd drop him off. Naturally I was figuring he'd want to go home, and then since I'd pulled him out of trouble and turned down his money he'd have to have me in for a drink and we'd be buddies.

He said, "Why don't we go to my apartment for a drink?" and gave his address to the autodriver (a Park Avenue address that sounded like a million) and the funny thing was that I could see him seeing through me and not caring. He was thinking: This guy sees I've got money; so he figures he's going to be my friend—okay, that's the only kind I'm ever going to have, and maybe he plays pinochle. I didn't like it but I figured I'd better go along.

He bought a new mask from the driver, but it turned out he didn't really need it, because it *was* a million-dollar address like I thought, and we could jump right out of the totally enclosed environment of the aircab into the big one of his building without even putting anything on. "Neat," I said, looking around his private lobby, and it really was neat, all hologram walls, real as hell, a big valley way up in the mountains somewhere, where you couldn't see a road or a house or anything at all, and the trees and bushes and weeds and everything were all green, like nothing was killing them.

"A piece of property I used to own," he said.

I said, "I bet it don't look like that now."

Then he said, "No, it doesn't . . . when I was trying to promote it I called it Beautyland—ever hear of it?" and when I shook my head one of the biggest damn androids I ever saw came out of the wallpaper— that was what it seemed like—and shook me down. He was brand new and his platinum trim said he had all the gadgets and he moved in that easy, gentle way they do when all their skin's two-centimeter armor plate.

I stayed mighty still, believe me, until he was finished; then I said, "That was some kind of password, huh? I should of said I heard of it."

Dives said, "Have you?"

"Like I said, no. But if you want me to lie a little that's okay." Then I thought it might be a good move to remind him of what I did for him, so I said, "Listen, why don't you take the big guy here with you when you go out, then you wouldn't need me," and the android nodded and said, *He is right they have hurt you again, Master.* He had the kind of deep voice they always give them.

The rich guy (that was a two-grand suit, by the way, if I ever saw one) just shrugged and said, "I think I owe them a chance at me from time to time. Come on in and we'll have that drink."

It was real class. The android took our verbal orders and relayed them to the Barmaster, then served them on a tray. Dives had brandy and I had vodka on the rocks, and when I picked it up he said, "You've been in prison, haven't you?" I nodded and told him they were called Social Reorientation Farms now and asked him how he knew, and he said he had spent some time on one himself. Naturally I asked him where, and when he had got out.

"Over a year ago. I was only there for six weeks—I had tried to kill myself, but it passed pretty quickly."

I told him that was lucky—I'd tried to make a killing and spent over eight years.

He wasn't paying much attention. He said, "I saw people drinking like that there. They fermented mash in the back of the laundry, but ice was nearly impossible to get, and when they had it they drank the way you do—holding the biggest piece in their mouths and drawing the liquor past it. That was why you didn't know about Beautyland; you were in prison."

I said I'd never try to defraud anyone else again; they'd gotten all that out of me.

"And I'll never try to take my own life again, either. At least, not directly." He pulled out a remote control for the android and hit the OFF button. I could see the thing turn off all right, and after a minute he threw the control into a far corner of the room. "That wasn't my only defense," he said, "but it was my principal one, and I won't use the others."

I said that was okay by me, but if someone came busting in I was going to make a dive for the control and turn it right back on again. I would have done it too—I've never had that much muscle on my side and I would like just once to see how it feels.

He said, "I don't think you'll want to turn him back on after you've heard me; I want to tell you about my valley."

I said, "Suppose after I've heard you I *don't* want to break your neck."

"Then we'll play chess. Or whatever you want. That valley belonged to me, and I loved it. You saw it."

I said, "Sure."

"But I couldn't live in it—to live in it would be to spoil it, to ruin it. You saw that. I thought of selling it to the government, but you know what has become of the national parks; developers offered me a lot of money for it—at least, what I thought was a lot of money then—but I knew what they were going to do if I sold my land to them. Meanwhile I had to take a job in a factory to live."

I was looking around at his apartment. I said, "Then you got a real bright idea."

"I thought I did. I thought I had figured out a way to make money out of the valley without destroying it. Using the land as collateral I got a loan, and with the money I had a biological survey made. Let me show you one of my ads."

He had it all set up and ready to roll. The TV wall went on and showed the same kind of picture that had been out in the lobby—I guess the same place—and one of those plastic voices said, "They call it BEAUTYLAND, and only you can save it." Then the picture turned to fire.

Dives said, "We had every tree, every damn plant, numbered. The idea was that we were going to sell them, item by item. There were eighteen rabbits in the valley and we named them all and got a picture of every one of them. There were six deer—I guess they may have been about the only wild deer left in the United States—and we named them too. I wanted three hundred thousand each for those deer; the highest-priced tree was a hundred and fifty thousand—it was an oak that must have been a couple of meters thick. See, the idea was that we were going to destroy anything that wasn't bought."

I said, "Give me that again."

"Anything the world didn't pay for—or somebody in it—I was going to burn. It all belonged to me, and they couldn't stop me. I had a flame projector made; you saw it a minute ago, because we used it in shooting that spot." He turned off the TV with a wave of his hand. "What they did pay for would be saved forever. None of this Mickey Mouse stuff the government does—we were going to build a wall around the place and keep everybody out. It could be photographed if you wanted from towers on the outside, but that was as close as anyone would be allowed to get. But first anything that wasn't paid for by somebody burned. You see, I thought someone would pay for all of it, or nearly all."

I asked, "How did you do?"

"We didn't," he said. "A few old ladies bought wild flowers and that was the end of it."

I waited for him to go on, and after a long time he said, "We called the best rabbit Benny Bunny, and a big part of the campaign was geared around the slogan Save Benny Bunny for Beautyland. Benny Bunny was supposed to cost fifty-five thousand. I got five hundred *toward* saving him from some elementary school in New Jersey; I sent it back and they wrote me later they used the money to buy some sparrow tapes."

"So you burned the stuff?"

"We burned it," he said, "yes."

I waited for him to tell me how he had swung it.

"I went back to the office I had rented," he said, "one morning after it had become apparent that the whole thing wasn't going to work. Our deadline was past, and our deadline extension was past, and the bank was closing in on me, though they must have known I didn't have any way to pay them off. I had talked to the media the night before and told them I didn't have the heart to burn the things myself—I was going to hire somebody to do it."

I kept on waiting.

"There was a line there, waiting for me to come. It went around the block twice—all kinds of people."

"Looking for jobs?"

"That's what they said, but that wasn't really it—I talked to some of them and they just wanted to do it. One of them—about the fifth or sixth one I talked to, I think—tried to bribe me. You can probably guess what came next."

"You put on a new campaign," I said.

"I didn't have to—I just announced it. I doubled and tripled the price of everything, but I was a sucker there—I could have gotten more for the deer and the rabbits. And the birds. They fought each other to pay my price for those."

I said, "You should have auctioned them."

"Yes, I should have, but it's too late now. We did it at night so the flames would show up on camera better—I got three million for the TV rights—and Benny Bunny got clear down onto one of the interstates before the man who had paid out a hundred and sixty-five thousand for the privilege nailed him. As it was he nearly lost him to a station wagon; he was the president of a big oil company, so I thought that was kind of ironic."

I said that I imagined there had been a lot of little quirky things like that.

He nodded and said, "I thought you might like to know how I made my money," and I told him I didn't give a damn as long as it was there.

MOTHER'S DAY

CAR SINISTER

Q: What do you get if you cross a racoon with a greyhound?
A: A furry brown animal that climbs trees and seats forty people.

—GRADE SCHOOL JOKE

There are three gas stations in our village. I suppose before I get any deeper into this I should explain that it really is a village, and not a suburb. There are two grocery stores (privately owned and so small my wife has to go to both when she wants to bake a cake), a hardware store with the post office in one corner, and the three gas stations.

Two of these are operated by major oil companies, and for convenience I'll call them the one I go to and the other one. I have a credit card for the one I go to, which is clean, well run, and trustworthy on minor repairs. I have no reason to think the other one is any different, in fact it looks just the same except for the colors on the sign, and I've noticed that the two of them exchange small favors when the need arises. They are on opposite sides of the main road (it is the kind of road that was called a highway in the nineteen thirties), and I suppose both managers feel they're getting their share.

The third station isn't like that at all; it looks quite different and sells a brand of gasoline I've never seen anywhere else. This third station is at the low end of the village, run by a man called Bosko. Bosko appears stupid although I don't think he really is, and always wears an army fatigue hat and a gray coat that was once part of a bus driver's uniform. Another man—a boy, really—helps Bosko. The boy's name is Bubber; he is usually even dirtier than Bosko, and has something wrong with the shape of his head.

I own a Rambler American and, as I said, always have it serviced at one of the major-brand stations. I might add that I work in the city, driving thirty miles each way, and the car is very important to me; so I would never have taken it to Bosko's if it hadn't been for that foolish business about my credit card. I lost it, you see. I don't know where.

Naturally I telegraphed the company, but before I got my new card I had to have the car serviced.

Of course, what I should have done was to go to my usual station and pay cash. But I wondered if the manager might not be curious and check his list of defaulting cards. I understand that the companies take great pains to keep these lists up to date, and since it had been two days since I'd wired them, it wasn't out of the question to suppose that my number would be there, and that he'd think I was a bad credit risk. A thing like that gets around fast in our village. I shouldn't really have worried about something like that, I know, but it was late and I was tired. And of course the other major oil company station would be even worse. The manager of my station would have seen me right across the road.

At any rate I was going on a trip the next day, and I thought of the old station at the low end of the village. I only wanted a grease job and an oil change. Hundreds, or at least dozens, of people must patronize the place every day. What could go wrong?

Bosko—I didn't know his name at the time, but I had seen him around the village and knew what he looked like—wasn't there. Only the boy, Bubber, covered with oil from an incredible car he had been working on. I suppose he saw me staring at it because he said, "Ain't you never seen one like that?"

I told him I hadn't, then tried to describe what I wanted done to my American. Bubber wasn't paying attention. "That's a *funny car* there," he said. "They uses 'em for drag races and shows and what not. Rears right up on his back wheels. Wait'll I finish with him and I'll show you."

I said, "I haven't time. I just want to leave my car to be serviced."

That seemed to surprise him, and he looked at my American with interest. "Nice little thing," he said, almost crooning.

"I always see it has the best of care. Could you give me a lift home now? I'll need my car back before eight tomorrow morning."

"I ain't supposed to leave when Bosko ain't here, but I'll see if I can find one that runs."

Cars, some of them among the strangest I had ever seen, were parked on almost every square foot of the station's apron. There was an American Legion parade car rebuilt to resemble a "forty and eight" boxcar, now rusting and rotting; a hulking candy-apple hot rod that looked usable, but which Bubber dismissed with, "Can't get no rings for her, she's overbored"; stunted little British minis with rickets; a Crosley, the first I had seen in ten years; a two-headed car with a hood, and I suppose an engine, at each end; and others I could not even put a name to. As we walked past the station for the second time in our search, I saw a sleek, black car inside and caught Bubber (soiling my fingers) by the sleeve. "How about that one? It looks ready to go."

Bubber shook his head positively and spat against the wall. "The Aston Martin? He's too damn mean."

And so I drove home, eventually, in a sagging school bus which had been converted into a sort of camper and had WABASH FAMILY GOSPEL SINGERS painted in circus lettering on its side. I spent the evening explaining the thing to my wife and went to bed rather seriously worried about whether or not I would have my car back by eight as well as about what Bubber's clothing would do to my upholstery.

I need not have concerned myself as it turned out. I was awakened about three (according to the illuminated dial of my alarm clock) by the sound of an engine in my driveway, and when I looked out through the Venetian blinds, I saw my faithful little Rambler parked there. I went back to sleep with most of my anxiety gone, listening to those strange little moans a warm motor makes as it cools. It seems to me they lasted longer than normal that night, mingling with my dreams.

Next morning I found a grimy yellow statement for twenty-five dollars on the front seat. Nothing was itemized; it simply read (when I finally deciphered the writing, which was atrocious) "for service."

As I mentioned above, I was leaving on a trip that morning, and I had no time to contest this absurd demand. I jammed it into the map compartment and contrived to forget it until I returned home a week later. Then I went to the station—Bosko was there, fortunately—and explained that there must have been some mistake. Bosko glanced at my bill and asked me again, although I had just told him, what it was I had ordered done. "I wanted the oil changed and the chassis greased," I repeated, "and the tank filled. You know, the car serviced."

I saw that that had somehow struck a nerve. Bosko froze for a moment, then smiled broadly and with a ceremonious gesture tore the yellow slip to bits which he allowed to sift through his fingers to the floor. "Bubber made a mistake, I guess, Colonel," he said with what struck me as false bonhomie. "This one's on the house. She behave okay while you had her out?"

I was rattled at being called Colonel (I have found since that Bosko applies that honorific to all his customers) and could only nod. As a matter of fact the American's performance had been quite flawless, the little car seeming, if anything, a bit more eager than usual.

"Well, listen," Bosko said, "you let me know if there's any trouble at all with her. And like I said, this one's on the house. We'd like your business."

My new card came, and I had almost forgotten this incident when my car began giving trouble in the mornings. I would start the engine as usual, and it would run for a few seconds, cough, and stop; and after this prove impossible to start again for ten or fifteen minutes. I took it to the station I usually patronize several times and they tinkered with it dutifully, but the next morning the same thing would occur. After this had been going on for three weeks or so, I remembered Bosko.

He was sympathetic. This, I have to admit, made me warm to him somewhat. The manager of my usual station had been pretty curt the third time I complained about my car's "morning trouble," as I called it. When I had described the symptoms to Bosko, he asked, "You smell gas when it happens, Colonel?"

"Yes, now that you mention it, I do. There's quite a strong gasoline odor."

He nodded. "You see, Colonel, what happens is that your engine is drawin' in the gas from the carb, then pukin' it back up at you. You know, like it was sick."

So my American had a queasy stomach mornings. It was a remarkable idea, but on the other hand one of the very few things I've ever been told by a mechanic that made sense. Naturally I asked Bosko what we could do about it.

"There's a few things, but really they won't any of them help much. The best thing is just live with it. It'll go away by itself in a while. Only I got something serious to tell you, Colonel. You want to come in my office?"

Mystified, I followed him into the cluttered little room adjoining the garage portion of the station and seated myself in a chair whose bottom was dropping out. To be truthful, I couldn't really imagine what he could have to tell me since he hadn't so much as raised the hood to look at my engine; so I waited with equanimity for him to speak. "Colonel," he said, "you got a bun in the oven—you know what I mean? Your car does, that is. She's *that way*."

I laughed, of course.

"You don't believe me? Well, it's the truth. See, what we got here," he lowered his voice, "is kinda what you would call a stud service. An' when you told Bubber you wanted her *serviced*, you never havin' come here before, that's what he thought you meant. So he, uh," Bosko jerked his head significantly toward the sleek, black Aston Martin in the garage, "he, you know, he *serviced* it. I was hopin' it wouldn't take. Lots of times it don't."

"This is ridiculous. Cars don't breed."

Bosko waggled his head at me. "That's what they'd like you to think in Detroit. But if you'd ever lived around there and talked to any of the union men, those guys would tell you how every year they make more and more cars with less and less guys comin' through the gate."

"That's because of automation," I told him. "Better methods."

"Sure!" He leveled a dirty finger at me. "Better methods is right. An' what's the best method of all, huh? Ain't it the way the farmer does? Sure there's lots of cars put together the old-fashioned way early in the year when they got to get their breedin' stock, but after that—well, I'm here to tell you, Colonel, they don't hire all them engineers up there for nothing. Bionics, they call it. Makin' a machine act like it was a' animal."

"Why doesn't everybody . . ."

He shushed me, finger to lips. " 'Cause they don't like it, that's why. There's a hell of a big license needed to do it legal, and even if you're willin' to put up the bread, you don't get one unless you're one of the big boys. That's why I try to keep my little operation here quiet. Besides, they got a way of makin' sure most people *can't*."

"What do you mean?"

"You know anything about horses? You know what a gelding is?"

I admit I was shocked, though that may sound foolish. I said, "You mean they . . . ?"

"Sure." Bosko made a scissors gesture with his arms, snapping them like a giant shears. "Ain't you ever noticed how they make all these cars with real hairy names, but when you get 'em out on the road, they ain't really got anything? Geldings."

"Do you think . . ." I looked (delicately, I hope) toward my American, "it could be repaired? What they call an illegal operation?"

Bosko spread his hands. "What for? Listen, Colonel, it would just cost you a lot of bread, and that little car of yours might never recover. Ain't it come through to you yet that if you just let nature take her course for a while yet, you're goin' to have yourself a new car for nothing?"

I took Bosko's advice. I should not have; it was the first time in my life I have ever connived at anything against the law; but the idea of having a second car to give my wife attracted me, and I must admit I was fascinated as well. I dare say that in time Bosko must have regretted having persuaded me; I pestered him with questions, and once even, by a little genteel blackmail, forced him to allow me to witness the Aston Martin in action.

For all its sleek good finish it was a remarkably unprepossessing car, with something freakish about it. Bosko told me it had been specially built for use on some British television program now defunct. I suppose the producers had wanted to project the most masculine possible image, and it was for this reason that it had been left reproductively intact—to fall, eventually, into Bosko's hands. When Bubber started the engine it made a sound such as I have never heard from any car in my life, a sort of lustful snarl.

The Aston Martin's bride for the night was a small and rather elderly Volks squareback, belonging I suppose to some poor man who could not afford to buy a new car through legal channels, or perhaps hoped to turn a small profit on his family's fecundity. I must say I felt rather sorry for her, forced to submit to a beast like the Aston Martin. In action all its appearance of feline grace proved a fraud; it experienced the same difficulties a swine breeder might expect with a huge champion boar, and had to be helped by Bosko with ramps and jacks while Bubber fought the controls.

The months of my American's time passed. Her gasoline consumption went up and up until I was getting barely eleven miles to the gallon. She acquired a swollen appearance as well, and became so deficient in endurance she could scarcely be forced up even a moderate hill, and overheated continually. When eight months had passed the plies on her tires separated, forming ugly welts in the sidewalls, but Bosko warned me not to replace them since the same problem would only occur again.

On the night of the delivery Bosko offered to allow me to observe, but I declined. Call it squeamishness, if you will. Late that night—very late—I walked past his station and stared from the sidewalk at the bright glow of a trouble light and the scuttling shadows within, but I felt no urge to let them know I was there. The next morning, before I had breakfast, Bosko was on the phone asking if I wanted to pick my cars up: "I'll drive your old one over if you'll give me a lift back." Then I knew that my American had come through the ordeal, and breathed somewhat more easily.

My first sight of her son was, I admit, something of a shock. It—I find it hard to call him *he*—is a deep, jungle green inherited from Heaven knows what remote ancestor, and his seats are covered in a long-napped sleazy stuff like imitation rabbit fur. I had expected—I don't know quite why—that he would be of some recognizable make: a Pontiac, or perhaps a Ford, since they are made in both England and America. He is nothing of the sort, of course, and I realize now that those *marques* with which we are familiar must be carefully maintained purebred lines. As it is I have searched him everywhere for some sort of brand name that would allow me to describe the car to prospective purchasers, but beyond a sort of trademark that appears in several places (a shield with a band or stripe running from left to right) there is nothing. Where part numbers or serial numbers appear, they are often garbled or illegible, or do not match.

It was necessary to license him of course, and to do this it was necessary to have a title. Through Bosko I procured one from an unethical used-car dealer for thirty dollars. It describes the car as a '54 Chevrolet; I wish it were.

No dealer I have found will give me any sort of price for it, and so I have advertised it each Sunday for the past eight months in the largest paper in the city where I work, and also in a small, nationally circulated magazine specializing in collector's cars. There have been only two responses: one from a man who left as soon as he saw the car, the other from a boy of about seventeen who told me he would buy him as soon as he could find someone who would lend him the money. Had I been more alert I would have taken whatever he had, made over the spurious title to him, and trusted him for the rest; but at the time I was still hoping to find a bona fide buyer.

I have had to turn my American over to my wife since she refuses to drive the new car, and the several mechanical failures he has already suffered have been extremely inconvenient. Parts in the conventional sense are nonexistent. Either alterations must be made which will allow the corresponding part from some known make to be used, or the part must be made by a job shop. This, I find, is one of the penalties of our —as I thought—unique automotive miscegenation; but when, a few weeks ago, I grew so discouraged I attempted to abandon the car, I discovered that someone else must have made the same crossing. When the police forced me to come and retrieve it, I found that the radiator, generator, and battery were missing.

ARMED FORCES DAY

THE BLUE MOUSE

"It's an awful thing you're doing," the old woman said, "an awful, terrible thing. How old are you, anyway? Have another cookie." Her voice was as thin as the wind that tossed her gray hair against the background of winter-gray hills.

"Eighteen." Lonnie accepted the cookie, with one in his mouth already and another in his throat. They were large, and the sour milk and brown sugar the old woman had used had given them a scratchy and persistent crumb. A big raisin occupied the center of each.

"You're but a little lad and not responsible," the old woman said, "but if you'd seen the half of all I have, you'd not be here killin' our boys."

Lonnie, whose two meters plus towered over her, nodded—knowing she would not listen if he tried to defend the Peace Force. A sip of the warm, weak tea she had given him softened cookies number one and two enough for him to swallow number three.

"And where would you be from?"

He gave her the name of his home city. From her blank expression he knew she had never heard of it. She said, "What country was it, I meant."

The crumbs clung to the front of his blue fatigue shirt, and he tried to brush them off. "Sector ten," he said.

She helped him absently, smoothing the wrinkled twill with age-crooked fingers. "And where is that?"

"South of nine, close to the Great Lakes. If you don't want us here putting down the unrest—" (it was always called "the unrest" in orientation lectures, and he felt an obligation, here alone by the old woman's tumbledown stone cottage, to represent the official view) "—why are you giving me the cookies and tea?"

"It said to do it on the tel. Our free channel. It says we does our part by tellin' you it's wrong that you should come here killin'. And it's easy enough to do—you're nice enough lads, the ones I've talked with." The wind was rising, and she took her free hand, the one not holding the blue-rimmed plate of cookies, away from his shirt to keep her skirt in place.

Lonnie said, "I don't kill anyone. I'm a Tech, not a Marksman."

"It's the same. You're carrying the bullets that will take the lives of boys here."

"It's not ammunition." He glanced toward the road, where his loaded truck stood with its launcher slanted at the sky. "Mostly it's winter clothes."

"It's the same," the old woman said stubbornly. (Up there the wild geese were calling, lost in the gray clouds. There was a feeling of rain.) "Never mind. You but think on it that our lads are only wanting to be free of the foreign law, and the greasy dark foreigners followin' your blue rag half 'round the world to suck our blood. Think on it, if you should find such a thing as a conscience about you."

Later, as Lonnie jolted along in the truck, the rain came. A sensor near the windshield detected it and sprayed out a detergent, transforming the drops into a cleansing film more optically flat and transparent than the polycarbonate windshield itself. Lonnie set the autodriver for MUD and switched it in. Occasionally, the insurgents cut the guide cables or pulled a slack section into a bog, but at such low speed he would be able to regain control if necessary, and he wanted to send a letter. He got out his Hallmark Voisriit.

"Dear Mother," he said. The feedback screen, showing the picture which on his mother's own viewer would accompany his voice, displayed a cartooned soldier ignoring exploding shells; the balloon over his head held the ezspeek words, "*Hii thair,*" and an exclamation point.

"October 15th. Dear Mother. I don't have a great deal to say, but I've some time on my hands right now and I wanted to tell you everything's all right here and really very quiet. It's damp and cold, but our tents are warm and dry. You asked if I still believed in what we're supposed to be doing. Yes I do, but I see it more clearly. It's not only whether or not we're going to let the world slip backward into nationalism and war, but—"

The truck topped a hill and he saw the wet plastic of the battalion tents. He had not realized there was so short a distance yet to go; sighing, he touched the *eeraas* button and slipped the Voisriit back into its leatheroid envelope, then took over from the autodriver.

The road dove between high tangles of wire, and the camp unfolded around him. The battalion supply tents, where he was going, were at the end of the road. Beyond them linked to the road by a rutted track, lay the tank park with its three hunchbacked hard-shell tanks and the combat cars. The Battalion Headquarters tents and the SAM-guarded helicopter pad flanked the road; and from it the company streets of the four Marksman companies branched at measured intervals, with that of his own Headquarters Company and the motor pool parking area further on.

Surrounding everything was the network of Marksman trenches and strong points, with computer-directed guns and launchers thrust forward to enfilade attackers, raking their advance from the side if they tried to overrun the trenches. Lonnie recalled that when he had first been assigned here he had thought these, with the wire and the mine fields, were impregnable. He had soon been enlightened by more experienced men. Leaving aside the chemical, viral, and nuclear weapons neither side dared use, there remained the ancient arithmetic of men. There were, all in all, blue-uniformed Techs and green-shirted Marksmen, a thousand United Nations soldiers defending this small outpost of the Peace Force. In the hills surrounding it, and in villages where they waited the order to take up arms, were perhaps fifty thousand insurgents.

He had helped the supply staff unload his truck and was about to see if it were still too early to get supper at the mess hall, when one of the supply clerks said casually, "Captain Koppel wants to see you." Koppel was Battalion Intelligence Officer.

"What for?"

"He didn't say. Just to send you over."

Lonnie nodded and put on his poncho, though he was already soaked from unloading without it. Rain slanted into his eyes as he left the tent.

A Marksman in green, matte-finished armor, with weary eyes like caves, moved cautiously aside for him. Techs, who did not fight, who according to the psychological tests administered at induction, *would not* fight, sometimes had been known to trip or strike a passing Marksman from behind. Marksmen were usually almost too exhausted to protest, and more often than might be expected were physically small. Lonnie himself—once (he told himself)—only once . . .

There had been five of them, friends from camp, full of beer and bravery after completing the "tough" training course. They had surprised two Marksmen on the gravel parking lot of a roadside joint with savage, wide-swung head punches until—

He blinked the image away, turned into the HQ tent, and saluted. "Tech Specialist Third Leonard P. Daws, sir."

"At ease, Daws." Captain Koppel was a blue-uniformed Tech like himself despite his rank, a man heavily forty with an intelligent, unworldly face that seemed designed for a clergyman. "You've just returned from Corps?"

"From Corps supply dump, sir."

"The road was clear?"

"Yes, sir."

"You saw no signs of the enemy?"

"No, sir. Only an old woman."

"Did you converse with her?"

Lonnie paused. "Only for a few minutes, sir. The orientation lectures always say that we're to behave well toward the civilian population and be friendly, so I thought it couldn't do much harm, sir."

The captain nodded. "Who initiated the contact, you or she?"

"I guess she did, sir. She has a cottage on the road about twenty kilometers up, and when she heard my truck coming she came out with a plate of cookies and some tea, so I stopped."

"I see. Go on."

"Well, that's about all there is to it, sir."

"Oh, come now. You're an intelligent young man, Daws—didn't somebody tell me you had some college?"

"A semester, sir, before I was inducted. Biology."

"Then you should be able to guess the sort of thing I want to know. Did this old lady of yours favor their side or ours? Did she pump you about anything? Did she try to subvert you?"

"Theirs, sir. I wouldn't say she really questioned me, but she more or less said I had ammunition in the truck, and I told her I didn't. Also, she asked what country I was from, and I told her Ten."

The captain pursed his lips. "I don't want you to get the wrong impression of our situation, Daws. It's not at all serious, and there's no question of our ability to maintain the integrity of our perimeter no matter what's thrown at us, but the guide cable has been cut. Did you know that?"

"No, sir. I came in on it for the last five kilometers or so and it seemed okay then."

"It was severed on the far side of the river, just over the bridge—we think. How long have you been in camp?"

"About an hour, sir. I helped unload before I came here."

"You should have come at once."

Lonnie stood a little straighter. The Supply sergeant and his men, he knew, had waited until he had helped unload before passing on Koppel's message. "I didn't think it was urgent, sir," he said.

"We sent out a repair crew and they ambushed them. Some of them surrendered and they killed them, too, Techs as well as Marksmen. You didn't see anything?"

"No, sir."

"Listen, Daws," the captain stood up, and walking around his desk put a hand on Lonnie's shoulder. "You have a gun mounted on that truck of yours, don't you?"

"An eighteen millimeter launcher, sir. The autodriver controls it once I turn it on. I would have used it if I'd seen anything, sir."

"I hope you would. Let me tell you something, Daws. If we win this fight it's going to be because we Techs won it, and if we lose it's going to be us who lost it."

He seemed to be waiting for an answer, so Lonnie said, "Yes, sir."

"Some of us think that because we're technical specialists, and our special skills make us too valuable to be risked in combat, we're too good to activate weapons when the need arises. I hope you know better."

"Sir—"

"Yes?"

"It isn't really that."

Koppel frowned. "Isn't really what?"

"All that about special skills. I mean, driving a truck—a truck that will mostly drive itself. It's because the tests showed they couldn't trust us in a fight but the public would be angry if we were deferred for that. It's not more of us they need, it's more of them."

"Daws, I think you ought to have a talk with the chaplain."

"You know it's true, sir. They only say all that so we won't resent the Marksmen so much, and even with all the propaganda, sometimes Supply won't give out things they have to Marksmen when they think they can get away with it. And last month when that mechanic in the motor pool got his foot mashed when the jack slipped, the medics let a Marksman bleed to death while they treated him."

"I am going to ask you again to talk to the chaplain, Daws. In fact, I'm going to order it. Sometime during the next three days. He'll tell me when you've come."

"Yes, sir."

"The injustices you spoke of *are* lamentable—if they actually occurred, which I doubt. But the motivation for them was the quite natural superiority felt by men who have difficulty in taking human life. The psychs know what they're doing, Daws."

"It isn't that either, sir." Something in Lonnie's throat was warning him to stop, but it was crushed by the memory of unconscious men sprawled on white gravel. "We can kill. We could kick a helpless man to death. What we can't do—"

"That will be enough! You're trying for a psycho discharge, aren't you, Daws? Well, you won't get it from me. You're dismissed!"

Lonnie saluted, waited a moment more with the vague feeling that Koppel might have something further to say, then made an about-face and left the tent.

It was raining hard now. A dark figure carrying more than the usual quantity of clattering mess gear was waiting under the eaves of the Aid tent. Brewer, of course. As Lonnie stepped into the rain he came forward, the wind whipping his poncho. "Ready for chow?"

Lonnie accepted his own mess gear.

"You got a chewing out in there, huh?"

"Could you hear it?"

"It shows on your face, Lon. Don't feel bad, this weather has everybody on edge—no air."

Lonnie stared at him, feeling stupid.

"No chopper strikes because they're afraid they might hit us instead. It's got all the crumby Markies so jumpy they're shooting at each other."

When they were inside the mess tent Lonnie asked, "You think anything will happen? Maybe this is what they've been waiting for."

Brewer shook his head, accepting a turkey leg from a KP server. Marksmen ate first, but the cooks, Techs themselves, held back the best pieces and biggest portions.

"There's a lot more of them out there than there are of us," Lonnie said.

Brewer snorted. "We could get reinforcements from Corps in six hours. Maybe less—four hours."

To himself Lonnie wondered.

It began at two minutes after midnight. Lonnie knew, because when he hit the dirt beside his cot, he struck his watch against one of the legs and the humming little fork inside went silent forever, leaving the hands upraised like a stout man and a thin one clutching each other for reassurance.

It began with rockets and big mortars, each detonation shaking the wet ground and lighting the camp with its flash, even through the rain. Shouting platoons of Marksmen splashed down the Headquarters Company street outside his tent on their way to their positions, and somewhere someone was screaming.

Then their own radar-eyed, computer-directed artillery had ranged the incoming rounds and begun to fire back. At almost the same moment, Lonnie heard the perimeter multilaunchers go into action, and flares burst overhead sending stark blue light through every crevice in the tent. He rolled under one hanging side curtain and sprinted for a sandbagged dugout nearby. It was dark and half full of water and entirely full of men, but he wedged in somehow.

No one spoke. As each rocket came whistling down he closed his eyes and, knowing how absurd it was, tensed. The blackness, the shrieking missiles and the explosions, the hip-high water and the ragged breathing of the men pressed against him seemed to endure for hours.

Abruptly, the darkness changed to dancing yellow light in which he could see the drawn faces around him. Someone with a flashlight stood in the doorway, and a voice from the back of the dugout yelled, "Turn that thing off."

Instead of obeying, the man with the light snapped, "Everybody outside. We need you at the tank park."

No one moved.

A second man appeared, and the first flicked his light on him long enough to show that he was holding an automatic rifle. "Come out," the first man said. "In a minute we're going to spray the place."

As they filed out a rocket struck somewhere to their left, and men threw themselves down in the mud in front of the dugout. Lonnie and several others did not, standing numbly erect in the firework glare of the flares while the soft earth trembled and shrapnel tore at the tents. The wind had died and the rain fell straight down, dripping from the rims of their helmets, washing the tops of their boots whenever they stood still.

When everyone was out—everyone, at least, who would obey the order to come out—the automatic rifleman fired a long burst through the doorway. Then, led by the man with the flashlight, with the automatic rifleman bringing up the rear, they started off.

The tank park had been a victim of its own design. Sheltered from surprise rockets or mortar strikes in a branch of the central valley, its one exit had been further narrowed by spider wire intended to defend it from infiltrating raiders. Now this exit was blocked by a combat car belly-deep in mud. Half a dozen men were already working to free it when they came up; the man with the flashlight, now seen to be a green-uniformed lieutenant not much older than Lonnie himself, waved his light toward a jumbled pile of tools. "Get it out. We have to bring the tanks into action or we don't have a chance. When you get it going and we can get them out, you can go back to your hole."

They worked frantically. A minim-dozer, floating on whining fans with only its thrust screws engaging the mud, leveled ruts and swept away the worst of the liquescent ooze while they drove in the suction probes of enthalpy pumps to freeze the stuff enough to give it traction. They shoved exploded aluminum mats under the combat car's churning triangular wheel assemblies and labored to lighten it by unbolting its foam-backed ceramic armor.

With a cassette of ammunition someone had flung him from the turret hatch, Lonnie stumbled through the mud—then, suddenly, lay facedown in it half deaf, a roaring in his ears and the cassette gone. He shook his head to clear it, opening and closing his mouth; the side of his face stung as though burned.

When he stood up he found his clothing had been ripped and scorched. Around him other survivors were rising as well; at their feet those who had not lived lay—some dismembered, some apparently untouched. A crater a meter deep and three meters wide gaped between the mired combat car and his own position, showing where the rocket had struck.

"Armor piercing," someone near him said. He looked around and recognized the lieutenant who had driven them from the dugout. "Armor piercing," the officer repeated half to himself. "Or it would have gone off higher up and gotten us all."

"Yes," Lonnie said.

The lieutenant looked around, noticing him. For a moment he seemed about to answer, but he shouted an order instead, to Lonnie and all the others.

Several obeyed, redoubling their efforts to free the combat car. Several merely stood staring. Two tried to help the wounded, and some others moved away from the car, the crater, and the shouting officer—moved away as inconspicuously as they could, a few walking backward, all looking for shadowed spots even darker than the rain-drenched darkness about the car.

The automatic rifleman saw one group and ran yelling toward them. They halted. Still running, the rifleman circled them until he barred their way, then—too quickly for Lonnie to see what had happened—he was down and the men he had tried to stop were jumping and stumbling across him, one carrying his rifle. The officer with the flashlight drew a pistol and fired, the shots coming so close together they sounded almost like a burst from an automatic weapon.

Lonnie was running and telling himself as he ran that it was dangerous to run, that the lieutenant with the flashlight would shoot him in the back. But by then it was too late; the tank park was somewhere behind him, and the ground beneath his pounding feet was no longer merely mud but a nightmare landscape of ditches and holes from which timbers and steel posts protruded.

Something pulled sharply and insistently at his wreck of a shirt. He stopped, turned around. There was no one there.

Something very swift passed close to his head. Stupidly, awkwardly, he got down. First to hands and knees, then prone, thinking as he did of a picnic at which he remembered lying belly-down in young grass. The thing, the bullet, had made an unvocalizable noise that was not a Voisriit BANG at all, but a sound suggesting a whip cracked very close to his ear. He thought of this as he lay in the oozing mud, and it came to him that the brief sound had in fact been hours of exposition packed into a millisecond; that it had been this compression that had made its strange rustle. It had told of Death, and he knew that he had heard and that he, who had been frightened merely by the thought of pain before—because he did not know Death—had understood. It had spoken, and the word spoken had been *never*. Never again, anything. Never again, even the luxury of being afraid. Never. Nothing.

He had seen his body, his own body, as it lay bloated and stinking; and much more . . .

His stomach was cold. He recalled being told of a fellow student at the university who had killed himself by swallowing dry ice, and thought it must have felt like that; but no, that would be flatulent as well, and he did not feel flatulent. Something splattered two meters in front, throwing up mud. The taste of brass was in his mouth.

A ditch—a trench he now realized—yawned not far to his right; he foundered toward it and rolled in.

He could stand now if he stooped. His hands touched the trench wall and felt the bulging burlap of sandbags, dripping wet. He wondered if the man who had shot at him (he was not certain whether it had been an insurgent or a Marksman) would throw a grenade. He would not see it in the darkness, he knew. He took a step forward and put his foot upon a man's hand. It jerked away and someone groaned, the motion and sound giving the impression—gone in an instant—that he had stepped on a rabbit or a rat. He crouched and heard the bubbling of a chest wound as the man tried to breathe. His fingers groped for the wound but found instead the thick straps of a sort of harness.

"Here," the wounded man whispered. "Here."

"In a minute," Lonnie said. "Let me get this off you." Then, mostly because he found talking somehow relieved his fear, "What is it anyway?"

"Fl . . . flame . . ." A whisper.

"Never mind." The straps were held by a central buckle. With it loosed, he could slide them away from the man's chest. His aid kit contained a self-adhesive dressing, and when he had located the wound he spread it in place. The bubbling stopped and he could hear the wounded man draw deep, choking breaths. "I'll get you to the aid station if I can," Lonnie said.

Weakly the man asked, "You're not one of our lads?"

"I guess not. U.N." He picked the man up, then crouched again as a flight of flechettes whizzed overhead.

"We have you, you know," the man said.

"What?" The flechettes, steel arrows like the darts men played with in bars here, had filled his mind.

"We have you. There's thousands more of ours coming, and my own lot almost did for you by ourselves a bit ago. Too many of yours won't fight."

Lonnie said, "The ratio's about the same on both sides—we know who ours are, that's all." He was answering with only a part of his thought, the rest concentrated on a new sound, a sound from the direction from which the flechettes had come. It was a scuffing and a breathing, the clinking of a hundred buckles and buttons against the fiberglass stocks of weapons, the husky voices of automatic rifle bolts as nervous men checked their loading by touch, then checked again. The squish of a thousand boots in mud.

"You think they can do that? Tell one lad has it and another doesn't?" The wounded man sounded genuinely curious, but there was a touch of scorn in his voice.

"Well, they examine the person and go by probabilities. They're very thorough."

"They did it to you?"

Lonnie nodded, but he was not thinking of the examination, the cold, long-wired sensors gummed to his skin. He said, "I was worrying about my mice. All the time I was answering the questions and looking at the holograph projections and everything, it was kind of in the back of my mind—you know, whether my mother would take care of them right while I was gone."

"Mice?" the wounded man asked, and then, "Here now, what're you doin'?"

"Fancy mice, with little rosettes of fur on them, and waltzing mice. I bred them." He had put the wounded man down and was running his fingers over the mechanism of the flamer the man had carried. "I remembered them just now, and I haven't thought about them for months. Now I think maybe I'd like to take them up again, if I get back. You know a lot of progress in medicine has come from studying the genetics of mice." The flamer seemed simple: two valves already opened, tubes leading to a sort of gun like the nozzle of a gasoline pump.

"Dirty job, I should think, cleaning up after them."

Lonnie said, "If you don't clean their cages, they die." Propping the flamer against the dripping wall of the trench, he backed into the harness and pulled the straps over his shoulders.

The blade of the wounded man's knife had been blackened, but the ground edge flashed in the faint light, and Lonnie threw up his arm in time to block the blow and wrench the knife from the man's weak fingers. "If you do something like that again," he said softly, "I'm going to pull off that patch I put on your chest."

After that he stood, his eyes just higher than the top of the trench, ignoring the man. He did not have to wait long.

The insurgents came raggedly but by the hundreds, firing as they advanced. He raised himself to his full height, glancing for some reason at his watch as he straightened up. The hands still stood at two minutes past midnight, unmoving, and that he felt must be correct. It was a new day.

His gouts of orange flame, hot as molten steel, held the straggling lines back until the three tanks came; and when they did he vaulted out of the trench and jogged forward with them, keeping twenty meters ahead until the canisters on his back were as empty and light as cardboard.

HOW I LOST THE SECOND WORLD WAR AND HELPED TURN BACK THE GERMAN INVASION

1 April, 1938

Dear Editor:

As a subscriber of some years standing—ever since taking up residence in Britain, in point of fact—I have often noted with pleasure that in addition to dealing with the details of the various *All New and Logical, Original Games* designed by your readers, you have sometimes welcomed to your columns vignettes of city and rural life, and especially those having to do with games. Thus I hope that an account of a gamesing adventure which lately befell me, and which enabled me to rub elbows (as it were) not only with Mr. W. L. S. Churchill—the man who, as you will doubtless know, was dismissed from the position of First Lord of the Admiralty during the Great War for his sponsorship of the ill-fated Dardanelles Expedition, and is thus a person of particular interest to all those of us who (like myself) are concerned with Military Boardgames—but also with no less a celebrity than the present *Reichschancellor* of Germany, Herr Adolf Hitler.

All this, as you will already have guessed, took place in connection with the great Bath Exposition; but before I begin my account of the extraordinary events there (events observed—or so I flatter myself—by few from as advantageous a position as was mine), I must explain, at least in generalities (for the details are exceedingly complex) the game of *World War,* as conceived by my friend Lansbury and myself. Like many others we employ a large world map as our board; we have found it convenient to mount this with wallpaper paste upon a sheet of deal four feet by six, and to shellac the surface; laid flat upon a commodious table in my study this serves us admirably. The nations siding with each combatant are determined by the casting of lots; and naval, land, and air units of all sorts are represented symbolically by tacks with heads of various colors; but in determining the *nature* of these units we have introduced a new principle—one not found, or so we believe, in any other game. It is that either contestant may at any time propose a new form of ship, firearm, or other weapon; if he shall urge its probability (not necessarily its utility, please note—if it prove not useful the loss is his only) with sufficient force to convince his opponent, he is allowed to convert such of his units as he desires to the new mode, and to have the exclusive use of it for three moves, after which his opponent may convert as well if he so chooses. Thus a player of *World War*, as we conceive it, must excel not only in the strategic faculty, but in inventive and argumentative facility as well.

As it happened, Lansbury and I had spent most of the winter now past in setting up the game and settling the rules for the movement of units. Both of us have had considerable experience with games of this sort, and knowing the confusion and ill feeling often bred by a rulebook treating inadequately of (what may once have appeared to be) obscure contingencies, we wrote ours with great thoroughness. On February 17 (Lansbury and I caucus weekly) we held the drawing; it allotted Germany, Italy, Austria, Bulgaria, and Japan to me, Britain, France, China, and the Low Countries to Lansbury. I confess that these alignments appear improbable—the literal-minded man might well object that Japan and Italy, having sided with Britain in the Great War, would be unlikely to change their coats in a second conflict. But a close scrutiny of history will reveal even less probable reversals (as when France, during the sixteenth century, sided with Turkey in what has been called the Unholy Alliance), and Lansbury and I decided to abide by the luck of the draw. On the twenty-fourth we were to make our first moves.

On the twentieth, as it happened, I was pondering my strategy when, paging casually through the *Guardian,* my eye was drawn to an announcement of the opening of the Exposition; and it at once occurred to me that among the representatives of the many nations exhibiting I might find someone whose ideas would be of value to me. In any event I had nothing better to do, and so—little knowing that I was to become a witness to history—I thrust a small memorandum book in my pocket and I was off to the fair!

I suppose I need not describe the spacious grounds to the readers of this magazine. Suffice it to say that they were, as everyone has heard, surrounded by an oval hippodrome nearly seven miles in length, and dominated by the Dirigible Tower that formed a most impressive part of the German exhibit, and by the vast silver bulk of the airship *Graf Spee*, which, having brought the chief functionary of the German Reich to Britain, now waited, a slave of the lamp of *Kultur* (save the Mark!) to bear him away again. This was, in fact, the very day that Reichschancellor Hitler—for whom the Exposition itself had opened early—was to unveil the "People's Car" exhibit. Banners stretched from poles and even across the main entry carried such legends as:

WHICH PEOPLE SHOULD HAVE A "PEOPLE'S CAR"
?????
THE ENGLISH PEOPLE!!

and

GERMAN CRAFTSMANSHIP
BRITISH LOVE OF FINE MACHINES

and even

IN SPIRIT THEY ARE AS BRITISH
AS THE ROYAL FAMILY.

Recollecting that Germany was the most powerful of the nations that had fallen to my lot in our game, I made for the German exhibit.

There the crowd grew dense; there was a holiday atmosphere, but within it a note of sober calculation—one heard workingmen discussing the mechanical merits (real and supposed) of the German machines, and their extreme cheapness and the interest-free loans available from the *Reichshauptkasse*. Vendors sold pretzels, *Lebkuchen*, and Bavarian creams in paper cups, shouting their wares in raucous Cockney voices. Around the great showroom where, within the hour, the Reichschancellor himself was to begin the "People's Car's" invasion of Britain by demonstrating the vehicle to a chosen circle of celebrities, the crowd was now ten deep, though the building (as I learned subsequently) had long been full, and no more spectators were being admitted.

The Germans did not have the field entirely to themselves, however. Dodging through the crowd were driverless model cars only slightly smaller (or at least so it seemed) than the German "People's Cars." These "toys," if I may so style something so elaborate and yet inherently frivolous, flew the rising-sun banner of the Japanese Empire from their aerials, and recited through speakers, in ceremonious hisses, the virtues of that industrious nation's produce, particularly the gramophones, wirelesses, and so on, employing those recently invented wonders, "transistors."

Like others, I spent a few minutes sightseeing—or rather, as I should say, craning myself upon my toes in an attempt to sightsee. But my business was no more with the "People's Car" and the German Reichschancellor than with the Japanese marionette motorcar, and I soon turned my attention to searching for someone who might aid me in the coming struggle with Lansbury. Here I was fortunate indeed, for I had no sooner looked around than I beheld a portly man in the uniform of an officer of the *Flugzeugmeisterei* buying a handful of Germanic confections from a hawker. I crossed to him at once, bowed, and after apologizing for having ventured to address him without an introduction, made bold to congratulate him upon the great airship floating above us.

"Ah!" he said. "You like dot fat sailor up there? Vell, he iss a fine ship, und no mistake." He puffed himself up in the good-natured German way as he said this, and popped a sweet into his mouth, and I could see that he was pleased. I was about to ask him if he had ever given any consideration to the military aspects of aviation, when I noticed the decorations on his uniform jacket; seeing the direction of my gaze he asked, "You know vat dose are?"

"I certainly do," I replied. "I was never in combat myself, but I would have given anything to have been a flyer. I was about to ask you, Herr—"

"Goering."

"Herr Goering, how you feel the employment of aircraft would differ if—I realize this may sound absurd—the Great War were to take place now."

I saw from a certain light in his eyes that I had found a kindred soul. "Dot iss a good question," he said, and for a moment he stood staring at me, looking for all the world like a Dutch schoolmaster about to give his star pupil's inquiry the deep consideration it deserved. "Und I vill tell you dis—vat ve had den vas nothing. Kites ve had, vith guns. If vor vas to come again now . . ." He paused.

"It is unthinkable, of course."

"*Ja*. Today *der Vaterland*, dot could not conquer Europe vith bayonets in dot vor, conquers all der vorld vith money und our liddle cars. Vith those things our leader has brought down die enemies of der party, und all der industry of Poland, of Austria, iss ours. Der people, they say, 'Our company, our bank.' But die shares are in Berlin."

I knew all this, of course, as every well-informed person does; and I was about to steer the conversation back toward new military techniques, but it was unnecessary. "But you," he said, his mood suddenly lightening, "und I, vot do ve care? Dot iss for der financial people. Do you know vat I" (he thumped himself on the chest) "vould do ven the vor comes? I would build *Stutzkampfbombers.*"

"Stutzkampfbombers?"

"Each to carry vun bomb! Only vun, but a big vun. Fast planes—" He stooped and made a diving motion with his right hand, at the last moment "pulling out" and releasing a Bavarian cream in such a way that it struck my shoe. "Fast planes. I vould put my tanks—you know tanks?"

I nodded and said, "A little."

"—in columns. The Stutzkampfbombers ahead of the tanks, the storm troops behind. Fast tanks too—not so much armor, but fast, vith big guns."

"Brilliant," I said. "A lightning war."

"Listen, mine friend. I must go und vait upon our *Führer,* but there iss somevun here you should meet. You like tanks—this man iss their father—he vas in your Navy in der vor, und ven der army vould not do it he did it from der Navy, und they told everybody they vas building vater tanks. You use dot silly name yet, and ven you stand on der outside talk about decks because uf him. He iss in there—" He jerked a finger at the huge pavilion where the Reichschancellor was shortly to demonstrate the "People's Car" to a delighted British public.

I told him I could not possibly get in there—the place was packed already, and the crowd twenty deep outside now.

"You vatch. Hermann vill get you in. You come vith me, und look like you might be from der newspaper."

Docilely I followed the big, blond German as he bulled his way—as much by his bulk and loud voice as by his imposing uniform—through the crowd. At the door the guard (in *Lederhosen*) saluted him and made no effort to prevent my entering at all.

In a moment I found myself in an immense hall, the work of the same Germanic engineering genius that had recently stunned the world with the *Autobahn.* A vaulted metallic ceiling as bright as a mirror reflected with lustrous distortion every detail below. In it one saw the tiled floor, and the tiles, each nearly a foot on a side, formed an enormous image of the small car that had made German industry preeminent over half the world. By an artistry hardly less impressive than the wealth and power which had caused this great building to be erected on the exposition grounds in a matter of weeks, the face of the driver of this car could be seen through the windshield—not plainly, but dimly, as one might actually see the features of a driver about to run down the observer; it was, of course, the face of Herr Hitler.

At one side of this building, on a dais, sat the "customers," those carefully selected social and political notables whose good fortune it would be to have the "People's Car" demonstrated personally to them by no less a person than the German nation's leader. To the right of this, upon a much lower dais, sat the representatives of the press, identifiable by their cameras and notepads, and their jaunty, sometimes slightly shabby, clothing. It was toward this group that Herr Goering boldly conducted me, and I soon identified (I believe I might truthfully say, "before we were halfway there") the man he had mentioned when we were outside.

He sat in the last row, and somehow seemed to sit higher than the rest; his chin rested upon his hands, which in turn rested upon the handle of a stick. His remarkable face, broad and rubicund, seemed to suggest both the infant and the bulldog. One sensed here an innocence, an unspoiled delight in life, coupled with that courage to which surrender is not, in the ordinary conversational sense "unthinkable," but is actually never thought. His clothes were expensive and worn, so that I would have thought him a valet save that they fit him perfectly, and that something about him forbade his ever having been anyone's servant save, perhaps, the King's.

"Herr Churchill," said Goering, "I have brought you a friend."

His head lifted from his stick and he regarded me with keen blue eyes. "Yours," he asked, "or mine?"

"He iss big enough to share," Goering answered easily. "But for now I leave him vith you."

The man on Churchill's left moved to one side and I sat down.

"You are neither a journalist nor a panderer," Churchill rumbled. "Not a journalist because I know them all, and the panderers all seem to know me—or say they do. But since I have never known that man to like anyone who wasn't one of the second or be civil to anyone except one of the first, I am forced to ask how the devil you did it."

I began to describe our game, but I was interrupted after five minutes or so by the man sitting in front of me, who without looking around nudged me with his elbow and said, "Here he comes."

The Reichschancellor had entered the building, and, between rows of *Sturmsachbearbeiter* (as the elite sales force was known), was walking stiffly and briskly toward the center of the room; from a balcony fifty feet above our heads a band launched into "Deutschland, Deutschland über Alles" with enough verve to bring the place down, while an American announcer near me screamed to his compatriots on the far side of the Atlantic that Herr Hitler was *here*, that he was even now, with commendable German punctuality, nearing the place where he was supposed to be.

Unexpectedly a thin, hooting sound cut through the music—and as it did the music halted as abruptly as though a bell jar had been dropped over the band. The hooting sounded again, and the crowd of onlookers began to part like tall grass through which an approaching animal, still unseen, was making its way. Another hoot, and the last of the crowd, the lucky persons who stood at the very edge of the cordoned-off area in which the Reichschancellor would make his demonstrations, parted, and we could see that the "animal" was a small, canary-yellow "People's Car," as the Reichschancellor approached the appointed spot from one side, so did this car approach him from the other, its slow, straight course and bright color combining to give the impression of a personality at once docile and pert, a pleasing and fundamentally obedient insouciance.

Directly in front of the notables' dais they met and halted. The "People's Car" sounded its horn again, three measured notes, and the Reichschancellor leaned forward, smiled (almost a charming smile because it was so unexpected), and patted its hood; the door opened and a blond German girl in a pretty peasant costume emerged; she was quite tall, yet—as everyone had seen—she had been comfortably seated in the car a moment before. She blew a kiss to the notables, curtsied to Hitler, and withdrew; the show proper was about to begin.

I will not bore the readers of this magazine by rehearsing yet again those details they have already read so often, not only in the society pages of the *Times* and other papers but in several national magazines as well. That Lady Woolberry was cheered for her skill in backing completely around the demonstration area is a fact already, perhaps, too well known. That it was discovered that Sir Henry Braithewaite could not drive only after he had taken the wheel is a fact hardly less famous. Suffice it to say that things went well for Germany; the notables were impressed, and the press and the crowd attentive. Little did anyone present realize that only after the last of the scheduled demonstrations was History herself to wrest the pen from Tattle. It was then that Herr Hitler, in one of the unexpected and indeed utterly unforseeable intuitive decisions for which he is famous (the order, issued from Berchtesgaden at a time when nothing of the kind was in the least expected, and, indeed, when every commentator believed that Germany would be content, at least for a time, to exploit the economic suzerainty she had already gained in Eastern Europe and elsewhere, by which every "People's Car" sold during May, June, and July would be equipped with Nordic Sidewalls at no extra cost comes at once to mind) having exhausted the numbers, if not the interest, of the nobility, turned toward the press dais and offered a demonstration to any journalist who would step forward.

The offer, as I have said, was made to the dais at large; but there was no doubt—there could be no doubt—for whom it was actually intended; those eyes, bright with fanatic energy and the pride natural to one who commands a mighty industrial organization, were locked upon a single placid countenance. That man rose and slowly, without speaking a word until he was face to face with the most powerful man in Europe, went to accept the challenge; I shall always remember the way in which he exhaled the smoke of his cigar as he said: "I believe this is an automobile?"

Herr Hitler nodded. "And you," he said, "I think once were of the high command of this country. You are Herr Churchill?"

Churchill nodded. "During the Great War," he said softly, "I had the honor—for a time—of filling a post in the Admiralty."

"During that time," said the German leader, "I myself was a corporal in the Kaiser's army. I would not have expected to find you working now at a newspaper."

"I was a journalist before I ever commenced politician," Churchill informed him calmly. "In fact, I covered the Boer War as a correspondent with a roving commission. Now I have returned to my old trade, as a politician out of office should."

"But you do not like my car?"

"I fear," Churchill said imperturbably, "that I am hopelessly prejudiced in favor of democratically produced products—at least, for the people of the democracies. We British manufacture a miniature car ourselves, you know—the Centurion."

"I have heard of it. You put water in it."

By this time the daises were empty. We were, to the last man and woman, and not only the journalists but the notables as well, clustered about the two (I say, intentionally, *two*, for greatness remains greatness even when stripped of power) giants. It was a nervous moment, and might have become more so had not the tension been broken by an unexpected interruption. Before Churchill could reply we heard the sibilant syllables of a Japanese voice, and one of the toy automobiles from Imperial Nippon came scooting across the floor, made as though to go under the yellow "People's Car" (which it was much too large to do), then veered to the left and vanished in the crowd of onlookers again. Whether it was madness that seized me at the sight of the speeding little car, or inspiration, I do not know—but I shouted, "Why not have a race?"

And Churchill, without an instant's delay, seconded me: "Yes, what's this we hear about this German machine? Don't you call it the race master?"

Hitler nodded. "Ja, it is very fast, for so small and economical a one. Yes, we will race with you, if you wish." It was said with what seemed to be perfect poise; but I noted, as I believe many others did, that he had nearly lapsed into German.

There was an excited murmur of comment at the Reichschancellor's reply, but Churchill silenced it by raising his cigar. "I have a thought," he said. "Our cars, after all, were not constructed for racing."

"You withdraw?" Hitler asked. He smiled, and at that moment I hated him.

"I was about to say," Churchill continued, "that vehicles of this size are intended as practical urban and suburban transportation. By which I mean for parking and driving in traffic—the gallant, unheralded effort by which the average Englishman earns his bread. I propose that upon the circular track which surrounds these exposition grounds we erect a course which will duplicate the actual driving conditions the British citizen faces—and that in the race the competing drivers be required to park every hundred yards or so. Half the course might duplicate central London's normal traffic snarl, while the other half simulated a residential neighborhood; I believe we might persuade the Japanese to supply us with the traffic using their driverless cars."

"Agreed!" Hitler said immediately. "But you have made all the rules. Now we Germans will make a rule. Driving is on the right."

"Here in Britain," Churchill said, "we drive on the left. Surely you know that."

"My Germans drive on the right and would be at a disadvantage driving on the left."

"Actually," Churchill said slowly, "I had given that some consideration before I spoke. Here is what I propose. One side of the course must, for verisimilitude, be lined with shops and parked lorries and charabancs. Let the other remain unencumbered for spectators. Your Germans, driving on the right, will go clockwise around the track, while the British drivers, on the left—"

"Go the other direction," Hitler exclaimed. "And in the middle—
ZERSTOREND GEWALT!"

"Traffic jam," Churchill interpreted coolly. "You are not afraid?"

The date was soon set—precisely a fortnight from the day upon
which the challenge was given and accepted. The Japanese consented
to supply the traffic with their drone cars, and the exposition officials to
cooperate in setting up an artificial street on the course surrounding the
grounds. I need not say that excitement was intense; an American firm,
Movietone News, sent not less than three crews to film the race, and
there were several British newsreel companies as well. On the appointed day excitement was at a fever pitch, and it was estimated that
more than three million pounds were laid with the bookmakers, who
were giving three to two on the Germans.

Since the regulations (written, largely, by Mr. Churchill) governing
the race and the operation of the unmanned Japanese cars were of importance, and will, in any event, be of interest to those concerned with
logical games, allow me to give them in summary before proceeding
further. It was explained to the Japanese operators that their task would
be to simulate actual traffic. Ten radio-controlled cars were assigned
(initially) to the "suburban" half of the course (the start for the Germans, the home stretch for the British team), while fifty were to operate in the "urban" section. Eighty parking positions were distributed
at random along the track, and the operators—who could see the entire
course from a vantage point on one of the observation decks of the dirigible tower—were instructed to park their cars in these for fifteen seconds, then move onto the course once more and proceed to the nearest
unoccupied position according to the following formula: if a parking
space were in the urban sector it was to be assigned a "distance value"
equal to its actual distance from the operator's machine, as determined
by counting the green "distance lines" with which the course was
striped at five-yard intervals—but if a parking position were in the suburban section of the track, its distance value was to be the counted distance plus two. Thus the "traffic" was biased—if I may use the expression—toward the urban sector. The participating German and English
drivers, unlike the Japanese, were required to park in every position
along the route, but could leave each as soon as they had entered it.
The spaces between positions were filled with immobile vehicles loaned
for the occasion by dealers and the public, and a number of London
concerns had erected mock buildings similar to stage flats along the
parking side of the course.

I am afraid I must tell you that I did not scruple to make use of my slight acquaintance with Mr. Churchill to gain admission to the paddock (as it were) on the day of the race. It was a brilliant day, one of those fine early spring days of which the west of England justly boasts, and I was feeling remarkably fit, and pleased with myself as well. The truth is that my game with Lansbury was going very satisfactorily indeed; putting into operation the suggestions I had received from Herr Goering I had overrun one of Lansbury's most powerful domains (France) in just four moves, and I felt that only stubbornness was preventing him from conceding the match. It will be understood then that when I beheld Mr. Churchill hurrying in my direction, his cigar clamped between his teeth and his old Homburg pulled almost about his ears, I gave him a broad smile.

He pulled up short, and said: "You're Goering's friend, aren't you—I see you've heard about our drivers."

I told him that I had heard nothing.

"I brought five drivers with me—racing chaps who had volunteered. But the Jerries have protested them. They said their own drivers were going to have to be Sturmsachbearbeiters and it wasn't sporting of us to run professionals against them; the exposition committee has sided with them, and now I'm going to have to get up a scratch team to drive for England, and those blasted SS are nearly professional caliber. I've got three men but I'm still one short even if I drive myself . . ."

For a moment we looked at one another; then I said: "I have never raced, but my friends all tell me I drive too fast, and I have survived a number of accidents; I hope you don't think my acquaintance with Herr Goering would tempt me to abandon fair play if I were enlisted for Britain."

"Of course not." Churchill puffed out his cheeks. "So you drive, do you? May I ask what marque?"

I told him I owned a Centurion, the model the British team would field; something in the way he looked at me and drew on his cigar told me that he knew I was lying—and that he approved.

I wish that my stumbling pen could do justice to the race itself, but it cannot. With four others—one of whom was Mr. Churchill—I waited with throbbing engine at the British starting line. Behind us, their backs toward us, were the five German Sturmsachbearbeiters in their "People's Cars." Ahead of us stretched a weirdly accurate imitation of a London street, in which the miniature Japanese cars already dodged back and forth in increasing disorder.

The starting gun sounded and every car shot forward; as I jockeyed my little vehicle into its first park I was acutely aware that the Germans, having entered at the suburban end of the course, would be making two or three positions to our one. Fenders crumpled and tempers flared, and I—all of us—drove and parked, drove and parked, until it seemed that we had been doing it forever. Sweat had long since wilted my shirt collar, and I could feel the blisters growing on my hands; then I saw, about thirty yards in front of me, a tree in a tub—and a flat painted to resemble, not a city shop, but a suburban villa. It dawned on me then—it was as though I had been handed a glass of cold champagne—that *we had not yet met the Germans.* We had not yet met them, and the demarcation was just ahead, the halfway point. I knew then that we had won.

Of the rest of the race, what is there to say? We were two hundred yards into the suburban sector before we saw the slanted muzzle of the first "People's Car." My own car finished dead last—among the British team—but fifth in the race when the field was taken as a whole, which is only to say that the British entries ran away with everything. We were lionized (even I); and when Reichschancellor Hitler himself ran out onto the course to berate one of his drivers and was knocked off his feet by a Japanese toy, there was simply no hope for the German "People's Car" in the English-speaking world. Individuals who had already taken dealerships filed suits to have their money returned, and the first ships carrying "People's Cars" to reach London (Hitler had ordered them to sail well in advance of the race, hoping to exploit the success he expected with such confidence) simply never unloaded. (I understand their cargo was later sold cheaply in Morocco.)

All this, I realize, is already well known to the public; but I believe I am in a position to add a postscript which will be of special interest to those whose hobby is games.

I had, as I have mentioned, explained the game Lansbury and I had developed to Mr. Churchill while we were waiting for the demonstrations of the "People's Car" to begin, and had even promised to show him how we played if he cared to come to my rooms; and come he did, though it was several weeks after the race. I showed him our board (the map shellacked over) and regretted that I could not also show him a game in progress, explaining that we had just completed our first, which (because we counted the Great War as *one*) we called World War Two.

"I take it you were victorious," he said.

"No, I lost—but since I was Germany that won't discomfort you, and anyway I would rather have won that race against the real Germans than all the games Lansbury and I may ever play."

"Yes," he said.

Something in his smile raised my suspicions; I remembered having seen a similar expression on Lansbury's face (which I really only noticed afterward) when he persuaded me that he intended to make his invasion of Europe by way of Greece; and at last I blurted out: "Was that race really fair? I mean to say—we did surprisingly well."

"Even you," Churchill remarked, "beat the best of the German drivers."

"I know," I said. "That's what bothers me."

He seated himself in my most comfortable armchair and lit a fresh cigar. "The idea struck me," he said, "when that devilish Japanese machine came scooting out while I was talking to Hitler. Do you remember that?"

"Certainly. You mean the idea of using the Japanese cars as traffic?"

"Not only that. A recent invention, the transistor, makes those things possible. Are you by any chance familiar with the operating principle of the transistor?"

I said that I had read that in its simplest form it was merely a small chip or flake of material which was conductive in one direction only.

"Precisely so." Churchill puffed his cigar. "Which is only to say that electrons can move through the stuff more readily in one direction than in another. Doesn't that seem remarkable? Do you know how it is done?"

I admitted that I did not.

"Well, neither did I before I read an article in *Nature* about it, a week or two before I met Herr Hitler. What the sharp lads who make these things do is to take a material called germanium—or silicon will do as well, though the transistor ends up acting somewhat differently—in a very pure state, and then add some impurities to it. They are very careful about what they put in, of course. For example, if they add a little bit of antimony the stuff they get has more electrons in it than there are places for them to go, so that some are wandering about loose all the time. Then there's other kinds of rubbish—boron is one of them—that makes the material have more spots for electrons than electrons to occupy them. The experts call the spots "holes," but I would call them "parking places," and the way you make your transistor is to put the two sorts of stuff up against each other."

"Do you mean that our track . . ."

Churchill nodded. "Barring a little terminological inexactitude, yes I do. It was a large transistor—primitive, if you like, but big. Take a real transistor now. What happens at the junction point where the two sorts of material come together? Well, a lot of electrons from the side that has them move over into the side that doesn't—there's so much more space there for them, you see."

"You mean that if a car—I mean an electron—tries to go the other way, from the side where there are a great many parking places—"

"It has a difficult time. Don't ask me why, I'm not an electrical engineer, but some aspects of the thing can't be missed by anyone, even a simple political journalist like myself. One is that the electron you just mentioned is swimming upstream, as it were."

"And we were driving downstream," I said. "That is, if you don't mind my no longer talking about electrons."

"Not at all. I pass with relief from the tossing sea of cause and theory to the firm ground of result and fact. Yes, we were driving with the current, so to speak; perhaps it has also occurred to you that our coming in at the urban end, where most of the Japanese cars were, set up a wave that went ahead of us; we were taking up the spaces, and so they were drawn toward the Germans when they tried to find some, and of course a wave of that sort travels much faster than the individuals in it. I suppose a transistor expert would say that by having like charges we repelled them."

"But eventually they would pile up between the teams—I remember that the traffic did get awfully thick just about when we passed through the Germans."

"Correct. And when that happened there was no further reason for them to keep running ahead of us—the Jerries were repelling them too by then, if you want to put it that way—and then the rules (my famous distance formula, if you recall) pulled them back into the urban area, where the poor Huns had to struggle with them some more while we breezed home."

We sat silent for a time; then I said, "I don't suppose it was particularly honest; but I'm glad you did it."

"Dishonesty," Churchill said easily, "consists in violating rules to which one has—at least by implication—agreed. I simply proposed rules I felt would be advantageous, which is diplomacy. Don't you do that when you set up your game?" He looked down at the world map on the table. "By the way, you've burnt your board."

"Oh, there," I said. "Some coals fell from Lansbury's pipe toward the end of the game—they cost us a pair of cities in south Japan, I'm afraid."

"You'd better be careful you don't burn up the whole board next time. But speaking of the Japanese, have you heard that they are bringing out an automobile of their own? They received so much attention in the press in connection with the race that they're giving it a name the public will associate with the toy motorcars they had here."

I asked if he thought that that would mean Britain would have to beat off a Japanese invasion eventually, and he said that he supposed it did, but that we Americans would have to deal with them first—he had heard that the first Japanese-made cars were already being unloaded in Pearl Harbor. He left shortly after that, and I doubt that I will ever have the pleasure of his company again, much though I should like it.

But my story is not yet finished. Readers of this magazine will be glad to learn that Lansbury and I are about to begin another game, necessarily to be prosecuted by mail, since I will soon be leaving England. In our new struggle, the United States, Britain, and China will oppose the Union of Soviet Socialist Republics, Poland, Romania, and a number of other Eastern European states. Since Germany should have a part in any proper war, and Lansbury would not agree to my having her again, we have divided her between us. I shall try to keep Mr. Churchill's warning in mind, but my opponent and I are both heavy smokers.

Sincerely,

"Unknown Soldier"

Editor's Note. While we have no desire to tear aside the veil of the *nom de guerre* with which "Unknown Soldier" concluded his agreeable communication, we feel we are yet keeping faith when we disclose that he is an American officer, of Germanic descent, no longer young (quite) and yet too young to have seen action in the Great War, though we are told he came very near. At present "Unknown Soldier" is attached to the American Embassy in London, but we understand that, as he feels it unlikely his country will ever again have need of military force within his lifetime, he intends to give up his commission and return to his native Kansas, where he will operate an agency for Buick motorcars. Best of luck, Dwight.

FATHER'S DAY

THE ADOPTED FATHER

John Parker's hands gripped the edge of the counter. "Do you mean," he said, "that although I paid for the deliveries, I can't see the records?"

"I mean," the nurse in the screen answered carefully, "that there are no more records, Mr. Parker. We have already given you copies of all those we have. Our records show the names, dates, and times of birth of your three children, their medical history here, and the medical history of Ms. Roberts. That is all we have."

"There must be more," John Parker said. To either side of him, women stood arguing with similar nurses in similar screens.

"There is no more, Mr. Parker. You have seen what we have. Ms. Roberts has been here three times. Your children were named—by her— Robert, Marian, and Tina. There were no complications. Ms. Roberts's confinements were paid for by the North American Division of World Assurance—not by you, as you appear to believe."

"You must fingerprint them," John Parker said. "For the police, if for no other reason. Or footprints. Don't you take footprints?"

"No, Mr. Parker," the nurse said. "That hasn't been done for many years. At birth the infant remains with its mother until its wrist has been banded. The band cannot be removed. There is no possibility of an exchange."

"Is there some way I can talk to a human being?" John Parker asked.

The nurse in the screen shook her head. "Not in my hospital, Mr. Parker. Not in any modern hospital."

Although he would have liked it very much if there had been, there was nothing modern about the foyer of John Parker's building. There was nothing old about it either, no suggestion of more gracious days. It was contemporary, in a period when *contemporary* meant the cheapest possible construction that would do the job, a period when a hundred million people drew unemployment benefits and the cost of labor was (John Parker smiled bitterly to himself) astronomical. Snow had been tracked onto the floor of this foyer, and a pouch of orange drink had been spilled in the elevator. John Parker pressed the button for the seventy-fifth floor, wondering why he did so.

A few days before, the elevator had stopped on the sixty-seventh, no doubt because some child had pushed UP, then dashed back into his own apartment. John Parker had not noticed. He had left the elevator and walked down a corridor precisely like his own. He had knocked on the door that should have been his, before he had seen the obscenity painted on it. Obscenities were no novelty, but this one had been old, the Day-Glo magenta paint flaking, and not his. He had walked back down the corridor to the elevator then and seen that he had gotten off at sixty-seven, eight floors too low.

Possibly it was my apartment after all, John Parker thought. I have done what the sign said.

The soles of his shoes were slightly sticky as he walked the corridor today. Now he read the graffiti, something he had not done for years. Yes, this was the seventy-fifth floor, to which a few new injunctions had been added. He searched it with his eyes—someone was assaulted in the building every month or so. He knocked at his own door, liberally besprinkled with short words, though most of the boys in this part of the building were supposed to be afraid of Robert.

"Yes?"

"Me. John." It was what he always said. He listened to Roseanne unfasten the chain and turn the bolt, then stepped into the warmth—struck again, as he had been every day for the past week, by how little Roseanne resembled him. Or, he thought, as he stared at his reflection in the window later, how little he resembled her. Weren't couples supposed to come to look alike? He and Roseanne had been together for nearly twenty years now.

Yet that was all right. Roseanne was no blood of his, not his sister, not his cousin. The children resembled neither of them, and that was not all right—not quite. Robert was tall and fair. Tina was fair, and would be tall. Both had blue eyes; his own were brown, Roseanne's hazel. Marian was small and dark, much smaller than he—smaller, for that matter than his mother or his sisters. Her eyes were brown, but darker than his own; her hair nearly black.

An accident of the genes? Quite possibly, and it did not really matter. But none of them thought the way he did, they all thought he was eccentric or worse, and that mattered a great deal. He got out a sheet of paper and squared it on his board, using the inexpensive little drafting machine his scholarship had supplied him with when he had entered the university. It had had to be repaired many times since then, but now, when he had long since lost sight of every human friend he had made there, it still functioned. He thought, This is the big day. This is the day I'm going to do the park.

"Another park?" Roseanne asked.

John Parker nodded, not looking up.

She leaned over his board as she always did, her hair just brushing his cheek. "That's a lovely one. What are these?"

"Habitats. It has a small zoo. African veldt here, pampas there. Andes over here. Refreshment complex—I'd like to have a real restaurant, but you can't put that in a drawing, and you know they'd never do it. Rest rooms. Security station. Petting zoo for the children."

"Maybe if you sent some of your plans to the mayor, he'd build them."

"You have sent him some," John Parker reminded her.

"I have, but you haven't." It was necessary to Roseanne's peace of mind that she believe him vaguely important.

"Perhaps someday I will," John Parker said.

"He was on TV just now. He looked very nice—you should have seen him. He asked everyone to cooperate with the police and refrain from vandalizing city property."

"I'm not a vandal," John Parker said.

Robert came in to borrow money. "Where's this one?" he asked. "On the moon?"

"Mars," John Parker said. "It would be perfectly possible to make Mars a world much like Earth. A cloud of finely powdered aluminum behind it would reflect back enough heat to raise the night temperature. Bringing down Demos and Phobus and a little of the asteroid belt would increase the planet's mass enough to let it hold an atmosphere, which you could make by breaking down the stony matter in the asteroids and moons. Pretty soon you'd turn the red planet green."

"What's this?"

"A hedge maze for children and lovers. There are seats, you see, and bowers. Sculpture the kids can climb on. They can wade in the pond too, and go up the tower in the middle to watch the people trying to find their way out. That's the goal."

"I bet I can solve it," Robert said. He put his finger on the drawing to trace the paths, but soon gave up.

John Parker had expected a screen and a computer persona at the agency. He was surprised and pleased to be ushered into the presence of a human being, a gray-haired woman who did not even look particularly motherly. "I'm here to inquire about adoption," John Parker said carefully.

"Certainly." The woman paused. "I take it you are—how should I put it?—one half of a couple?"

John Parker shook his head.

Her hand went toward a button on her desk. "Perhaps we should have one of the legal staff present."

He covered the button with his own hand and smiled. "That won't be necessary. Really it won't, Ms. —?"

"Harris. You needn't be married, you understand, Mr. Parker."

John Parker nodded.

"And of course the other member of the couple can be of your own gender—we don't inquire. But there must be two persons willing to make a home, willing to take responsibility for the welfare of the child."

"I don't want to adopt a child. I want to be adopted myself."

Ms. Harris stared at him.

"I'm not being facetious. I want a group of children to take me as their father. I'm over forty, I have a good job and no criminal record."

"You want them to adopt you," Ms. Harris said.

John Parker nodded. "Is that ever done?"

Ms. Harris shook her head slowly. "I don't think so. I've never heard of it. I'll bring it up at the next board meeting. It might be a good idea."

"So much can be done with our minds now," John Parker said. "Implanted learning and so on. It should be possible to erase whole areas of experience. After it was over, the man could forget it wasn't his own family." He leaned forward. "Honestly, Ms. Harris, didn't they think of that long ago?"

Too quickly to be stopped, Ms. Harris's hand stabbed one of the buttons. John Parker rose, got his overcoat, and walked out. No one attempted to stop him.

He got off at the sixty-seventh floor and went down the corridor counting doors. The old obscenity had been partially obscured by a new purple one. He knocked on it.

There was no answer.

He knocked again, louder. There was still no reply, and he thumped the door with his fist, and at last began to kick it. At the thirteenth or possibly the fifteenth kick, wood shattered and it flew open.

The strange living room was cool. Not as cold as the corridor outside, but not nearly as warm as his own. It had been an ordinary enough living room once, perhaps—two chairs, a sofa, the television, an end table. Yet it appeared (John Parker smiled to himself) that now someone was actually living in it. There was an untidy knot of blankets at one end of the sofa, a half-full glass of water on the end table, crumpled foil packages on the floor. He thought, If only I were enough of a detective, I could tell how long it's been since anyone was here—but there are no detectives now, only police. . . .

The back of the television felt slightly warm, but he might have been wrong.

In the kitchen, the sink was filled with dirty plates and gummy cups and glasses. A full canister of synthetic coffee and three unopened packages of irradiated food lay in one of the cabinets; they were HAM AND LIMA BEANS, LIVER AND ONIONS, and SMOKED TONGUE WITH AU GRATIN POTATOES. "A kid," John Parker said under his breath. He went into the living room again. "Come on out. I know you're in here." He did not, not really.

There was only one bedroom, and he wondered why the child did not sleep in it. When he opened the door, it was like opening the door of the foyer. Worse. A blast of icy wind hit him. He stepped inside, leaving the door open so he could keep an eye on the one to the corridor.

A dead woman lay in the bed. Her face was uncovered, her eyes open. John Parker pulled down the sheet. She wore only a nightgown; there was no blood, and there were no marks on her neck. He tossed an empty pill bottle into a dresser drawer and slid it closed, then pulled the sheet over her face, obscurely glad he had not had to touch her.

In the living room again, he shut the bedroom door behind him. The bathroom was locked; he told himself he should have thought of the bathroom to begin with. "Come out," he said. "It's no use. I'll just break the lock." He turned on the television and sat down on the sofa.

Twenty minutes passed before he heard the rattle of the knob. Without turning his head he said, "Come on out. I won't hurt you, and I might be able to help you. You're almost out of groceries."

It was a boy, small and dark as Marian. "How'd you know?" he said.

"That you were in here? Somebody was. The nightbolt was out in your front door—I could see it through the crack, and it has to be turned from inside. A grown-up would have answered when I knocked, or at least yelled for help when I kicked the door. Then too, I looked at what you ate. There'd been soft drinks, but they were all gone and you were drinking water. You never made coffee, and the meals you've got left are the kind my own kids—" John Parker stopped, unable to finish the sentence. "I suppose I'm lucky I wasn't arrested. I don't know what made me come here, except that I'd been here once before. For some reason I thought I'd find something out here. You try to go back . . ."

"What are you going to do, Mister?"

"I don't know," John Parker said slowly.

"Ain't you a blue?"

John Parker shook his head. "I'm an architect. Why didn't you *go* to the police, or somebody, instead of just staying here and playing games with the elevators? If you'd told your teacher at school, it would have called some social agency."

"They would have taken me away from here," the boy said. "I didn't want to go."

"So you just opened the window and closed off the bedroom. How long ago?"

"I don't know."

The boy began to cry; the sobs shook him like convulsions, and for the first time John Parker realized how young he was. He picked him up. The room was still cold, and he opened his overcoat, wrapping it about them both. "Less than three weeks anyway. It hasn't been this cold for longer than that. What's your name?"

"Mitch." More sobs. "Why'd Mama die?"

"Heart attack, probably. Bad food, bad air. People die young, Mitch, but she's gone and that's the thing to remember, and whatever it was that hurt her can't hurt her anymore. Did you ever play some game when you knew the other kid was going to beat you?"

Interested, Mitch looked up and nodded.

"Then remember how when he *does* beat you, the game is over and you can go away. Dying's like that. Your mother's gone away, and she's finished with whatever it was."

"Do you know my father?"

"Perhaps," John Parker said. "Who is your father?"

"I don't know his name. He lives here in this building."

"Do you think it could be me?"

Mitch shook his head. "I don't think so. Mama showed him to me once."

"And that's why you stayed. You've been trying to find him."

"Do you know who he is?"

"No," John Parker said. "But I know what he is. Do you know that, Mitch?"

"No," the boy said softly.

John Parker set him down and began to pace the room. "He's someone like you. That's what makes him your father. Take my own children. If I have any, they'll be more or less like me—in logic, that's called a tautology. If you're crazy, your kids are crazy too, and crazy in more or less the same way you are. That's what makes them your kids." His foot sent a yellow envelope skittering across the floor. He retrieved it and tore it open: *"This is your FINAL warning. If we do not receive. . . ."* "They're going to throw you out of here," John Parker said. "How long ago did this come?"

"I don't know."

"Today?"

Mitch shook his head.

"Yesterday?"

"Maybe." Mitch shrugged.

"There are probably two or three more in the series after this, but there may not be two, and anyway it's possible you've already got them. Did your mother keep any writing paper?"

Mitch went into the little kitchen and brought a stack of cheap white stationery from a drawer. "We only need one envelope," John Parker said. He wrote the Housing Authority's address on it and added a stamp from the supply he carried in his check folder, then dropped the bill in.

"Are you going to pay?"

"Your mother must have been at least four months behind," John Parker said, "and I can't afford to. But this will buy us some time." He tore out a check and crossed off his own name and Roseanne's, then drew a line through the account number and wrote in a fictitious one. He made the check out for the amount specified on the bill, and signed it *Robert Roberts-Parker,* explaining, "The bank's computer will read my account number anyway—it's printed in magnetic ink. When I send the check back, they'll credit my account and go looking for Robert, who'll be hard to find since he doesn't have an account and isn't in the telephone directory. With any luck, they'll spend a while on the number I gave them too."

Mitch stared at him without comprehension.

"Eventually they'll disallow the check and send you more letters. Something may have turned up by then. If it hasn't, we'll have to think up another game." John Parker thrust the check into the envelope and licked the flap. "It's a great principle—you could call it the principle of adventure or even the principle of play. Robert—that's the young man who just paid your rent—tried to solve my maze and couldn't, even after I told him that the tower was for the kids to climb, and the pond was for them to wade in. You have to wade across the pond to reach the tower, of course. He saw a barrier when he should have seen an invitation. I'll show you that maze sometime. You like to play, Mitch?"

The boy nodded.

"Me too." John Parker crossed to the window and stared at the dark sky beyond the glass. "That's coal smoke, the technology of the nineteenth century brought into the twenty-first and hard at work. They could have conquered the solar system and harnessed the sun, but they did this instead, because there was no fun involved. Their great-grandfathers had done it, and they knew it would work. *Tom Swift and His Steam Everything.* I've got most of the Tom Swift books, Mitch, and I'll let you read them when you're a little older. Coal makes great buttons for snowmen, though."

"Are we going to look for my father now?"

"As soon as I fix your lock," John Parker said. He found epoxy in the kitchen and re-created the wood around the shattered socket. "That'll set in three or four hours," he told the boy. "If no one pushes on your door before then, this place will be all right. Tonight we'll do something about your mama, put her where the right people will find her and take care of her."

In the elevator, he grasped the boy's shoulder. "You know what we've been doing wrong, Mitch? We've been looking seriously—me for my own kids, you for your dad. Looking seriously only finds little things, and those aren't little things. We have to have fun. Then maybe we'll both find what we want. I know a place that has a heated pool. Let's go swimming."

The elevator jolted to a stop. Three young men were waiting in the foyer. One held a tire iron, one a doubled length of chain. John Parker thrust a hand into his coat pocket. "This fires high-energy gamma rays," he said levelly. "You don't feel a thing now, but within six weeks you'll develop leukemia and in six more you'll be dead."

The three hesitated, and he flipped open a match box with his other hand. "I'm calling in Star Patrol to pick up the pieces," he announced.

When they were safely outside, John Parker told Mitch, "See, you just learned something—be crazy. Nobody bothers the crazy people." He paused. "In the end, maybe it's the crazy people who win after all. Is swimming okay? You like to swim?"

Mitch nodded, his eyes shining.

John Parker raised the match box to his lips. "We're in trouble down here," he whispered, "but don't beam us up quite yet." The hand that a moment before had been a radiation pistol was hailing a cab.

LABOR DAY

FORLESEN

When Emanuel Forlesen awoke, his wife was already up preparing breakfast. Forlesen remembered nothing, knew nothing but his name, for an instant did not remember his wife, or that she was his wife, or that she was a human being, or what human beings were supposed to look like.

At the time he woke he knew only his own name; the rest came later and is therefore suspect, colored by rationalization and the expectations of the woman herself and the other people. He moaned, and his wife said: "Oh, you're awake. Better read the orientation."

He said, "What orientation?"

"You don't remember where you work, do you? Or what you're supposed to do."

He said, "I don't remember a damn thing."

"Well, read the orientation."

He pushed aside the gingham spread and got out of bed, looking at himself, noticing first the oddly deformed hands at the ends of his legs, then remembering the name for them: *shoes*. He was naked, and his wife turned her back to him politely while she prepared food. "Where the hell am I?" he asked.

"In our house." She gave him the address. "In our bedroom."

"We cook in the bedroom?"

"We sure do," his wife said. "There isn't any kitchen. There's a parlor, the children's bedroom, this room, and a bath. I've got an electric frypan, a tabletop electric oven, and a coffeepot here; we'll be all right."

The confidence in her voice heartened him. He said, "I suppose this used to be a one-bedroom house, and we made the kitchen into a place for the kids."

"Maybe it's an old house, and they made the kitchen into the bathroom when they got inside plumbing."

He was dressing himself, having seen that she wore clothing, and that there was clothing too large for her piled on a chair near the bed. He said, "Don't you know?"

"It wasn't in the orientation."

At first he did not understand what she had said. He repeated, "Don't you know?"

"I told you, it wasn't in there. There's just a diagram of the house, and there's this room, the children's room, the parlor and the bath. It said that door there"—she gestured with the spatula—"was the bath, and that's right, because I went in there to get the water for the coffee. I stay here and look after things and you go out and work, that's what it said. There was some stuff about what you do, but I skipped that and read about what I do."

"You didn't know anything when you woke up either," he said.

"Just my name."

"What's your name?"

"Edna Forlesen. I'm your wife—that's what it said."

He walked around the small table on which she had arranged the cooking appliances, wanting to look at her. "You're sort of pretty," he said.

"You are sort of handsome," his wife said. "Anyway you look tough and strong." This made him walk over to the mirror on the dresser and try to look at himself. He did not know what he looked like, but the man in the mirror was not he. The image was older, fatter, meaner, more cunning, and stupider than he knew himself to be, and he raised his hands (the man in the mirror did likewise) to touch his features; they were what they should have been and he turned away. "That mirror's no good," he said.

"Can't you see yourself? That means you're a vampire."

He laughed, and decided that that was the way he always laughed when his wife's jokes weren't funny. She said, "Want some coffee?" and he sat down.

She put a cup in front of him, and a pile of books. "This is the orientation," she said. "You better read it—you don't have much time."

On top of the pile was a mimeographed sheet, and he picked that up first. It said—

Welcome to the planet Planet.

You have awakened completely ignorant of everything. Do not be disturbed by this. It is NORMAL. Under no circumstances ever allow yourself to become excited, confused, angry, or FEAR-

FUL. *While you possess these capacities, they are to be regarded as incapacities.*

Anything you may have remembered upon awakening is false. The orientation books provided you contain information of inestimable value. Master it as soon as possible, BUT DO NOT BE LATE FOR WORK. If there are no orientation books where you are, go to the house on your right (from the street). DO NOT GO TO THE HOUSE ON YOUR LEFT.

If you cannot find any books live like everyone else.

The white paper under this paper is your JOB ASSIGNMENT. The yellow paper is your TABLE OF COMMONLY USED WAITS AND MEASURES. Read these first; they are more important than the books.

"Eat your egg," his wife said. He tasted the egg. It was good but slightly oily, as though a drop of motor oil had found its way into the grease in which she had fried it. His *Job Assignment* read—

Forlosen, E.

(To his wife he said, "They got our name wrong.")

Forlosen, E. You work at Model Pattern Products, 19000370 Plant Prkwy, Highland Industrial Park. Your duties are supervisory and managerial. When you arrive punch in on the S&M clock (beige) NOT the Labor clock (brown). The union is particular about this. Go to the Reconstruction and Advanced Research section. To arrive on time leave before 060.30.00.

The yellow paper was illegible save for the title and first line: *There are 240 ours in each day.*

"What time is it?" he asked his wife.

She glanced at her wrist. "Oh six oh ours. Didn't they give you a watch?"

He looked at his own wrist—it was bare, of course. For a few moments Edna helped him search for one; but it seemed that none had been provided, and in the end he took hers, she saying that he would need it more than she. It was big for a woman's watch, he thought, but very small for a man's. "Try it," she said, and he obediently studied the tiny screen. The words, "The Time Is" were cast in the metal at its top; below them, glimmering and changing even as he looked: "060.07.43." He took a sip of coffee and found the oily taste was there too.

The book at the top of the pile was a booklet really, about seven inches by four with the pages stapled in the middle. The title, printed in black on a blue cover of slightly heavier paper, was *How to Drive*.

Remember that your car is a gift. Although it belongs to you and you are absolutely responsible for its acts (whether driven by yourself or others, or not driven) and maintenance (pg 15), do not:

1. *Deface its surface.*
2. *Interfere with the operation of its engine, or with the operation of any other part.*
3. *Alter it in such a way as to increase or diminish the noise of operation.*
4. *Drive it at speeds in excess of 40 miles/our.*
5. *Pick up hitchhikers.*
6. *Deposit a hitchhiker at any point other than a Highway Patrol Station.*
7. *Operate it while you are in an unfit condition. (To be determined by a duly constituted medical board.)*
8. *Fail to halt and render medical assistance to persons injured by you, your car, or others (provided third parties are not already providing such assistance).*
9. *Stop at any time or for any reason at any point not designated as a stopping position.*
10. *Wave or shout at other drivers.*
11. *Invade the privacy of other drivers—as by noticing or pretending to notice them or the occupants of their vehicles.*
12. *Fail to return it on demand.*
13. *Drive it to improper destinations.*

He turned the page. The new page was a diagram of the control panel of an automobile, and he noted the positions of Windshield, Steering Wheel, Accelerator, Brake, Reversing Switch, Communicator, Beverage Dispenser, Urinal, Defecator, and Map Compartment. He asked Edna if they had a car, and she said she thought they did, and that it would be outside.

"You know," he said, "I've just noticed that this place has windows."

Edna said, "You're always jumping up from the table. Finish your breakfast."

Ignoring her, he parted the curtains. She said, "Two walls have windows and two don't. I haven't looked out of them." Outside he saw sunshine on concrete; a small, yellow, somehow hunched-looking automobile; and a house.

"Yeah, we've got a car," he said. "It's parked right under the window."

"Well, I wish you'd finish breakfast and get to work."

"I want to look out of the other window."

If the first window had been, as it appeared to be, at one side of the house, then the other should be at either the back or the front. He opened the curtains and saw a narrow, asthmatic brick courtyard. On the bricks stood three dead plants in terra cotta jars; the opposite side of the court, no more than fifteen feet off, was the wall of another house. There were two widely spaced windows in this wall, each closed with curtains; and as he watched (though his face was only at the window for an instant) a man pushed aside the curtains at the nearer window and looked at him. Forlesen stepped back and said to Edna: "I saw a man; he looked afraid. A bald man with a wide, fat face, and a gold tooth in front, and a mole over one eyebrow." He went to the mirror again and studied himself.

"You don't look like that," his wife said.

"No, I don't—that's what bothers me. That was the first thing I thought of—that it would be myself, perhaps the way I'm going to look when I'm older. I've lost a lot of my hair now and I could lose the rest of it, in fact, I suppose I will. And I could break a tooth in front and get a gold one—"

"Maybe it wasn't really a mole," Edna said. "It could have been just a spot of dirt or something."

"It could have been." He had seated himself again, and as he spoke he speared a bite of egg with his fork. "I suppose it's even possible that I could grow a mole I don't have now, and I could put on weight. But that wasn't me; those weren't my features, not at any age."

"Well, why should it be you?"

"I just felt it should, somehow."

"You've been reading that red book." Edna's voice was accusing.

"No, I haven't even looked at it." Curious, he pushed aside brown and purple pamphlets, fished the red book out of the pile, and looked at it. The cover was of leather and had been blind-tooled in a pattern of thin lines. Holding it at a slant to the light from the window he decided he could discern, in the intricacies of the pattern, a group of men surrounding a winged being. "What is it?" he said.

"It's supposed to tell you how to be good, and how to live—everything like that."

He riffled the pages, and noted that the left side of the book—the back of each leaf—was printed in scarlet in a language he did not understand. The right side, printed in black, seemed by its arrangement on the page to be a translation.

> *Of the nature of Death and the Dead we may enumerate twelve kinds. First there are those who become new gods, for whom new universes are born. Second those who praise. Third those who fight as soldiers in the unending war with evil. Fourth those who amuse themselves among flowers and sweet streams with sports. Fifth those who dwell in gardens of bliss, or are tortured. Sixth those who continue as in life. Seventh those who turn the wheel of the Universe. Eighth those who find in their graves their mothers' wombs and in one life circle forever. Ninth ghosts. Tenth those born again as men in their grandsons' time. Eleventh those who return as beasts or trees. And last those who sleep.*

"Look at this," he said, "this can't be right."

"I wish you'd hurry. You're going to be late."

He looked at the watch she had given him. It read 060.26.13, and he said, "I still have time. But look here—the black is supposed to say the same thing as the red, but look at how different they are: where it says, 'And last those who sleep,' there's a whole paragraph opposite it; and across from, 'Fourth those who amuse themselves . . .' there are only two words."

"You don't want any more coffee, do you?"

He shook his head, laid down the red book, and picked up another; its title was *Food Preparation in the Home*. "That's for me," his wife said. "You wouldn't be interested by that."

Contents
Introduction—Three Meals a Day
Preparing Breakfast
Preparing Luncheon
Preparing Supper
Helpful Hints for Homemakers

He set the book down again, and as he did so its cheap plastic cover popped open to the last page. At the bottom of the Hints for Homemakers, he read: *Remember that if he does not go you and your children will starve.* He closed it and put the sugar bowl on top of it.

"I wish you'd get going," his wife said.

He stood up. "I was just leaving. How do I get out?"

She pointed to one of the doors, and said, "That's the parlor. You go straight through that, and there's another door that goes outside."

"And the car," Forlesen said, more than half to himself, "will be around there under the window." He slipped the blue *How To Drive* booklet into one of his pockets.

The parlor was smaller than the bedroom, but because it held no furniture as large as the bed or the table it seemed nearly empty. There was an uncomfortable-looking sofa against one wall, and two bowlegged chairs in corners; an umbrella stand and a dusty potted palm. The floor was covered by a dark, patterned rug, and the walls by flowered paper. Four strides took him across the room; he opened another, larger and heavier door and stepped outside. A moment after he had closed the door he heard the bolt snick behind him; he tried to open it again, and found, as he had expected, that he was locked out.

The house in which he seemed to have been born stood on a narrow street paved with asphalt. Only a two-foot concrete walkway separated it from the curb; there was no porch, and the doorway was at the same level as the walk, which had been stenciled at intervals of six feet or so with the words GO TO YOUR RIGHT—NOT TO YOUR LEFT. They were positioned in such a way as to be upside down to a person who had gone to the left. Forlesen went around the corner of his house instead and got into the yellow car—the instrument panel differed in several details from the one in the blue book. For a moment he considered rolling down the right window of the car to rap on the house window, but he felt sure that Edna would not come. He threw the reversing switch instead, wondering if he should not do something to bring the car to life first. It began to roll slowly backward at once; he guided it with the steering wheel, craning his neck to look over his shoulder.

The narrow street seemed deserted. He switched into Front and touched the accelerator pedal with his foot; the car inched forward, picking up speed only slowly even when he pushed the pedal to the floor. The street was lined with small brick houses much like the one he had left; their curtains were drawn, and small cars like his own but of various colors were parked beside the houses. Signs stood on metal poles cast into the asphalt of the road, spaced just sufficiently far apart that each was out of sight of the next. They were diamond-shaped, with black letters on an orange ground, and each read HIDDEN DRIVES.

His communicator said: *"If you do not know how to reach your destination, press the button and ask."*

He pressed the button and said, "I think I'm supposed to go to a place called Model Pattern Products."

"Correct. Your destination is 19000370 Plant Parkway, Highland Industrial Park. Turn right at the next light."

He was about to ask what was meant by the word *light* in this connotation, when he saw that he was approaching an intersection and that over it, like a ceiling fixture unaccompanied by any ceiling, was suspended a rapidly blinking light which emitted at intervals of perhaps a quarter second alternating flashes of red and green. He turned to the right; the changing colors gave an illusion of jerky motion, belied by the smooth hum of the tires. The flickering brought a sensation of nausea, and for a moment he shut his eyes against it; then felt the car nosing up, tilting under him. He opened his eyes and saw that the new street onto which he had turned was lifting beneath him, becoming, ahead, an air-borne ribbon of pavement that traced a thin streak through the sky. Already he was higher than the tops of the trees. The roofs of the houses—little tarpaper things like the lids of boxes—were dwindling below. He thought of Edna in one of those boxes (he found he could not tell which one) cooking a meal for herself, perhaps smoothing the bed in which the two of them had slept, and knew, with that sudden insight which stands in relation to reason as reason does to instinct, that she would spend ours, most of whatever day there was, looking out the parlor window at the empty street; he found that he both pitied and envied her, and stopped the car with some vague thought of returning home and devising some plan by which they could either stay there together or go together to wherever it was he was being sent. "Model Pattern Products," he said aloud. What was that?

As though it were answering him the speaker said, "Why have you stopped? Do you require mechanical assistance?"

"Wait a minute, I'm not sure if I do or not." He got out of the car and walked to the low rail at the edge of the road and looked down. Something, he felt sure, must be supporting the mass of concrete and steel upon which he stood, but he could not see what it was, only the houses and trees and the narrow asphalt streets below. The sunlight striking his face when he looked up again gave him an idea, and he hurried across the road and bent over the rail on the opposite side. There, as he had anticipated, the shadow of the road, long in the level morning sunshine, lay stretched across the roofs and streets. Under it, very closely spaced, were yet other shadows; but these were so broken by the irregular shapes upon which they were thrown by the sun that he could not be sure if they were the shadows of things actually straight, or if the casters of these shadows (whatever they might be) were themselves bowed, twisted, and deformed.

He was still studying them when the humming sound of wheels

drew his attention back to the flying roadway upon which he stood. A car, painted a metallic and yet peculiarly pleasing shade of blue, was speeding toward him. Unaccustomed to estimating the speeds of vehicles, he wondered for an instant whether or not he had time to recross the road and reach his own car again, and was torn between the fear of being run down if he tried and that of being pinned against the rail where he stood, should the blue car swerve too near. Then he realized that the blue car was slowing as it approached him—that he himself was, so to speak, its destination. Its door, he saw, was painted with a fantastic design, a mingling of fabulous beasts with plants and what appeared to be wholly abstract symbols.

A man was seated in the blue car, and as Forlesen watched he leaned across the seat toward him, rolling down the window. "Hey, bud, what are you doing outside your car?"

"I was looking over the railing," Forlesen said. He indicated the sheer drop beside him. "I wanted to see how the road got up in the air like this."

"Get back in."

Forlesen was about to obey, when in a remote corner of his field of vision he detected a movement, a shifting in that spot of ground below toward which he had been looking a moment before, and thus toward which (as is the habit of vision) his gaze was still to some degree drawn. He swung around to look at it, and the man in the blue car said again, "Get back in your car, bud." And then: "I'm telling you, you better get back."

"Come here," Forlesen said. "Look at this." He heard the door of the other car open and assumed the driver was coming to join him, then felt something—it might have been the handlebar of a bicycle against which he had accidentally backed—prodding him in the spine, just above his belt. He moved away from it with his attention still riveted on the shadows below, but it followed him. He turned and saw that the driver had, as he had supposed, left the blue car, and that he wore a loose, broad-sleeved blue shirt with a metal badge pinned to the fabric off-center. Also that he wore no trousers, his sexual organs being effectively concealed by the length of the shirt, and that from under the shirt six or more plastic tubes led back to the blue car, some of the color of straw and others of the dark red color of blood; and that he held a pistol, and that it had been the muzzle of this pistol which he (Forlesen) had felt a moment before pressing against his back. "Get in there," the man from the blue car said a third time.

Forlesen said, "All right," and did as he was told; but found (to his own very great surprise) that he was not frightened.

When he was behind the wheel of his own car again, the man from the blue car re-entered it, and (so it appeared to Forlesen) seemed to holster his gun beneath the car's dashboard. "I'm back in my car now," Forlesen said. "Can I tell you what it was I saw?"

The man in the blue car said to his speaker: "This is two oh four twelve forty-three. Subject has returned to his vehicle. Repeat—subject has returned to his vehicle."

"Those pillars or columns or whatever they are that hold this road up—one of them moved, or at least its shadow did. I saw it."

The man in the blue car muttered something under his breath.

"Are they falling down?" Forlesen asked. "Have you been noticing cracks?"

The speaker in his car said: "Information received indicates an unauthorized stop. Continue toward your destination at once." He noticed that the speaker in the blue car seemed to be talking to its driver as well; but he could not hear what was being said. After a moment (his own speaker had fallen silent) he heard the driver say, "Yes, ma'am. Over and out." Then the pistol was aimed at him once more, this time at his face, through the window of the blue car. The driver said, "You roll that thing, bud, and you roll it now or I shoot."

Forlesen stepped on the accelerator, and his car began to move forward, slowly at first, then picking up speed until he felt sure it was traveling much faster than a man could run. In the mirror above the windshield he could see the blue car; it did not turn—as he had supposed it might—to follow him, but after a delay continued to descend the road he himself was going up.

He had supposed that this road would lead him to Model Pattern Products (whatever that might be), but when he had been following it for some time it joined another, similar but far wider, highway. There were now multiple lines of traffic all going in the same direction, and by traveling in the fast lane he could avoid looking over the side. It was a relief he accepted gratefully; he had a good head for heights, but he had found himself studying the long shadows of the supports whenever the twistings of the road put them on the side upon which he drove.

With that distraction out of the way he discovered that he enjoyed driving, though the memory of the twisted columns remained in the back of his mind. Yet the performance of the yellow car was deeply satisfying: it sped to the top of the high, white, billowing undulations of the highway with a power slight yet sure, and descended in a way

that made him almost believe himself a hawk—or the operator of some
fantastic machine that could itself soar like a bird—or even such a
winged being as had appeared on the cover of the red book. The clear
sky, which lay now to the right and left of the highway as well as
above it, promoted these fantasies; and its snowy clouds might almost
have been other highways like the one on which he traveled—indeed,
from time to time he seemed to see moving dots of color on them, as
though cars like his own, but immensely remote, dashed over plains
and precipices of vapor. He used the defecator and the urinal, dis-
pensed himself a sparkling green beverage; the car was a cozy and secret place of retirement, a second body, his palace and his fortress; he
imagined himself a mouse descending a clear stream in half an egg-
shell, the master of a comet enfolding a hollow world.

He had been traveling in this way for a long while when he saw the
hitchhiker. The man did not stand at the side of the road where
Forlesen would have expected to see a pedestrian if, indeed, he had anticipated seeing any at all; but balanced himself on the high divider
that separated the innermost lane from those on which traffic moved in
the opposite direction. As he was some distance ahead, Forlesen was
able to observe him for several minutes before reaching the point at
which he stood.

He appeared to be a tall man, much stooped; and despite the ludi-
crousness of his position, his attitude suggested a certain dignity. His
hands and arms were in constant motion—not only as he sought to
maintain his balance, but because he mimed to each car that passed his
desire to ride, acting out in pantomime the car's stopping—his haste to
reach it—his opening the door and seating himself—his gratitude.

Nor did he care, apparently, in which direction he rode. While
Forlesen watched, he turned around and for a few moments sought to
attract the attention of a passing vehicle on the opposite side; then, as
though he realized that he was unlikely to have better fortune there
than in the direction he had chosen originally, turned back again. His
clothing was stiffly old-fashioned; once fairly good perhaps, but now
worn and dusty. When Forlesen stopped before this scarecrow figure
and motioned toward the seat beside him, the hitchhiker seemed so
startled at having gotten a ride at last that he wondered if he were
going to get in. Traffic zoomed and swirled around them like a summer
storm.

With his long legs folded high and the edge of the dashboard pressing against his shins he looked (Forlesen thought) like a cricket. An
old cricket, for despite his agility and air of alertness the hitchhiker was

old, his mouth full of crooked and stained old teeth and new white straight ones which were surely false, his bright, dark eyes surrounded by wrinkles, the hand he extended crook-fingered and calloused. "Name's Abraham Beale." Bad teeth in a good smile.

"Emanuel Forlesen," Forlesen said, taking the hand as he started the car rolling again. "Where are you going, Mr. Beale?"

"Anywhere." Beale was craning his neck to look out the small window in the back of the car. "Glad you didn't git hit," he said. " 'Fraid you would."

"I'm sure they could see I had stopped," Forlesen said, "and there are plenty of other lanes."

"Half of them's asleep. More'n half. You're awake, so I guess you thought everybody was, ain't that right?"

"They're driving; I'd think they'd run off the road if they were sleeping."

Beale was dusting his high-crowned, battered old hat with his big hands, patting and brushing it gently as though it were a baby animal of some delicate and appealing kind, a young rabbit or a little coati mundi. "I could see them," he said. "From where I was up there. Most of them didn't even see me—off in cloudland somewheres."

"I'm going to Model Pattern Products," Forlesen said.

The older man shook his head, and, having finished with his hat, set it on one knee. "I already tried there," he said, "nothin' for me." In a slightly lower voice, the voice of a man who is ashamed but feels he should not be, he added: "Lost my old job. I been trying to hook on somewhere else."

"I'm sorry to hear that." Forlesen found, somewhat to his surprise, that he *was* sorry. "What did you do?"

"About everything. There ain't much I can't turn a hand to. By rights I'm a lawyer, but I've soldiered some and worked stock out West, and lumberjacked, and once I fired on the railroad. And I'm a pretty good reaper mechanic if I do say so myself." Beale took a round tin box of snuff from one of the pockets of his shabby vest and put a pinch of the brown contents under his lip, then offered the box to Forlesen.

"You've had an interesting time," Forlesen said, waving it away. "I would have guessed you were a farmer, I think, if I had had to guess."

"Well, I've followed a plow and I ain't ashamed to say it. I was raised on the farm—oldest of thirteen children, and we all helped. I'd farm again if I had the land; it would be something. You know what? My dad, he left the old place to me, and the same day I got the letter that said I was to have it—from a esteemed colleague there, you know, a old fellow named Abner Bunter, we used to call him Banty, my dad'd had him do his will for him, me not being there—I got another that said the state was taking her for a highway. Had it and lost it between rippin' up one envelope and the other. I remember when it happened I went out and bought a cigar; I had been workin' but I couldn't work no more, not right then."

"Didn't they pay you for it?" Forlesen asked. He had been coming up behind a car the color of sour milk, and changed lanes as he spoke, shooting into an opening that allowed him to pass.

"You bet. There was a check in there," Beale said. "I planted her, but she didn't grow."

Forlesen glanced at him, startled.

"Hey!" The older man slapped his leg. "You think I'm touched. I meant I invested her."

"Well, I'm sorry you lost your money," Forlesen said.

"I didn't exactly lose it." Beale rubbed his chin. "It just sort of come to nothing. I still got it—draw the interest every year, they post her in the book for me—but there ain't nothing left." He snapped his fingers. "Tell you what it's like. We had a tree once on the farm, a apple tree—McIntoshes I think they were. Well, it never did die, but every winter it would die back a little bit, first one limb and then another, until there wasn't hardly anything left. Dad always thought it would come back, so he never did grub it out; but I don't believe it ever bore after I was big enough to go to school; and I remember the year I left home he cut a switch of it for Avery—Avery was the youngest of us brothers, he was always getting into trouble, like I recollect one time he let one of Dad's blueslate gamecocks in the pen with our big Shanghai rooster; said he thought the blueslate was too full of himself, and the big one would take him down a piece; well, what happened was the blueslate ripped him right up the front; any fool could have told him; looked like he was going to clean him without picking first. Dad was mad as hell—he thought the world of that rooster, and he used to feed him cake crumbs right out of his hand."

"What happened to the apple tree?" Forlesen asked.

"That's what I said myself," Beale said. Forlesen waited for him to continue, but he did not. The miles (hundreds of miles, Forlesen thought) slipped by; at long intervals the speaker announced the time: "It is oh sixty-three, oh sixty-five, oh sixty-eight thirty ours." The road dropped by slow degrees until they were level with the roofs of buildings, buildings whose roofs were jagged sawblades fronted with glass.

Forlesen said, "Model Pattern Products is in an industrial park—the Highland Industrial Park; maybe you'll be able to get a job there."

Beale nodded slowly. "I been looking out for something that looked to be in my line," and after a moment added, "I guess I didn't finish tellin' you 'bout my check I got, did I? Look here." His left hand fumbled inside his shabby coat, and Forlesen noticed that the elbows were so threadbare that his shirt could be seen through the fabric as though the man himself had begun to be slightly transparent, at least in his external and nonessential attributes. After a moment he held out a small, dun-colored bankbook, opening it dextrously with the fingers of one hand, but to the wrong page, an empty and unused page, which he presented for Forlesen's inspection. "That's all there is," he said. "I never drew a nickel, and I put the interest, most times, right smack back in; and that's all that's left. That's Dad's farm, them little numbers in the book."

Forlesen said, "I see."

"They didn't cheat me," Beale continued, "that was a good hunk of money when they give it to me, big money. But it's went down and down since till it's only little money, and little money ain't hardly worth nothing. Listen, you're young yit—I suppose you think two dollars is twice as much as one? Like, if you're paid one and some other feller gits two, he's got twice as much as you? Or the other way around?"

"I suppose so," Forlesen said.

"Well, you're right. Now suppose you've got—I won't ask you to tell me, I'll just strike upon a figure here from your general age and appearance and whatnot—five thousand dollars. And the other's got fifty thousand. Would you say he had ten times what you did?"

"Yes."

"That's where you're wrong; he's got fifty times, a hundred times what you do—maybe two hundred. Ain't you never noticed how a man with fifty thousand cold behind him will act? Like you're nothin' to him, you don't even weigh in his figuring at all."

Forlesen smiled. "Are you saying five thousand times ten isn't fifty thousand?"

"Look at it this way: you take your dollar to the store and you can git a dozen of eggs and a can of beans and a plug of tobacco. The other takes his two and gits two dozen of eggs, two cans of beans, and two plugs—ain't that right? But a man that has big money don't pay fifteen cents a plug like you and me; he can buy by the case if he feels inclined, and if he gits very much he gits it cheap as the store. Another thing—some things he can buy you and me can't git at all. It ain't that we can buy less, we can't git even a little bit of it. Let me give you an example: the railroads and the coal mines buy your state legislatures, right? Sure they do, and everybody knows it. Now there's thousands and thousands of people on the other side of them, and those thousands of people, if you was to add their money up, would be worth more. But they can't buy the legislature at all, ain't that right?"

"Go on," Forlesen said.

"Well, don't that prove that little money's power to buy certain things is zero? If it had any at all, thousands and thousands times it would make those people the kings of the state, but the actual fact is they can't do a thing—thousands time nothing is still nothing." Suddenly Beale turned, staring out the window of the car, and Forlesen realized that while they had been talking the road had descended to the ground. Still many-laned, it passed now through a level landscape dotted with great, square buildings which, despite their size, made no pretense of majesty or grace, but seemed in every case intentionally ugly. They were constructed of the cheapest materials, mostly corrugated metal and cinderblock, and each was surrounded by a high, rusty, wire fence, with a barren area of asphalt or gravel beyond it as though to provide (Forlesen knew the thought was ridiculous) a clear field of fire for defenders within.

"Hold up!" Beale said urgently. "Hold up a minute there." He gripped Forlesen's right arm, and Forlesen jockeyed the car to the outermost lane of traffic, then onto the rutted clay at the shoulder of the road.

"Look 'e there!" Beale said, pointing down a broad alley between two of the huge buildings.

Forlesen looked as directed. "Horses."

"Mustangs! Never been broke, you can tell that from looking at 'em. Whoever's got 'em's going to need some help." Beale opened the car door, then turned and shook Forlesen's hand. "Well, you've been a friend," he said, "and if ever I can do anything for you just you ask." Then he was gone, and Forlesen sat, for a moment, looking at the billboard-sized sign above the building into which the horses were being driven. It showed a dog's head in a red triangle on a field of black, without caption of any kind.

The speaker said: "Do not stop en route. You are still one and one half aisles from Model Pattern Products, your place of employment."

Forlesen nodded and looked at the watch his wife had given him. It was 069.50.

"You are to park your car," the speaker continued, "in the Model Pattern Products parking lot. You are not to occupy any position marked VISITORS, or any position marked with a name not your own."

"Do they know I'm coming?" Forlesen asked, pressing the button.

"An employee service folder has already been made out for you," the speaker told him. "All that needs to be done is to fill in your name."

The Model Pattern Products parking lot was enclosed by a high fence; but the gates were open, and the hinges so rusted that Forlesen, who stopped in the gateway for a moment thinking some guard or watchman might wish to challenge him, wondered if they had ever been closed; the ground itself, covered with loose gravel the color of ash, sloped steeply; he was forced to drive carefully to keep his car from skidding among the concrete stops of brilliant orange provided to prevent the parked cars from rolling down the grade; most of these were marked either with some name not his or with the word VISITOR, but he eventually discovered an unmarked position (unattractive, apparently, because smoke from a stubby flue projecting from the back of an outbuilding would blow across it) and left his car. His legs ached.

He was thirty or forty feet from his car when he realized he no longer had the speaker to advise him; several people were walking toward the gray metal building that was Model Pattern Products, but all were too distant for him to talk to them without shouting, and something in their appearance suggested that they would not wait for him to overtake them in any case. He followed them through a small door and found himself alone.

An anteroom held two time clocks, one beige, the other brown. Remembering the instruction sheet, he took a blank timecard from the rack and wrote his name at the top, then pushed it into the beige machine and depressed the lever. A gong sounded. He withdrew the card and checked the stamped time: 069.56. A thin, youngish woman with large glasses and a sharp nose looked over his shoulder. "You're late," she said. (He was aware for an instant of the effort she was making to read his name at the top of the card.) "Mr. Forlesen."

He said, "I'm afraid I don't know the starting time."

The woman said: "Oh seventy ours sharp, Mr. Forlesen. Start oh seventy ours sharp, coffee for your subdivision one hundred ours to one hundred and one. Lunch one hundred and twenty to one hundred and forty-one. Coffee, your subdivision, one fifty to one fifty-one P.M. Quit one seventy ours at the whistle."

"Then I'm not late," Forlesen said. He showed her his card.

"Mr. Frick likes everyone to be at least twenty minutes early, especially supervisory and management people. The real go-getters—that's what he calls them—the real go-getters—try to be early. I mean, earlier than the regular early. Oh sixty-nine twenty-five, something like that. They unlock their desks and go upstairs for early coffee, and sometimes they play cards; it's fun."

"I'm sorry I missed it," Forlesen said. "Can you tell me where I'm supposed to go now?"

"To your desk," the woman said, nodding. "Unlock it."

"I don't know where it is."

"Well, of course you don't, but I can't assign you to your desk—that's up to Mr. Fields, your supervisor." After a moment she added, "I know where you're going to go, but he has the keys."

Forlesen said, "I thought I was a supervisor."

"You are," the woman told him, "but Mr. Fields is—you know—a real supervisor. Anyway, nearly. Do you want to talk to him now?"

Forlesen nodded.

"I'll see if he'll see you now. You have Creativity Group today, and Leadership Training. And Company Orientation, and Bet-Your-Life— that's the management managing real life pseudo-game—and one inter-departmental training-transfer."

"I'll be glad to get the orientation anyway," Forlesen said. He followed the woman, who had started to walk away. "But am I going to have time for all that?"

"You don't get it," she told him over her shoulder, "you give it. And you'll have lots of time for work besides—don't worry. I've been here a long time already. I'm Miss Fawn. Are you married?"

"Yes," Forlesen said, "and I think we have children."

"Oh. Well, you look it. Here's Mr. Fields's office, and I nearly forgot to tell you you're on the Planning and Evaluation Committee. Don't forget to knock."

Forlesen knocked on the door to which the woman had led him. It was of metal painted to resemble wood, and had riveted to its front a small brass plaque which read: "Mr. D'Andrea."

"Come in!" someone called from inside the office.

Forlesen entered and saw a short, thickset, youngish man with close-cropped hair sitting at a metal desk. The office was extremely small and had no windows, but there was a large, brightly colored picture on each wall—two photographs in color (a beach with rocks and waves, and a snow-clad mountain) and two realistic landscapes (both of rolling green countryside dotted with cows and trees).

"Come in," the youngish man said again. "Sit down. Listen, I want to tell you something—you don't have to knock to come in this office. Not ever. My door—like they say—is always open. What I mean is, I may keep it shut to keep out the noise and so forth out in the hall, but it's always open to you."

"I think I understand," Forlesen said. "Are you Mr. Fields?" The plaque had somewhat shaken his faith in the young woman with glasses.

"Right—Ed Fields at your service."

"Then I'm going to be working for you. I'm Emanuel Forlesen." Forlesen leaned forward and offered his hand, which Fields walked around the desk to take.

"Glad to meet you, Manny. Always happy to welcome a new face to the subdivision." For an instant, as their eyes met, Forlesen felt himself weighed in invisible scales and, he thought, found slightly wanting. Then the moment passed, and a few seconds later he had difficulty believing it had ever been. "Remember what I told you when you came in—my door is always open," Fields said. "Sit down." Forlesen sat, and Fields resumed his place behind the desk.

"We're a small outfit," Fields said, "but we're sharp." He held up a clenched fist. "And I intend to make us the sharpest in the division. I need men who'll back my play all the way, and maybe even run in front a little. Sharpies. That's what I call 'em—sharpies. And you work with me, not for me."

Forlesen nodded.

"We're a team," Fields continued, "and we're going to function as a team. That doesn't mean there isn't a quarterback, and a coach—" he pointed toward the ceiling "—up there. It does mean that I expect every man to bat two fifty or better, and the ones that don't make three hundred had better be damn good field. See what I mean?"

Forlesen nodded again and asked, "What does our subdivision do? What's our function?"

"We make money for the company," Fields told him. "We do what needs to be done. You see this office? This desk, this chair?"

Forlesen nodded.

"There's two kinds of guys that sit here—I mean all through the company. There's the old hasbeen guys they stick in here because they've been through it all and seen everything, and there's the young guys like me that get put here to get an education—you get me? Sometimes the young guys just never move out, then they turn into the old ones. That isn't going to happen to me, and I want you to remember that the easiest way for you to move up yourself is to move into this spot right here. Someday this will all be yours—that's the way to think of it. That's what I tell every guy in the subdivision—someday this'll all be yours." Fields reached over his head to tap one of the realistic landscapes. "You get what I mean?"

"I think so."

"Okay, then let me show you your desk and where you're gonna work."

As they dodged among windowless, brightly lit corridors, it struck Forlesen that though the building was certainly ventilated—some of the corridors, in fact, were actually windy—the system could not be working very well. A hundred odors, mostly foul, but some of a sickening sweetness, thronged the air; and though most of the hallways they traveled were so cold as to be uncomfortable, a few were as stuffy as tents left closed all day beneath a summer sun.

"What's that noise?" Forlesen asked.

"That's a jackhammer busting concrete. You're going to be in the new wing." Fields opened a green steel door and led the way down a narrow, low-ceilinged passage pungent with the burnt-metal smell of arc welding; the tiled floor was gritty with cement dust, and Forlesen wondered, looking at the unpainted walls, how they could have gotten so dirty when they were clearly so new. "In here," Fields said.

It was a big room, and had been divided into cubicles with rippled glass partitions five feet high. The effect was one of privacy, but the cubicles had been laid out in such a way as to allow anyone looking through the glass panel in the office door to see into them all. The windows were covered with splintering boards, and the floor sufficiently uneven that it was possible to imagine it a petrified sea, though its streaked black-and-gray pattern was more suggestive of charred wood. "You're in luck," Fields said. "I'd forgotten, or I would have told you back in the office. You get a window desk. Right here. Sitting by the window makes it kind of dark, but you only got the one other guy on the side of you over there, that's nice, and you know there's always a certain prestige goes with the desk that's next to the window."

Forlesen asked, "Wouldn't it be possible to take some of the glass out of these partitions and use it in the windows?"

"Hell, no. This stuff is partition glass—what you need for a window is window glass. I thought you were supposed to have a lot of science."

"My duties are supposed to be supervisory and managerial," Forlesen said.

"Don't ever let anybody tell you management isn't a science." Fields thumped Forlesen's new desk for emphasis and got a smudge of dust on his fist. "It's an art, sure, but it's a science too."

Forlesen, who could not see how anything could be both, nodded.

Fields glanced at his watch. "Nearly oh seventy-one already, and I got an appointment. Listen, I'm gonna leave you to find your way around."

Forlesen seated himself at his desk. "I was hoping you'd tell me what I'm supposed to do here before you left."

Fields was already outside the cubicle. "You mean your responsibilities; there's a list around somewhere."

Forlesen had intended to protest further, but as he started to speak he noticed an optical illusion so astonishing that for the brief period it was visible he could only stare. As Fields passed behind one of the rippled glass partitions on his way to the door, the distortions in the glass caused his image to change from that of the somewhat dumpy and rumpled man with whom Forlesen was now slightly familiar; behind the glass he was taller, exceedingly neat, and blank-faced. And he wore glasses.

When he was gone Forlesen got up and examined the partitions carefully; they seemed ordinary enough, one surface rippled, the other smooth, the tops slightly dusty. He looked at his empty desk through the glass; it was a vague blur. He sat down again, and the telephone rang. "Cappy?"

"This is Emanuel Forlesen." At the last moment it occurred to Forlesen that it might have been better to call himself "Manny" as Fields had—that it might seem more friendly and less formal, particularly to someone who was looking for someone he addressed so casually; but, as the thought entered his mind, something else, not a thought but one of those deeper feelings from which our thoughts have, perhaps, evolved, contradicted it so he repeated his name, bearing down on the first syllable: *"Ee-manuel Forlesen."*

"Isn't Cappy Dillingham there?"

"He may be in this office," Forlesen said, "that is, his desk may be here, but he's not here himself, and this is my telephone—I just moved into the office."

"Take a message for him, will you? Tell him the Creativity Group meeting is moved up to oh seventy-eight sharp. I'm sorry it had to be so early, but Gene Fine has got a bunch of other stuff and we couldn't figure out anything else to do short of canceling. And we couldn't get a room so we're meeting in the hall outside the drilling and boring shop. There's definitely going to be a film. Have you got that?"

"I think so," Forlesen said. "Oh seventy-eight, hall outside the drillroom, movie." He heard someone behind him and turned to look. It was Miss Fawn, so he said, "Do you know where Mr. Dillingham is? I'm taking a call for him."

"He died," Miss Fawn said. "Let me talk to them." She took the receiver. "Who's calling, please? . . . Mr. Franklin, Mr. Dillingham died . . . Last night . . . Yes, it is. Mr. Forlesen is taking his place in your group—you should have gotten a memo on it . . . On Mr. Dillingham's old number; you were just talking to him. He's right here. Wait a moment." She turned back to Forlesen: "It's for you."

He took the telephone and a voice in the earpiece said, "Are you Forlesen? Listen, this is Ned Franklin. You may not have been notified yet, but you're in our Creativity Group, and we're meeting—wait a minute, I've got a memo on it under all this crap somewhere."

"Oh seventy-eight," Forlesen said.

"Right. I realize that's pretty early—"

"We wouldn't want to try to get along without Gene Fine," Forlesen said.

"Right. Try to be there."

Miss Fawn seemed to be leaving. Forlesen turned to see how she would appear in the rippled glass as he said, "What are we going to try and create?"

"Creativity. We create creativity itself—we learn to be creative."

"I see," Forlesen said. He watched Miss Fawn become pretty while remaining sexless, like a mannequin. He said, "I thought we'd just take some clay or something and start in."

"Not that sort of creativity, for crap's sake!"

"All right," Forlesen said.

"Just show up, okay? Mr. Frick is solidly behind this and he gets upset when we have less than full attendance."

"Maybe he could get us a meeting room then," Forlesen suggested. He had no idea who "Mr. Frick" was, but he was obviously important.

"Hell, I couldn't ask Mr. Frick that. Anyway, he never asks where we had the meeting—just how many came and what we discussed, and whether we feel we're making progress."

"He could be saving it."

"Yeah, I guess he could. Listen, Cappy, if I can get us a room I'll call you, okay?"

"Right," said Forlesen. He hung up, wondered vaguely why Miss Fawn had come, then saw that she had left a stack of papers on a corner of his desk. "Well, the hell with you," he said, and pushed them toward the wall. "I haven't even looked at this desk yet."

It was a metal desk, and somewhat smaller, older, and shabbier than the one in Fields's office. It seemed odd to Forlesen that he should find old furniture in a part of the building which was still—judging from the sounds that occasionally drifted through the walls and window boards— under construction; but the desk, and his chair as well, were unques- tionably nearing the end of their useful lives. The center desk drawer held a dead insect, a penknife with yellowed imitation ivory sides and a broken blade, a drawing of a bracket (very neatly lettered, Forlesen no- ticed) on crumpled tracing paper, and a dirty stomach mint. He threw this last away (his wastebasket was new, made of plastic, and did not seem to fit in with the other furnishings of the office) and opened the right-hand side drawer. It contained an assortment of pencils (all more or less chewed), a cube of art gum with the corners worn off, and some sheets of blank paper with one corner folded. The next drawer down yielded a wrinkled brown paper bag that disgorged a wad of wax paper, a stale half cookie, and the sharp smell of apples; the last two drawers proved to be a single file drawer in masquerade; there were five empty file folders in it, including one with a column of twenty-seven figures written on it in pencil, the first and lowest being 8,750 and the last and highest 12,500; they were not totaled. On the left side of the desk what looked like the ends of four more drawers proved to be a device for con- cealing a typewriter; there was no typewriter.

Forlesen closed it and leaned back in his chair, aware that inventory- ing the desk had depressed him. After a moment he remembered Fields's saying that he would find a list of his responsibilities in the office, and discovered it on the top of the stack of papers Miss Fawn had left with him. It read:

MANAGEMENT PERSONNEL

> *Make M.P.P. Co. profitable and keep it profitable.*
>
> *Assist in carrying out corporate goals.*
>
> *Maintain employee discipline by reporting violators' names to their superiors.*
>
> *Help keep costs down.*
>
> *If any problems come up help to deal with them in accord with company policy.*
>
> *Training, production, sales, and public relations are all super- vised by management personnel.*

Forlesen threw the paper in the waste basket.

The second paper in the stack was headed: SAMPLE LEADERSHIP PROBLEM #105, and read:

A young woman named Enid Fenton was hired recently as clerical help. Her work has not been satisfactory, but because clerical help has been in short supply she has not been told this. Recently a reduction in the work load in her department made it possible to transfer three girls to another department. Miss Fenton asked for one of the transfers and when told that they had already been assigned to others behaved in such a manner as to suggest (though nothing was actually said) that she was considering resignation. Her work consists of keypunching, typing, and filing. Should her supervisor:

☐ Discharge her.

☐ Indicate to her that her work has been satisfactory but hint that she may be laid off.

☐ Offer her a six week leave of absence (without pay) during which she may obtain further training.

☐ Threaten her with a disciplinary fine.

☐ Assign her to assist one of the older women.

☐ Ask the advice of the other members of his Leadership group, following it only if he agrees the group has reached a correct decision in this case.

☐ Reassign her to small-parts assembly.

NOTE: QUESTIONS CONCERNING THIS SAMPLE LEADERSHIP PROBLEM SHOULD BE ADDRESSED TO ERIC FAIRCHILD—EX 8173.

After reading the problem through twice Forlesen picked up his telephone and dialed the number. A female voice said, "Mr. Fairchild's office."

Forlesen identified himself, and a moment later a masculine voice announced, "Eric Fairchild."

"It's about the leadership problem—number one oh five?"

"Oh, yes." (Fairchild's voice was hearty; Forlesen imagined him slapping backs and challenging people to Indian-wrestle at parties.) "I've had quite a few calls about that one. You can check as many answers as you like if they're not mutually exclusive—okay?"

"That wasn't what I was going to ask," Forlesen said. "This girl's work—"

"Wait a minute," Fairchild said. And then, much more faintly, "Get me the Leadership file, Miss Fenton."

"What did you say?" Forlesen asked.

"Wait a minute," Fairchild said again. "If we're going to dig into this thing in depth I want to have a copy of the problem in front of me. Thank you. Okay, you can shoot now. What did you say your name was?"

"Forlesen. I meant after you said 'Wait a minute,' the first time. I thought I heard you call your secretary Miss Fenton."

"Ha ha ha."

"Didn't you?"

"My secretary's name is Mrs. Fairchild, Mr. Forlesen—no, she's not my wife, if that's what you're thinking, Mr. Frick doesn't approve of nepotism. She's just a nice lady who happens to be named Mrs. Fairchild, and I was addressing Miss Fetton, who is filling in for her today."

"Sorry," Forlesen said.

"You wanted to ask about problem one hundred and five?"

"Yes, I wanted to ask—well, for one thing, in what way is the young woman's work unsatisfactory?"

"Just what it says on the sheet, whatever that is. Wait a minute, here it is—*Her work has not been satisfactory, but because clerical help has been in short supply she has not been told this.*"

"Yes," Forlesen said, "but in what way has it been unsatisfactory?"

"I see what you're getting at now, but I can't very well answer that, can I? After all, the whole essence of Leadership Training involves presenting the participants with structured problems—you see what I mean? This is a structured problem. Miss Fenton, could I trouble you to go down to the canteen and get me some coffee? Take it out of petty cash. Now if I explained something like that to you, and not to the others, then it would have a different structuring for you than for them. You see?"

"Well, it seemed to me," Forlesen said, "that one of the first things to do would be to take Miss Fenton aside and explain to her that her work *was* unsatisfactory, and perhaps hear what she had to say."

"Miss who?"

"Fetton, the girl in the problem."

"Right, and I see what you mean. However, since it specifically says what I read to you, and nothing else more than that, then if I was to tell you something else it would be structured different for you than for the other fellows. See what I mean?"

After thinking for a moment Forlesen said, "I don't see how I can check any of the boxes knowing no more than I do now. Is it all right if I write my own solution?"

"You mean, draw a little box for yourself?"

"Yes, and write what I said after it—I mean, what I outlined to you a minute ago. That I'd talk to her."

"I don't think there's room on the paper for all that, fella. I mean, you said quite a bit."

Forlesen said, "I think I can boil it down."

"Well, we can't allow it anyway. These things are scored by a computer and we have to give it an answer—what I'm driving at is, the number of your answer. Like the girl codes in the I.D. number of each participant and then the problem number, and then the answer number, like *one* or *two* or *three*. Or then if she puts like twenty-*three* it knows you answered *two* AND *three*. That would be *indicate to her that her work has been satisfactory but hint that she may be laid off, and offer her a six-week leave of absence without pay during which she may obtain further training.* You get it?"

"You're telling me that that's the right answer," Forlesen said. "Twenty-three."

"Listen, hell no! *I* don't know what the right answer is, only the machine does; maybe there isn't any right answer at all. I was just trying to give you a kind of a hint—what I'd do if I was in your shoes. You want to get a good grade, don't you?"

"Is it important?"

"I would say that it's important—I think it's important to any man to know he did something like this and he did good—wouldn't you say so? But like we said at the start of the course, your grade is your personal thing. We're going to give grades, sure, on a scale of seven hundred and fifty-seven—that's the top—to forty-nine, but nobody knows your grade but you. You're told your own grade and your class standing and your standing among everybody here who's ever taken the course—naturally that doesn't mean much, the problems change all the time—but what you do with that information is up to you. You evaluate yourself. I know there have been these rumors about Mr. Frick coming in and asking the computer questions, but it's not true—frankly I don't think Mr. Frick even knows how to program. It doesn't just talk to you, you know."

"I didn't get to attend the first part of the course," Forlesen said. "I'm filling in for Cappy Dillingham. He died."

"Sorry to hear that. Old age, I guess."

"I don't know."

"Probably that was it. Hell, it seems like it was only yesterday I was talking to him about his grade after class—he had some question about one oh four, I don't even remember what it was now. Old Cappy. Wow."

"How was he doing?" Forlesen asked.

"Not too hot. I had him figured for about a five-fifty, give or take twenty—but listen, if you had seen the earlier stuff you wouldn't be asking these questions now. You'd of been guided into it—see what I mean?"

Forlesen said: "I just don't see how I can mark this. I'm going to return the unmarked sheet under protest."

"I told you, we can't score something like that."

Forlesen said, "Well, that's what I'm going to do," and hung up.

His desk said: "You're a sharp one, aren't you? He's going to call you back."

Forlesen looked for the speaker but could not find it.

"I heard you talking to Franklin too; and I saw you throw away the Management Responsibilities list. Do you know that in a lot of the offices here you find that framed and hung on the wall? Some of them hang it where they can see it, and some of them hang it where their visitors can see it."

"Which kind get promoted?" Forlesen asked. He had decided the speaker was under the center desk drawer, and was on his hands and knees looking for it.

"The kind that fit in," the desk said.

Forlesen said, "What kind of an answer is that?" The telephone rang and he answered it.

"Mr. Forlesen, please." It was Fairchild.

"Speaking."

"I was wondering about number one oh five—have you sent it back yet?"

"I just put it in my outbox," Forlesen said. "They haven't picked it up yet." Vaguely he wondered if Miss Fawn was supposed to empty the outbox, or if anyone was; perhaps he was supposed to do it himself.

"Good, good. Listen, I've been thinking about what you said—do you think that if I told you what was wrong with this girl you'd be able to size her up better? The thing is, she just doesn't fit in; you know what I mean?"

"No," Forlesen said.

"Let me give you an example. Guys come in the office all the time, either to talk to me or just because they haven't anything better to do. They kid around with the girls, you know? Okay, this girl, you never know how she's going to take it. Sometimes she gets mad. Sometimes she thinks the guy really wants to get romantic, and she wants to go along with it."

"I'd think they'd learn to leave her alone," Forlesen said.

"Believe me, they have. And the other girls don't like her—they come in to me and say they want to be moved away from her desk."

"Do they say why?"

"Oh, hell, no. Listen, if you'd ever bossed a bunch of women you'd know better than that; the way they always put it is the light isn't good there, or it's too close to the keypunch—too noisy—or it's too *far* from the keypunch and they don't wanna have to walk that far, or they want to be closer to somebody they *do* like. But you know how it is—I've moved her all around the damn office and everybody wants to get away; she's Typhoid Mary."

"Make her your permanent secretary," Forlesen said.

"*What?*"

"Just for a while. Give your mother a special assignment. That way you can find out what's wrong with this girl, if anything is, which I doubt."

"You're crazy, Forlesen," Fairchild said, and hung up.

The telephone rang again almost as soon as Forlesen set the receiver down. "This is Miss Fawn," the telephone said. "Mr. Freeling wants to see you, Mr. Forlesen."

"Mr. Freeling?"

"Mr. Freeling is Mr. Fields's chief, Mr. Forlesen; and Mr. Fields is your chief. Mr. Freeling reports to Mr. Flint, and Mr. Flint reports directly to Mr. Frick. I am Mr. Freeling's secretary."

"Thank you," Forlesen said, "I was beginning to wonder where you fit in."

"Right out of your office, down the hall to the 'T,' left, up the stairs, and along the front of the building. Mr. Freeling's name is on the door."

"Thank you," Forlesen said again.

Mr. Freeling's name was on the door, in the form of a bronzelike plaque. Forlesen, remembering D'Andrea's brass one, saw at once that Mr. Freeling's was more modern and up-to-date, and realized that Mr. Freeling was more important than D'Andrea had been; but he also realized that D'Andrea's plaque had been real brass and that Mr. Freeling's was plastic. He knocked, and Miss Fawn's voice called, "Come in." He came in, and Miss Fawn threw a switch on her desk and said, "Mr. Forlesen to see you, Mr. Freeling."

And then to Forlesen: "Go right in."

Mr. Freeling's office was large and had two windows, both overlooking the highway. Forlesen found that he was somewhat surprised to see the highway again, though it looked just as it had before. The pictures on the walls were landscapes much like Fields's, but Mr. Freeling's desk, which was quite large, was covered by a sheet of glass with photographs under it; and these were all of sailboats, and of groups of men in shorts and striped knit shirts and peaked caps.

"Sit down," Mr. Freeling said. "Be with you in a minute." He was a large, sunburned, squinting man, beginning to go gray. The chair in front of his desk had wooden arms and a vinyl seat made to look like ostrich hide. Forlesen sat down, wondering what Mr. Freeling wanted; and after a time it came to him that what Mr. Freeling wanted was for him to wonder this, and that Mr. Freeling would have been wiser to speak to him sooner. Mr. Freeling had a pen in his hand and was reading a letter—the same letter—over and over; at last he signed it with a scribble and laid it and the pen flat on his desk. "I should have called you in earlier to say welcome aboard," he said, "but maybe it was better to give you a chance to drop your hook and get your jib in first. Are you finding em pee pee a snug harbor?"

"I think I would like it better," Forlesen said, "if I knew what it was I'm supposed to be doing here."

Freeling laughed. "Well, that's easily fixed—Bert Fields is standing watch with you, isn't he? Ask him for a list of your responsibilities."

"It's Ed Fields," Forlesen said, "and I already have the list. What I would like to know is what I'm supposed to be doing."

"I see what you mean," Freeling said, "but I'm afraid I can't tell you. If you were a lathe operator I'd say *make that part,* but you're a part of management, and you can't treat managerial people that way."

"Go ahead," Forlesen told him. "I won't mind."

Freeling cleared his throat. "That isn't what I meant, and, quite frankly, if you think anyone here is going to feel any compulsion to be polite to you, you're in for squalls. What I meant was that if I knew what you ought to be doing I'd hire a clerk to do it. You're where you are because we feel—rightly or wrongly—that you can find your own work, recognize it when you see it, and do it or get somebody else to. Just make damn sure you don't step on anybody's toes while you're doing it, and don't make more trouble than you fix. Don't rock the boat."

"I see," Forlesen said.

"Just make damn sure before you do anything that it's in line with policy, and remember that if you get the unions down on us we're going to throw you overboard quick."

Forlesen nodded.

"And keep your hand off the tiller. Look at it this way—your job is fixing leaks. Only the sailor who's spent most of his life down there in the hold with the oakum and . . . uh . . . Fastpatch has the experience necessary to recognize the landmarks and weathersigns. But don't you patch a leak somebody else is already patching, or has been told to patch, or is getting ready to patch. Understand? Don't come running to me with complaints, and don't let me get any complaints about you. Now what was it you wanted to see me about?"

"I don't," Forlesen said. "You said you wanted to see me."

"Oh. Well, I'm through."

Outside Forlesen asked Miss Fawn how he was supposed to know what company policy was. "It's in the air," Miss Fawn said tartly, "you breathe it." Forlesen suggested that it might be useful if it were written down someplace, and she said, "You've been here long enough to know better than that, Mr. Forlesen; you're no kid anymore." As he left the office she called, "Don't forget your Creativity Group."

He found the drilling room only after a great deal of difficulty. It was full of drill presses and jig bores—perhaps thirty or more—of which only two were being used. At one, a white-haired man was making a hole in a steel plate; he worked slowly, lifting the drill from time to time to fill the cavity with oil from a squirt-can beside the machine. At the other a much younger man sang as he worked, an obscene parody of a popular song. Forlesen was about to ask if he knew where the Creativity Group was meeting when he felt a hand on his shoulder. He turned and saw Fields, who said, "Looks like you found it. Come on, I'm going to make this one come hell or high water. Right through the door on the other side there."

They threaded their way through the drill presses, most of which seemed to be out of order in some way, and were about to go through the door Fields had indicated, when Forlesen heard a yell behind them. The younger man had burned his hand in trying to change the smoking drill in his machine. "That's a good operator," Fields said. "He pushes everything right along—you know what I mean?" Forlesen said he did.

The creativity meeting, as Franklin had told him, was in the corridor. Folding metal chairs had been set up in groupings that looked intentionally disorganized, and a small motion picture screen stood on an easel. Franklin was wrestling with a projector resting (pretty precariously, Forlesen thought) on the seat of the rearmost chair; he had the look of not being as young as he seemed, and after he had introduced himself they sat down and watched him. From time to time others joined them, and people passing up and down the hall, mostly men in gray work clothing, ignored them all, threading their way among the tin chairs without seeming to see them and stepping skillfully around the screen, from which, from time to time, flashed faint numerals 1, 2, and 3, or the legend:

Creativity Means Jobs.

After a while Fields said, "I think we ought to get started."

"You go ahead," Franklin told him. "I'll have this going in a minute."

Fields walked to the front of the group, beside the screen, and said: "Creativity group twenty-one is now in session. I'm going to ask the man in front to write his name on a piece of paper and pass it back. Everybody sign, and do it so we can read it, please. We're going to have a movie on creativity—"

"*Creativity Means Jobs,*" Franklin put in.

"Yeah, *Creativity Means Jobs,* then a free-form critique of the movie. Then what, Ned?"

"Open discussion on creativity in problem study."

"You got the movie yet?"

"Just a minute."

Forlesen looked at his watch. It was oh seventy-eight forty-five.

Someone at the front of the group, close to where Fields was now standing, said: "While we have a minute I'd like to get an objection on record to this phrase *creativity in problem study.* It seems to me that what it implies is that creativity is automatically going to point you toward some solution you didn't see before, and I feel that anyone who believes that's going to happen—anyway in most cases—doesn't know what the hell they're talking about."

Fields said, "Everybody knows creativity isn't going to solve your problems for you."

"I said point the way," the man objected.

Someone else said, "What creativity is going to do for you in the way of problem study is point the way to new ways of seeing your problem."

"Not necessarily successful," the first man said.

"Not necessarily successful," the second man said, "if by successful what you mean is permitting you to make a non-trivial elaboration of the problem definition."

Someone else said, "Personally I feel problem definitions don't limit creativity," and Fields said: "I think we're all agreed on that when they're *creative* problem definitions. Right, Ned?"

"Of creative problems."

"Right, of creative problems. You know, Ned told me one time when he was talking to somebody about what we do at these meetings this fellow said he thought we'd just each take a lump of clay or something and, you know, start trying to make some kind of shape." There was laughter, and Fields held up a hand good-naturedly. "Okay, it's funny, but I think we can all learn something from that. What we can learn is, most people when we talk about our Creativity Group are thinking the same way this guy was, and that's why, when we talk about it we got to make certain points, like for one thing creativity isn't ever what you do alone, right? It's your creative *group* that gets things going—hey, Ned, what's the word I want?"

"Synergy."

"Yeah, and teamwork. And second, creativity isn't about making new things—like some statue or something nobody wants. What creativity is about is solving company problems—"

Franklin called, "Hey, I've got this ready now."

"Just a minute. Like you take the problem this company had when Adam Bean that founded it died. The problem was—should we go on making what we used to when he was alive, or should we make something different? That problem was solved by Mr. Dudley, as I guess everybody knows, but he wouldn't have been able to do it without a lot of good men to help him. I personally feel that a football team is about the most creative thing there is."

Someone brushed Forlesen's sleeve; it was Miss Fawn, and as Fields paused, she said in her rather shrill voice, "Mr. Fields! Mr. Fields, you're wanted on the telephone. It's quite important." There was something stilted in the way she delivered her lines, like a poor actress, and after a moment Forlesen realized that there was no telephone call, that she had been instructed by Fields to provide this interruption and thus give him an excuse for escaping the meeting while increasing the other participants' estimate of his importance. After a moment more he understood that Franklin and the others knew this as well as he, and that the admiration they felt for Fields—and admiration was certainly there, surrounding the stocky man as he followed Miss Fawn out—had its root in the daring Fields had shown, and in the power implied by his securing the cooperation of Miss Fawn, Mr. Freeling's secretary.

Someone had dimmed the lights. *Creativity Means Jobs* flashed on the screen, then a group of men and women in what might have been a schoolroom in a very exclusive school. One waved his hand, stood up, and spoke. There was no sound, but his eyes flashed with enthusiasm; when he sat down, an impressive-looking woman in tweeds rose, and Forlesen felt that whatever she was saying must be unanswerable, the final word on the subject under discussion; she was polite and restrained and as firm as iron, and she clearly had every fact at her fingertips.

"I can't get this damn sound working," Franklin said. "Just a minute."

"What are they talking about?" Forlesen asked.

"Huh?"

"In the picture. What are they discussing?"

"Oh, I got it," Franklin said. "Wait a minute. They're talking about promoting creativity in the educational system."

"Are they teachers?"

"No, they're actors—let me alone for a minute, will you? I want to get this sound going."

The sound came on, almost coinciding with the end of the picture; while Franklin was rewinding the film Forlesen said, "I suppose actors would have a better understanding of creativity than teachers would at that."

"It's a re-creation of an actual meeting of real teachers," Franklin explained, "they photographed it and taped it, then had the actors reproduce the debate."

Forlesen decided to go home for lunch. Lunch ours were one hundred twenty to one hundred forty-one—twenty-one ours should be enough, he thought, for him to drive there and return, and to eat. He kept the pedal down all the way, and discovered that the signs with HIDDEN DRIVES on their faces had SLOW CHILDREN on their backs.

The brick house was just as he remembered it. He parked the car on the spot where he had first seen it (there was a black oil stain there) and knocked at the door. Edna answered it, looking not quite as he remembered her. "What do you want?" she said.

"Lunch."

"Are you crazy? If you're selling something, we don't want it."

Forlesen said, "Don't you know who I am?"

She looked at him more closely. He said, "I'm your husband Emanuel."

She seemed uncertain, then smiled, kissed him, and said, "Yes you are, aren't you. You look different. Tired."

"I am tired," he said, and realized that it was true.

"Is it lunchtime already? I don't have a watch, you know. I haven't been able to keep track. I thought it was only the middle of the morning."

"It seemed long enough to me," Forlesen said. He wondered where the children were, thinking that he would have liked to see them.

"What do you want for lunch?"

"Whatever you have."

In the bedroom she got out bread and sliced meat, and plugged in the coffeepot. "How was work?"

"All right. Fine."

"Did you get promoted? Or get a raise?"

He shook his head.

"After lunch," she said. "You'll get promoted after lunch."

He laughed, thinking that she was joking.

"A woman knows."

"Where are the kids?"

"At school. They eat their lunch at school. There's a beautiful cafeteria—everything is stainless steel—and they have a dietician who thinks about the best possible lunch for each child and makes them eat it."

"Did you see it?" he asked.

"No, I read about it. In here." She tapped Food Preparation in the Home.

"Oh."

"They'll be home at one hundred and thirty—that's what the book says. Here's your sandwich." She poured him a cup of coffee. "What time is it now?"

He looked at the watch she had given him. "A hundred and twenty-nine thirty."

"Eat. You ought to be going back soon."

He said, "I was hoping we might have time for more than this."

"Tonight, maybe. You don't want to be late."

"All right." The coffee was good, but tasted slightly oily; the sandwich meat salty and dry and flavorless. He unstrapped the watch from his wrist and handed it to her. "You keep this," he said. "I've felt badly about wearing it all morning—it really belongs to you."

"You need it more than I do," she said.

"No I don't; they have clocks all over, there. All I have to do is look at them."

"You'll be late getting back to work."

"I'm going to drive as fast as I can anyway—I can't go any faster than that no matter what a watch says. Besides, there's a speaker that tells me things, and I'm sure it will tell me if I'm late."

Reluctantly she accepted the watch. He chewed the last of his sandwich. "You'll have to tell me when to go now," he said, thinking that this would somehow cheer her.

"It's time to go already," she said.

"Wait a minute—I want to finish my coffee."

"How was work?"

"Fine," he said.

"You have a lot to do there?"

"Oh, God, yes." He remembered the crowded desk that had been waiting for him when he had returned from the creativity meeting, the supervision of workers for whom he had been given responsibility without authority, the ours spent with Fields drawing up the plan which, just before he left, had been vetoed by Mr. Freeling. "I don't think there's any purpose in most of it," he said, "but there's plenty to do."

"You shouldn't talk like that," his wife said, "you'll lose your job."

"I don't, when I'm there."

"I've got nothing to do," she said. It was as though the words themselves had forced their way from between her lips.

He said, "That can't be true."

"I made the beds, and I dusted and swept, and it was all finished a couple of ours after you had gone. There's nothing."

"You could read," he said.

"I can't—I'm too nervous."

"Well, you could have prepared a better lunch than this."

"That's *nothing*," she said. "Just *nothing*." She was suddenly angry, and it struck him, as he looked at her, that she was a stranger, that he knew Fields and Miss Fawn and even Mr. Freeling better than he knew her.

"The morning's over," he said. "I'm sorry I can't give it back to you, but I can't; what I did—that was nothing too."

"Please," she said, "won't you go? Having you here makes me so nervous."

He said, "Try and find something to do."

"All right."

He wiped his mouth on the paper she had given him and took a step toward the parlor; to his surprise she walked with him, not detaining him, but seeming to savor his company now that she had deprived herself of it. "Do you remember when we woke up?" she said. "You didn't know at first that you were supposed to dress yourself."

"I'm still not sure of it."

"Oh, you know what I mean."

"Yes," he said, and he knew that he did, but that she did not.

The signs said NO TURN, and Forlesen wondered if he were really compelled to obey them, if the man in the blue car would come after him if he did not go back to Model Pattern Products. He suspected that he would, but that nothing he could do would be worse than M.P.P. itself. In front of the dog-food factory a shapeless brown object fluttered in the road, animated by the turbulence of each car that passed and seeming to attack it, throwing itself with desperate, toothless courage at the singing, invulnerable tires. He had almost run over it before he realized what it was—Abraham Beale's hat.

The parking lot was more rutted than he had remembered; he drove slowly and carefully. The outbuilding had been torn down, and another car, startlingly shiny (Forlesen did not believe his own had ever been that well polished, not even when he had first looked out the window at it) had his old place; he was forced to take another, farther from the plant. Several other people, he noticed, seemed to have gone home for lunch as he had—some he knew, having shared meeting rooms with them. He had never punched out on the beige clock, and did not punch in.

There was a boy seated at his desk, piling new schoolbooks on it from a cardboard box on the floor. Forlesen said hello, and the boy said that his name was George Howe, and that he worked in Mr. Forlesen's section.

Forlesen nodded, feeling that he understood. "Miss Fawn showed you to your desk?"

The boy shook his head in bewilderment. "A lady named Mrs. Frost —she said she was Mr. Freeling's secretary; she had glasses."

"And a sharp nose."

George Howe nodded.

Forlesen nodded in reply, and made his way to Fields's old office. As he had expected, Fields was gone, and most of the items from his own desk had made their way to Fields's—he wondered if Fields's desk sometimes talked too, but before he could ask it Miss Fawn came in.

She wore two new rings and touched her hair often with her left hand to show them. Forlesen tried to imagine her pregnant or giving suck and found that he could not, but knew that this was a weakness in himself and not in her. "Ready for orientation?" Miss Fawn asked.

Forlesen ignored the question and asked what had happened to Fields.

"He passed on," Miss Fawn said.

"You mean he died? He seemed too young for it; not much older than I am myself—certainly not as old as Mr. Freeling."

"He was stout," Miss Fawn said with a touch of righteous disdain. "He didn't get much exercise and he smoked a great deal."

"He worked very hard," Forlesen said. "I don't think he could have had much energy left for exercise."

"I suppose not," Miss Fawn conceded. She was leaning against the door, her left hand toying with the gold pencil she wore on a chain, and seemed to be signaling by her attitude that they were old friends, entitled to relax occasionally from the formality of business. "There was a thing—at one time—between Mr. Fields and myself. I don't suppose you ever knew it."

"No, I didn't," Forlesen said, and Miss Fawn looked pleased.

"Eddie and I—I called him Eddie, privately—were quite discreet. Or so I flatter myself now. I don't mean, of course, that there was ever anything improper between us."

"Naturally not."

"A look and a few words. Elmer knows; I told him everything. You are ready to give that orientation, aren't you?"

"I think I am now," Forlesen said. "George Howe?"

Miss Fawn looked at a piece of paper. "No, Gordie Hilbert."

As she was leaving, Forlesen asked impulsively where Fields was.

"Where he is buried, you mean? Right behind you."

He looked at her blankly.

"There." She gestured toward the picture behind Forlesen's desk. "There's a vault behind there—didn't you know? Just a small one, of course; they're cremated first."

"Burned out."

"Yes, burned up and then they put them behind the pictures—that's what they're for. The pictures, I mean. In a beautiful little cruet. It's a company benefit, and you'd know if you'd read your own orientation material—of course, you can be buried at home if you like."

"I think I'd prefer that," Forlesen said.

"I thought so," Miss Fawn told him. "You look the type. Anyway, Eddie bought the farm—that's an expression the men have."

At one hundred and twenty-five hours he was notified of his inter-departmental training transfer. His route to his new desk took him through the main lobby of the building, where he observed that a large medallion set into the floor bore the face (too solemn, but quite unmistakable) of Abraham Beale, though the name beneath it was that of Adam Bean, the founder of the company. Since he was accompanied by his chief-to-be, Mr. Fleer, he made no remark.

"It's going to be a pleasure going down the fast slope with you," Mr. Fleer said. "I trust you've got your wax ready and your boots laced."

"My wax is ready and my boots are laced," Forlesen said; it was automatic by now.

"But not too tight—wouldn't want to break a leg."

"But not too tight," Forlesen agreed. "What do we do in this division?"

Mr. Fleer smiled and Forlesen could see that he had asked a good question. "Right now we're right in the middle of a very successful crash program to develop a hardnosed understanding of the ins and outs of the real, realistic business world," Mr. Fleer said, "with particular emphasis on marketing, finance, corporate developmental strategy, and risk appreciation. We've been playing a lot of Bet-Your-Life, the management-managing real-life pseudogame."

"Great," Forlesen said enthusiastically; he really felt enthusiastic, having been afraid that it would be more creativity.

"We're in the center of the run," Mr. Fleer assured him, "the snow is fast, and the wind is in our faces."

Forlesen was tempted to comment that his boots were laced and his wax ready, but he contented himself at the last moment with nodding appreciatively and asking if he would get to play.

"You certainly will," Mr. Fleer promised him. "You'll be holding down Ffoulks's chair. It's an interesting position—he's heavily committed to a line of plastic toys, but he has some military contracts for field rations and biological weapons to back him up. Also he's big in aquarium supplies—that's quite a small market altogether, but Ffoulks is big in it, if you get what I mean."

"I can hardly wait to start," Forlesen said. "I have a feeling that this may be the age of aquariums." Fleer pondered this while they trudged up the stairs.

Bet-Your-Life, the management-managing real-life pseudogame, was played on a very large board laid out on a very big table in a very large meeting room. Scattered all over the board were markers and spinners and decks of cards, and birdcages holding eight- and twelve-sided dice. Scattered around the room, in chairs, were the players: two were arguing and one was asleep; five others were studying the board or making notes, or working out calculations on small hand-held machines that were something like abacuses and something like cash registers. "I'll just give you the rule book, and have a look at my own stuff, and go," Mr. Fleer said. "I'm late for the meeting now." He took a brown pamphlet from a pile in one corner of the room and handed it to Forlesen, who (with some feeling of surprise) noticed that it was identical to one of the booklets he had found under his job assignment sheet upon awakening.

Mr. Fleer had scrawled a note on a small tablet marked with the Bet-Your-Life emblem. He tore the sheet off as Forlesen watched, and laid it in an empty square near the center of the board. It read: BID 17 ASK 18 1/4 SNOWMOBILE 5 1/2 UP 1/2 OPEN NEW TERRITORY SHUT DOWN COAL OIL SHOES FLEER. He left the room, and Forlesen, timing the remark in such a way that it might be supposed that he thought him out of earshot, said, "I'll bet he's a strong player."

The man to his left, to whom the remark was nominally addressed, shook his head. "He's overbought in sporting goods."

"Sporting goods seem like a good investment to me," Forlesen said. "Of course I don't know the game."

"Well, you won't learn it reading that thing—it'll only mix you up. The basic rule to remember is that no one has to move, but that anyone can move at any time if he wants to. Fleer hasn't been here for ten ours—now he's moved."

"On the other hand," a man in a red jacket said, "this part of the building is kept open at all times, and coffee and sandwiches are brought in every our—some people never leave. I'm the referee."

A man with a bristling mustache, who had been arguing with the man in the red jacket a moment before, interjected, "The rules can be changed whenever a quorum agrees—we pull the staple out of the middle of the book, type up a new page, and slip it in. A quorum is three quarters of the players present but never seven or less."

Forlesen said hesitantly, "It's not likely three quarters of those present would be seven, is it?"

"No, it isn't," the referee agreed. "We rarely have that many."

The man with the mustache said, "You'd better look over your holdings."

Forlesen did so, and discovered that he held 100 percent of the stock of a company called International Toys and Foods. He wrote BID 34 ASK 32 FFOULKS on a slip and placed it in the center of the board. "You'll never get thirty-two for that stuff," the man with the mustache said, "it isn't worth near that."

Forlesen pointed out that he had an offer to buy in at thirty-four but was finding no takers. The man with the mustache looked puzzled, and Forlesen used the time he had gained to examine the brown pamphlet. Opening it at random he read: *"We're a team," Fields continued, "and we're going to function as a team. That doesn't mean that there isn't a quarterback, and a coach" he pointed toward the ceiling, "up there. It does mean that I expect every man to bat two fifty or better, and the ones that don't make three hundred had better be damn good Fields. You see what I mean?"*

"I buy five hundred, and I'm selling them to you."

Forlesen nodded again and asked, "What does our subdivision do? What's our function?"

"I said I'm going to buy five hundred shares, and then I'm going to sell them back to you."

"Not so fast," Forlesen said. "You don't own any yet."

"Well, I'm buying." The man with the mustache rummaged among his playing materials and produced some bits of colored paper. Forlesen accepted the money and began to count it.

The man with the red jacket said: "Coffee. And sandwiches. Spam and Churkey." The man with the mustache went over to get one, and Forlesen went out the door.

The corridor was deserted. There had been a feeling of airlessness in the game room, an atmosphere compounded of stale sweat and smoke and the cold, oily coffee left to stagnate in the bottom of the paper hot-cups; the corridor was glacial by comparison, filled with quiet wind and the memory of ice. Forlesen stopped outside the door to savor it for a second, and was joined by the man with the mustache, munching a sandwich. "Nice to get out here for a minute, isn't it?" he said.

Forlesen nodded.

"Not that I don't enjoy the game," the man with the mustache continued. "I do. I'm in Sales, you know."

"I didn't. I thought everyone was from our division."

"Oh no. There's several of us Sales guys, and some Advertising guys. Brought in to sharpen you up. That's what *we* say."

"I'm sure we can use some sharpening."

"Well, anyway, I like it—this wheeling and dealing. You know what Sales is—you put pressure on the grocers. Tell them if they don't stock the new items they're going to get slow deliveries on the standard stuff, going to lose their discount. A guy doesn't learn much financial management that way."

"Enough," Forlesen said.

"Yeah, I guess so." The man with the mustache swallowed the remainder of his sandwich. "Listen, I got to be going; I'm about to clip some guy in there."

Forlesen said, "Good luck," and walked away, hearing the door to the game room open and close behind him. He went past a number of offices, looking for his own, and up two flights of steps before he found someone who looked as though she could direct him, a sharp-nosed woman who wore glasses.

"You're looking at me funny," the sharp-nosed woman said. She smiled with something of the expression of a blindfolded schoolteacher who has been made to bite a lemon at a Halloween party.

"You remind me a great deal of someone I know," Forlesen said, "Mrs. Frost." As a matter of fact the woman looked exactly like Miss Fawn.

The woman's smile grew somewhat warmer. "Everyone says that. Actually we're cousins—I'm Miss Fedd."

"Say something else."

"Do I talk like her too?"

"No. I think I recognize your voice. This is going to sound rather silly, but when I came here—in the morning, I mean—my car talked to me. I hadn't thought of it as a female voice, but it sounded just like you."

"It's quite possible," Miss Fedd said. "I used to be in Traffic, and I still fill in there at times."

"I never thought I'd meet you. I was the one who stopped and got out of his car."

"A lot of them do, but usually only once. What's that you're carrying?"

"This?" Forlesen held up the brown book; his finger was still thrust between the pages. "A book. I'm afraid to read the ending."

"It's the red book you're supposed to be afraid to read the end of," Miss Fedd told him. "It's the opposite of a mystery—everyone stops before the revelations."

"I haven't even read the beginning of that one," Forlesen said. "Come to think of it, I haven't read the beginning of this one either."

"We're not supposed to talk about books here, not even when we haven't anything to do. What was it you wanted?"

"I've just been transferred into the division, and I was hoping you'd help me find my desk."

"What's your name?"

"Forlesen. Emanuel Forlesen."

"Good. I was looking for you—you weren't at your desk."

"No I wasn't," Forlesen said. "I was in the Bet-Your-Life room—well, not recently."

"I know. I looked there too. Mr. Frick wants to see you."

"Mr. Frick?"

"Yes. He said to tell you he was planning to do this a bit later today, but he's got to leave the office a little early. Come on."

Miss Fedd walked with short, mincing steps, but so rapidly that Forlesen was forced to trot to keep up. "Why does Mr. Frick want to see me?" He thought of the way he had cheated the man with the mustache, of the time he had baited Fairchild on the telephone, of other things.

"I'm not supposed to tell," Miss Fedd said. "This is Mr. Frick's door."

"I know," Forlesen told her. It was a large door—larger than the other doors in the building, and not painted to resemble metal. Mr. Frick's plaque was of silver (or perhaps platinum), and had the single word *Frick* engraved in an almost too-tasteful script. A man Forlesen did not know walked past them as they stood before Mr. Frick's tasteful plaque; the man wore a hat and carried a briefcase, and had a coat slung over his arm.

"We're emptying out a little already," Miss Fedd said. "I'd go right in now if I were you—I think he wants to play golf before he goes home."

"Aren't you going in with me?"

"Of course not—he's got a group in there already, and I have things to do. Don't knock, just go in."

Forlesen opened the door. The room was very large and crowded; men in expensive suits stood smoking, holding drinks, knocking out their pipes in bronze ashtrays. The tables and the desk—yes, he told himself, there is a desk, a very large desk next to the window at one end, a desk shaped like the lid of a grand piano—the tables and the desk all of dark heavy tropical wood, the tables and the desk all littered with bronze trophies so that the whole room seemed of bronze and black wood and red wool. Several of the men looked at him, then toward the opposite end of the room, and he knew at once who Mr. Frick was: a bald man standing with his back to the room, rather heavy, Forlesen thought, and somewhat below average height. He made his way through the smokers and drink holders. "I'm Emanuel Forlesen."

"Oh, there you are." Mr. Frick turned around. "Ernie Frick, Forlesen." Mr. Frick had a wide, plump face, a mole over one eyebrow, and a gold tooth. Forlesen felt that he had seen him before.

"We went to grade school together," Mr. Frick said. "I bet you don't remember me, do you?"

Forlesen shook his head.

"Well, I'll be honest—I don't think I would have remembered you; but I looked up your file while we were getting set for the ceremony. And now that I see you, by gosh, I do remember—I played prisoner's base with you one day; you used to be able to run like anything."

"I wonder where I lost it," Forlesen said. Mr. Frick and several of the men standing around him laughed, but Forlesen was thinking that he could not possibly be as old as Mr. Frick.

"Say, that's pretty good. You know, we must have started at about the same time. Well, some of us go up and some don't, and I suppose you envy me, but let me tell you I envy you. It's lonely at the top, the work is hard, and you can never set down the responsibility for a minute. You won't believe it, but you've had the best of it."

"I don't," Forlesen said.

"Well, anyway I'm tired—we're all tired. Let's get this over with so we can all go home." Mr. Frick raised his voice to address the room at large. "Gentlemen, I asked you to come here because you have all been associated at one time or another, in one way or another, with this gentleman here, Mr. Forlesen, to whom I am very happy to present this token of his colleagues' regard."

Someone handed Mr. Frick a box, and he handed it to Forlesen, who opened it while everyone clapped. It was a watch. "I didn't know it was so late," Forlesen said.

Several people laughed; they were already filing out.

"You've been playing Bet-Your-Life, haven't you?" Mr. Frick said. "A fellow can spend more time at that than he thinks."

Forlesen nodded.

"Say, why don't you take the rest of the day off? There's not much of it left anyhow."

Outside, others, who presumably had not been given the remainder of the day off by Mr. Frick, were straggling toward their cars. As Forlesen walked toward his, feeling as he did the stiffness and the pain in his legs, a bright, new car pulled onto the lot and a couple got out, the man a fresh-faced boy, really; the girl a working-class girl, meticulously made up and dressed, cheaply attractive and forlorn, like the models in the advertisements of third-rate dress shops. They went up the sidewalk hand in hand to kiss, Forlesen felt sure, in the time clock room, and separate, she going up the steps, he down. They would meet for coffee later, both uncomfortable, out of a sense of duty; meet for lunch in the cafeteria, he charging her meal to the paycheck he had not yet received.

The yellow signs that lined the street read YIELD; orange and black machines were eating the houses just beyond the light. Forlesen pulled his car into his driveway, over the oil spot. A small man in a dark suit was sitting on a wood and canvas folding stool beside his door, a black bag at his feet; Forlesen spoke to him but he did not answer. Forlesen shrugged and stepped inside.

A tall young man stood beside a long, angular object that rested on a sort of trestle in the center of the parlor. "Look what we've got for you," he said.

Forlesen looked. It was exactly like the box his watch had come in, save that it was much larger: of red-brown wood that seemed almost black, lined with pinkish-white silk.

"Want to try her out?" the young man said.

"No, I don't." Forlesen had already guessed who the young man must be, and after a moment he added a question: "Where's your mother?"

"Busy," the young man said. "You know how women are . . . Well, to tell the truth she doesn't want to come in until it's over. This lid is neat—watch." He folded down half the lid. "Like a Dutch door." He folded it up again. "Don't you want to try it for size? I'm afraid it's going to be tight around the shoulders, but it's got a hell of a good engine."

"No," Forlesen said, "I don't want to try it out." Something about the pinkish silk disgusted him. He bent over it to examine it more closely; and the young man took him by the hips and lifted him in as though he were a child, closing the lower half of the lid; it reached to his shirt pockets and effectively pinioned his arms. "Ha, ha," Forlesen said.

The young man sniffed. "You don't think we'd bury you before you're dead, do you? I just wanted you to try it out, and that was the easiest way. How do you like it?"

"Get me out of this thing."

"In a minute. Is it comfortable? Is it a good fit? It's costing us quite a bit, you know."

"Actually," Forlesen said, "it's more comfortable than I had foreseen.

The bottom is only thinly padded, but I find the firmness helps my back."

"Good, that's great. Now have you decided about the Explainer?"

"I don't know what you mean."

"Didn't you read your orientation? Everyone's entitled to an Explainer—in whatever form he chooses—at the end of his life. He—"

"It seems to me," Forlesen interrupted, "that it would be more useful at the beginning."

"—may be a novelist, aged loremaster, National Hero, warlock, or actor."

"None of those sounds quite right for me," Forlesen said.

"Or a theologian, philosopher, priest, or doctor."

"I don't think I like those either."

"Well, that's the end of the menu as far as I know," his son said. "I'll tell you what—I'll send him in and you can talk to him yourself; he's right outside."

"That little fellow in the dark suit?" Forlesen asked. His son, whose head was thrust out the door already, paid no attention.

After a moment the small man came in carrying his bag, and Forlesen's son placed a chair close to the coffin for him and went into the bedroom. "Well, what's it going to be," the small man asked, "or is it going to be nothing?"

"I don't know," Forlesen said. He was looking at the weave of the small man's suit, the intertwining of the innumerable threads, and realizing that they constituted the universe in themselves, that they were serpents and worms and roots, the black tracks of forgotten rockets across a dark sky, the sine waves of the radiation of the cosmos. "I wish I could talk to my wife."

"Your wife is dead," the small man said. "The kid didn't want to tell you. We got her laid out in the next room. What'll it be? Doctor, priest, philosopher, theologian, actor, warlock, National Hero, aged loremaster, or novelist?"

"I don't know," Forlesen said again. "I want to feel, you know, that this box is a bed—and yet a ship, a ship that will set me free. And yet . . . it's been a strange life."

"You may have been oppressed by demons," the small man said. "Or revived by unseen aliens who, landing on the Earth eons after the death of the last man, have sought to re-create the life of the twentieth century. Or it may be that there is a small pressure, exerted by a tumor in your brain."

"Those are the explanations?" Forlesen asked.

"Those are some of them."

"I want to know if it's meant anything," Forlesen said. "If what I suffered—if it's been worth it."

"No," the little man said. "Yes. No. Yes. Yes. No. Yes. Yes. Maybe."

OPENING DAY

AN ARTICLE
ABOUT HUNTING

As we had arranged earlier by vidphone, I met Mr. Roman Cowly in the lobby of the administration building of Federal Farm_____. Mr. Cowly, who has held the office of District Commissioner of Ecology since his appointment in 1982, is a tall, robust man of about fifty. He shook my hand cordially when I introduced myself. "Glad you could make it. So you feel that your readers will be interested in a closeup look at the science of wildlife management, do you?"

I assured him I did.

"Well, I think you'll find our modern, scientific methods quite a revelation if you're not already 'up on them' as we say. You understand," he led me through the building as he spoke, having already introduced me to the Farm Manager, Mr. Swint, "we are not simply going to hunt *any* bear tomorrow. We will be 'thinning out' a particular one who has been doing a great deal of damage."

I assured him that I understood this, and ventured to ask him the purpose of the numerous low white-painted buildings I saw behind the farm's main structure.

"Those are poultry houses," Mr. Swint, the farm manager, informed us. "Poultry and apples are the principal products of our farm here. We also raise a little corn for poultry feed—that's what's known as diversified farming."

I said, "Has the bear been killing the poultry?"

"No," said Mr. Swint, "he's been after the apples." He took us into the orchard and showed us several spots where the bear had been feeding on rotten apples that had dropped to the ground, and even in some cases biting at ripe apples while they still hung on the tree. "You wouldn't think he could reach up that high and get them, would you?" Mr. Swint said, pulling down the remains of an apple for me to examine. "He's a regular monster, this one."

The tracks, or "spore," of the bear were considerably confused, but

Commissioner Cowly was able to show me several clear prints and two places where the animal had vomited meals composed largely of half digested apples. "It's the spray that does that," Mr. Swint said. "Of course nobody ought to eat so many apples at one time, but you can't tell a bear that."

I asked if he thought it was a grizzly bear.

"No," Commissioner Cowly explained, "we're fairly certain this is simply the common black bear," (Euarctos americanus) "and not a Grizzly." (Ursus horribilis.) "Of course it could be the brown or 'cinnamon' color phase." (Also E. americanus. Color distinctions are not ridgidly enforced among American bears.)

Mr. Swint explained that the grizzly bear was no longer found in this area, and I asked why this was so.

"They had to be controled because they killed sheep," he explained. "Fortunately that could be done pretty easily because they went back to a dead sheep again and again until they had eaten the entire carcass. If you couldn't find a sheep a bear had killed but knew bears were in the vicinity you could shoot a couple yourself and put the poison in them." He added that sheep had never done well in this locality and that he had none on the farm.

In a section of the orchard close to the surrounding woods I was shown two pits being dug. One would hold the "marker"—as the man charged with the duty of "marking" the offending bear with an indelible luminous orange dye sprayed from an aerosol can is called—and the other myself. Because of the necessity of sawing and chopping through a number of large roots the work was proceeding slowly, but I was assured that it would be complete before nightfall. It had been my understanding that Commissioner Cowly himself was to be the "marker," that night, but he informed me that due to unexpected business he would be unable to join the hunt proper until next morning, and that Mr. Swint would take his place.

While this was still under discussion we were interrupted by the sound of a truck stopping in front of the main building. This proved to be Mr. Alexander ("Sandy") Banks, a Preditor Control Agent of Commissioner Cowly's, and the truck contained six of the commission's best trained hunting dogs. These were "domiciled" in the back, which had been transformed into a sort of kennel with chickenwire. Mr. Banks had not been scheduled to put in an appearance until the next day, but had become confused about the nature of his orders—for which he was subjected to a bit of good-natured joshing from Commissioner Cowly, who was inclined to treat the error humorously no matter how often Banks explained it.

Later I was shown the dogs Mr. Banks had brought, and Commissioner Cowly explained that such a pack was not simply flung together fortuitously. "Every animal you see there," he explained, "is an expert, with his own particular function to perform in the pack. Sandy will show them to you if you like."

I was eager to see them, and "Sandy" accordingly pulled the dogs one by one from the truck so that I could examine them at close range.

"This here is 'Wanderer,'" he said as he led out the first animal, a sad and very dignified looking hound of more than ordinary stature. "You notice how I led him out first? That's because he's what we call the head dog or 'boss' dog. He's part foxhound and a quarter coon dog and half bloodhound on his mother's side." When I stepped cautiously away from "Wanderer" Commissioner Cowly added, "You don't have to be afraid of him; Wanderer's a very gentle dog. If he were to catch this bear he'd just lick his face, wouldn't he, 'Sandy'?"

"Sandy" nodded. "People don't know it, but bloodhound blood's the gentlest blood there is. We got Wanderer to hunt for kids that gets lost, and when he finds them he don't do no more than lick their faces. He's so gentle, is what we say, he squats to pee." Sandy tied Wanderer to the bumper of the truck and drew out two hounds together. "These here's 'Nip' and 'Tuck,' the twins," he informed me. "Nip's a bluetick, and 'Tuck,' he's a redbone hound." Nip and Tuck were duly tied to separate trees, where they howled softly until Mr. Swint quieted them with a rock.

"This here is 'Sweet Sue,'" Mr. Banks informed me, drawing another hound from the truck. "Sweet Sue" was diminutive in size, possessed of a melting glance, and indubitably female and the recent mother of puppies. The three male dogs seemed at least mildly intrigued at her appearance, despite the hours of her company in the back of the truck. Sandy didn't bother to tie up "Sweet Sue," and she frisked around his feet as he extracted the last dog, a white bull terrier with a torn ear, from its confines. "My catch dog," he explained. "'Lance' 'll tree anything that won't tree for the hounds or fight it 'til I come." The bull terrier grinned in that peculiarly unprincipled way bull terriers have. His teeth would have done credit to a small shark.

"You see," Commissioner Cowly said, "as I told you, each of these animals is a specialist. Fascinating, isn't it?"

On the way back to the pits, which he wished to examine (Commissioner Cowly having decided that although Mr. Banks had not been instructed to appear until the day following he should, since he was not available for duty here, remain to "mark the bear") I asked "Sandy" what part Sweet Sue would be expected to play in the hunt.

"Sweet Sue is just a general all around good hound dog," Sandy said. "But I mostly bring her to encourage the others and make them braver; of course when she's in heat I got to keep her locked up. Now, like you see, she's just whelped—I drowned them—and that's because a while ago I let her go too long. It was a fruit case, just like this here one, except that it was a possum doin' it. I put the dogs after him and waited for them to yell 'treed,' which they never did, and along about sunup I give up myself and went back to the truck figuring they had about run that rascal into the next county. But the joke was on me because that night the possum was back again and took some more, but them dogs didn't come draggin' back for a week and when I saw the look that was on their faces I knowed but by then it was too late. Also that 'Sweet Sue' is a good dog for rabbits."

That night after Commissioner Cowly had returned to his office Mr. Banks and I established ourselves in the pits. It was necessary that this be done early, since the bear might well "spy out" the orchard before deserting the safety of the woods, so six o'clock found us in position, our locations artfully concealed beneath screens or "blinds" of leafy branches from the apple trees. A gentle rain was falling.

I had taken the precaution of filling a thermos with hot coffee from the kitchen, but I resolved to limit myself to a single cup an hour. My other equipment consisted of my camera, flashgun, and bulbs; and an extra can of the florescent spray paint—this last for emergency use only, since I was not the official marker and there could conceivably be legle difficulties about hunting a bear marked by someone not directly associated with the Bureau of Wildlife Management. "Sandy" Banks (in the other pit, not fifteen feet from where I crouched, but in the rain and the darkness how far it seemed!) I knew, had a paint can like mine (save that his was full), and a Kap-Tscher gun which fired (by means of a powerful latex spring) "hypodermic darts," each consisting of a four-inch needle about as thick as a knitting needle, a "mainbody" or syringe containing a carefully calculated dose of powerful tranquilizing drug (a tricky business this, since too small a quantity would fail to quiet the bear, while an overdose of even a few milligrams would be fatal), plastic quidance feathers, and a small siren with a blinking light (battery powered) to assist the huntsman in locating the immobilized animal. In addition, although this was somewhat against instructions (Commissioner Cowly wished to donate the animal to a National Park)

Banks had, I knew, an old military assult rifle; he had showed me this weapon in strictest confidence after I had assured him repeatedly that I would not mention its existance in this article, since exposure would almost certainly mean the loss of his position.

After the first four or five hours the wait grew monotonous. The rain that had been falling all afternoon turned somewhat heavier, and it occurred to me that our blinds—that is, the mats of apple tree limbs that covered our holes—would have been much more effective in shedding water if they had been made with a pitch in the center, such as is found in the roof of a small house or a tent. It might even be possible (I intend to experiment with this idea at the next opportunity) to actually *use* a small tent, erecting it over one's pit and covering the canvas with branches; it would not, of course, be possible then to part the leaves from inside to look out, but this might be taken care of by cutting holes in the walls of the tent as needed. If the wait were to be of long duration I might even have a stove or a little fire.

I had been crouched under the blind about six hours when I discovered that there were apples still clinging to the limbs that made up my shelter. I picked one and, recalling what Mr. Swint had told us about the sprays used on them, washed it with what was left of my coffee, which was cold by this time anyway. Since it was now completely dark this was a tricky operation, but I discovered that each apple had a little recessed area (I call this a "well") surrounding the stem, and I contrived to fill this with the cold coffee and wash the remainder of the surface by dabbling my fingers in this natural "reservoir."

I had treated a second apple in this same way and was groping through the leafy "blind" for a third when my fingers stumbled on something which, at first contact, I might almost have taken for a raw oyster. I raised myself to a sort of half crouch (I had been sitting) and thrust aside the leaves to see what it was, and found myself staring at what at first seemed—before I had found my mental focus, so to speak— to be the face of a man suffering from a gross deformity of the nose and jaws, so that the lower part of his face protruded in a way that was grotesque and pathetic in the extreme. An instant later I realized that I was "eyeball to eyeball" with the bear, and with what I still feel to have been considerable presence of mind I yelled to inform "Sandy" Banks of my discovery and threw myself backward (that is, back down into the pit) as forcefully as I could, thus putting an additional eighteen or twenty inches between myself and the animal, should he choose to attack.

The bear, who must have understood that he was to be hunted as soon as he heard me call to Banks, at once displayed the extreme agility which renders all his kind such formidable antagonists. With a peculiar cry I can only describe as approximating the note of a large dog kicked unexpectedly while asleep he flung his head and shoulders in the direction opposite me so vigorously that he was able to continue in a sort of rolling motion until his hind feet were high in the air, and, following through, bring them down *behind* his head so that he had, in the twinkling of an eye, revolved his entire body, which must have weighed several hundred pounds, through a full three hundred and sixty degrees of arc.

He then showed (all this took place, as you must realized, in less than a few seconds) yet another of the remarkable abilities with which nature has armed his tribe: the ability to "charge" or sprint at an exceedingly high speed from what is called a "standing start"—or even, as in this case, beginning from a movement already in progress with considerable celerity in the opposite direction. Fortunately for me this charge was directed not toward myself but at Sandy Banks' position. Lying flat, as I was, in my own, I was unable to see just what occurred, but I distinctly heard the crash as Banks' "blind" gave way beneath the weight of the bear. I ran to get help.

By this time it was pitch dark, and the rain, which was increasing in force, had rendered the footing extremely trecherous, so that the first four or five persons I encountered were apple trees. I could hear shouting in the distance however, and I assumed from this that Mr. Swint (the farm Manager) had been appraised of the bear's presence and was coming to our assistance. In the hope of encountering him on the way I decided to dash straight for the main farm building, but had taken only a few strides when I fell into a hole filled with water and brush.

After a few moments' reflection I realized that this must necessarily be either Banks' pit or my own, since (to the best of my knowledge) there was no other similar construction in the orchard. It was the work of seconds to determine that if it were indeed Banks' the bear was no longer present.

We started on the bear's trail a few hours after dawn the next morning. Though I had been unable to mark the bear properly (my aerosol marking can, which had been in my hip pocket, had unfortunately discharged while I was evading him) Banks had succeeded (as he himself said) in "giving it to him right in the face" when he encountered the creature in the orchard while coming back to resume his post after a brief sojourn at the main farm building. Anticipating the return of

Commissioner Cowly in the morning he had, a few seconds before, prudently "misplaced" his assult rifle in the mud; and since he had left the Kap-Tscher gun in his "blind" he had possessed nothing except the marking spray ("and his legs" as he humorously remarked) with which to defend himself from the bear. Luckily these had proved sufficient.

Wet weather, as Commissioner Cowly explained to me before we set out, holds scent and is thus ideal for displaying the talents of trailing dogs. This day was ideal, the rain of the night preceeding having continued almost until our "jump off" time, when it gave way to sleet. The dogs were whimpering with excitement as they were led out, and had several times to be restrained from returning to the truck. "Wanderer" as "Commissioner Cowly" explained to me, would be put on the scent first. "The best method," he told me (to quote him directly), "of working with a bloodhound is to allow him to smell some possession or article of clothing of the prey he is to seek; a handkerchief, underwear, or a dirty sock is ideal." I was about to ask if it would be necessary to "start" the dogs with a tuft of hair torn from the bear's pelt (since it would be manifestly impossible to use an article of clothing—properly so called—except, possibly, in the case of a fugitive circus bear) when I noticed Banks carrying a soiled handkerchief. For a moment, I confess, I felt incredulity; but it soon developed that the handkerchief was Banks' own, and contained one of the bear's droppings (technically called a "spore"), a number of which had been discovered near the spot where I had inadvertantly touched his nose. "Wanderer" took one long sniff and howeled mournfully—the overture of the hunting song of the pack!

It was good to be alive that morning in the rain-grey woods, where the icicles shaped themselves at the tip of every leaf. The dogs were soon out of sight, and we—Commissioner Cowly, Mr. Swint, Banks, and I—followed them by sound alone, Banks interpreting every note of the canine chorus for us: "Hear that," he (Alexander "Sandy" Banks, the Preditor Control Agent employed by the Wildlife Management Commission) would say, "that's Nip!" Or, "That's Tuck!"

We had traversed nearly three miles of rough, wooded country (bears are extraordinary travelers despite their normally relaxed and even indolent dispositions, and when pursued by half a dozen or so large dogs followed by men with guns will often keep up the chase hour after hour until they are ready to drop, although on other occasions they may seek to escape by climbing trees, hitching rides on trains, or other such slights) when the hounds met their first check. We found them milling about in an open lumbering "cut" (informally used, after the lumbering operations were complete, for solid wastes disposal) through which a small stream ran. "They've lost the scent," Commissioner Cowly explained, "and are casting for it." At that moment Sweet Sue "got the part," and raising her head she voiced a series of yelps more highly pitched and feminine than those of the larger dogs and, having thus announced her discovery, disappeared into the trees. "Gawdam dog's on a rabbit track," "Sandy" Banks commented.

"I don't believe it," I replied. "I think she has found the bear."

I should have known better than to pit my slender skills against those of such an experienced woodsman as (Sandy) Banks. "Bear went down that creek," he explained to me, "t' throw off the dogs. The scent," (spore) "won't last on running water."

It seemed obvious that the ice was too thin to have supported the weight of the bear, and I pointed this out to Banks, but he directed my attention to a series of holes, each about a foot long and six inches in width, in which the ice was just beginning to re-form. "Them's his steps," he said. "You notice how they're only about as far apart as a bear would walk? And if you'll look real close at the back edges of them you'll see blood where he cut hisself."

Traces of this sort (technically known as "spore") are most important, and I was stepping out onto the ice to examine them for myself when, quite unexpectedly, the trecherous surface gave way beneath one of my boots, which was plunged to the calf into the icy water. Fortunately the tough leather saved my Achilles' tendon from injury, but before I could draw it out the boot was filled to the top. This occasioned a good laugh all around, but it was one in which, since I was already feeling somewhat ill (I believe as a result of the apples I had eaten the preceeding night), I was unable to join as heartily as I would have wished. "Got a boot full of water, don't you," Mr. Swint remarked when the laughter had subsided. "You better take it off."

I was already attempting to do this, and eventually, with the help of a knife I borrowed from Banks, I succeeded, dumped out the freezing water, and squeezed out my sock. My foot, I noticed, had become an interesting blue color.

At that moment a small gray rabbit came dashing out of the woods, dodging backward and forward in that erratic way rabbits have, and throwing up sprays of icy water as it passed. Mr. Swint threw my boot at him, and Commissioner Cowly a stick, the latter so well aimed that it broke the animal's back. We were just going over to look at him (before he dragged himself to safety, for he was still able to make fairly good time by pulling himself along with his front paws, and the dogs did not seem to have noticed him) when "Sweet Sue" emerged from the woods with remarkable speed, followed by what I at first took to be a much larger dog. Before Banks could bring the Kap-Tscher gun into play both animals had disappeared into the trees again. It was (or had been) the bear.

All was not lost, however. Old "Wanderer" picked up the trail as soon as it was pointed out to him by Banks, and in a trice he—with Nip and "Tuck" not far behind, and trailed by Lancelot (the bull terrier) who up until then had appeared somewhat disenchanted with the entire proceeding—was running on a headhigh scent. In a few minutes their baying was transformed into shrill yelping. "They've got him!" Commissioner Cowly exclaimed, crouching to halt Wanderer who, having apparently been savagely used by the bear, was just then running past us in the opposite direction. Maddened by excitement the dog fastened to his hand, and it was necessary for Mr. Swint to kick him ("Wanderer") several times before he would let go.

A few steps further and we were at the spot where "Bruin" had taken his stand. Salt water from an oil drilling operation had killed fifty or a hundred acres of timber here, and his back was protected by a huge, dead oak. Here he stood ready to maul with utmost vicuiousness any of the dogs who ventured to attack him. I raised my camera for a picture, and as I did so I could see from the expression of dispair that crossed that coal black face that he believed it to be a gun. His look of relief when the camera made only a harmless click was quite comic. It was at this moment, however, that "Sweet Sue" who, more than any of the other dogs had been holding him at bay, standing (brave dog!) squarely before him and keeping up a constant high-pitched yipping, was seized by the hindquarters by "Launcelot" the bull terrier, who perhaps feared that she was getting too close to the bear. Unfortunately, with that "dead game" instinct of his race the white dog did not release her even when he had succeeded in dragging her backward several yards into a clump of withered bushes, and for a few seconds it appeared that the bear might attack us. Banks saved the day, putting four Kap-Tscher darts into the brute in rapid succession, after which Mr. Swint and I took turns until the supply of darts was exhausted. Even so, Commissioner Cowly, always solicitous for the welfare of anyone even remotely connected to his department, insisted on Banks striking the head of the now unconscious bear with a large stone before he would declare it officially "safe." Then—too soon it seemed!—the hunt was over. The quarry lay still, and the thought came to me, as it always does at the end of such adventures, When and Where shall I ever again find such friends or such sport? And will anybody buy this? There was no sound in all the woods save the thrashing and panting of the five dogs in the dead bushes and the soft hiss of "Banks'" spray can as he "marked" the bear.

HOMECOMING DAY

THE CHANGELING

I suppose whoever finds these papers will be amazed at the simplicity of their author, who put them under a stone instead of into a mailbox or a filing cabinet or even a cornerstone—these being the places where most think it wise to store up their writings. But consider, is it not wiser to put papers like these into the gut of a dry cave as I have done?

For if a building is all it should be, the future will spare it for a shrine; and if your children's sons think it not worth keeping, will they think the letters of the builders worth reading? Yet that would be a surer way than a filing cabinet. Answer truly: Did you ever know of papers to be read again once they entered one of these, save when some clerk drew them out by number? And who would seek for these?

There is a great, stone-beaked, hook-billed snapping turtle living under the bank here, and in the spring, when the waterfowl have nested and brooded, he swims beneath their chicks more softly than any shadow. Sometimes they peep once when he takes their legs, and so they have more of life than these sheets would have once the clacking cast iron jaw of a mailbox closed on them.

Have you ever noted how eager it is to close when you have pulled out your hand? You cannot write *The Future* on the outside of an envelope; the box would cross that out and stamp *Dead Letter Office* in its place.

Still, I have a tale to tell; and a tale untold is one sort of crime:

I was in the army, serving in Korea, when my father died. That was before the North invaded, and I was supposed to be helping a captain teach demolition to the ROK soldiers. The army gave me compassionate leave when the hospital in Buffalo sent a telegram saying how sick he was. I suppose everyone moved as fast as they could, I know I did, but he died while I was flying across the Pacific. I looked into his coffin where the blue silk lining came up to his hard, brown cheeks and crowded his working shoulders; and went back to Korea. He was the last family I had, and things changed for me then.

There isn't much use in my making a long story of what happened afterward; you can read it all in the court-martial proceedings. I was one of the ones who stayed behind in China, neither the first nor the last to change his mind a second time and come home. I was also one of the ones who had to stand trial; let's say that some of the men who had been in the prison camp with me remembered things differently. You don't have to like it.

While I was in Ft. Leavenworth I started thinking about how it was before my mother died, how my father could bend a big nail with his fingers when we lived in Cassonsville and I went to the Immaculate Conception School five days a week. We left the month before I was supposed to start the fifth grade, I think.

When I got out I decided to go back there and look around before I tried to get a job. I had four hundred dollars I had put in Soldier's Deposit before the war, and I knew a lot about living cheap. You learn that in China.

I wanted to see if the Kanakessee River still looked as smooth as it used to, and if the kids I had played softball with had married each other, and what they were like now. Somehow the old part of my life seemed to have broken away, and I wanted to go back and look at that piece. There was a fat boy who was tongue-tied and laughed at everything, but I had forgotten his name. I remembered our pitcher, Ernie Cotha, who was in my grade at school and had buck teeth and freckles; his sister played center field for us when we couldn't get anybody else, and closed her eyes until the ball thumped the ground in front of her. Peter Palmieri always wanted to play Vikings or something like that, and pretty often made the rest of us want to too. His big sister Maria bossed and mothered us all from the towering dignity of thirteen. Somewhere in the background another Palmieri, a baby brother named Paul, followed us around watching everything we did with big, brown eyes. He must have been about four then; he never talked, but we thought he was an awful pest.

I was lucky in my rides and moved out of Kansas pretty well. After a couple of days I figured I would be spending the next night in Cassonsville, but it seemed as though I had run out of welcomes outside a little hamburger joint where the state route branched off the federal highway. I had been holding out my thumb nearly three hours before a guy in an old Ford station wagon offered me a lift. I'd mumbled, "Thanks," and tossed my AWOL bag in back before I ever got a good look at him. It was Ernie Cotha, and I knew him right away—even though a dentist had done something to his teeth so they didn't push his lip out any more. I had a little fun with him before he got me placed, and then we got into a regular school reunion mood talking about the old times.

I remember we passed a little barefoot kid standing alongside the road, and Ernie said, "You recollect how Paul always got in the way, and one time we rubbed his hair with a cow pile? You told me next day how you caught blazes from Mama Palmieri about it."

I'd forgotten, but it all came back as soon as he mentioned it. "You know," I said, "it was a shame the way we treated that boy. He thought we were big shots, and we made him suffer for it."

"It didn't hurt him any," Ernie said. "Wait till you see him; I bet he could lick us both."

"The family still live in town?"

"Oh sure." Ernie let the car drift off the blacktop a little, and it threw up a spurt of dust and gravel before he got it back on. "Nobody leaves Cassonsville." He took his eyes from the road for a moment to look at me. "You knew Maria's old Doc Witte's nurse now? And the old people have a little motel on the edge of the fairgrounds. You want me to drop you there, Pete?"

I asked him how the rates were, and he said they were low enough, so, since I'd have to bunk down somewhere, I told him that would be all right. We were quiet then for five or six miles, before Ernie started up again.

"Say, you remember the big fight you two had? Down by the river. You wanted to tie a rock to a frog and throw him in, and Maria wouldn't let you. That was a real scrap."

"It wasn't Maria," I told him, "that was Peter."

"You're nuts," Ernie said. "That must have been twenty years ago. Peter wasn't even born then."

"You must be thinking of another Peter," I said. "I mean Peter Palmieri, Maria's brother."

Ernie stared at me until I thought he was going to run us into the ditch. "That's who I mean too," he said, "but little Peter's only a kid eight, maybe nine." He glanced back at the road. "You're thinking of Paul, only it was Maria you had the fight with; Paul was just a toddler."

We were quiet again for a few minutes after that, and it gave me time to remember that tussle on the river bank. I recalled that four or five of us had walked up to the point where we always tied the skiff we used to cross over to our rocky, useless island in the middle of the channel. We meant to play pirates or something, but the skiff had dragged loose from its moorings and was gone. Peter had tried to get the rest of us to search downstream for it, but everyone was too lazy. It was one of those hot, still summer days when the dust floats in the air; the days that make you think of threshing. I caught a frog somehow and hit upon the idea for an experiment.

Then I remembered that Ernie was at least partially right. Maria had tried to stop me and I had hit her in the eye with a stone. But that wasn't the big fight. It was Peter who came to avenge Maria then, Peter with whom I rolled snarling and scratching, trying to get a grip on his sweat-slick body in the prickly weeds. Ernie was right about Paul's being no more than an infant, and there had been a scrap with Maria; but it was Peter who'd finally made me cut the string from the frog's leg and let it go. Side by side we had watched the little green animal hop back toward the water, and then, when it was only one jump away from dear safety, I had lashed out and suddenly, swiftly, driven the broad blade of my scout knife through him and pinned him to the mud.

The Palmieris' place was called The Cassonsville Tourist Lodge. There were ten white cottages and a house with a café jutting out of the front to support a big sign that said *EAT* like Buddha commanding the grasshopper.

Mama Palmieri surprised me by recognizing me at once and smothering me with kisses. She herself had hardly changed at all. Her hair had gone gray at the temples, but most of it was still the glossy black it had been; and while she had always been fat, she was no fatter now. Maybe not quite so solid looking. I don't think Papa really remembered me, but he gave me one of his rare smiles.

He was a small, dark, philosophical man who seldom spoke, and I suppose people meeting the two of them for the first time would assume that Mama dominated her husband. The truth was that she regarded him as infallible in every crisis. And for practical purposes Mama was almost right; he had the inexhaustible patience and rockbound common sense of a Sicilian burro—all the qualities that have made that tough, diminutive animal the traditional companion of wandering friars and desert rats.

The Palmieris wanted me to stay in Maria's room (she had gone to Chicago to attend some sort of nurses' convention and was not due back until the end of the week) as a guest, and insisted that I eat with the family. I made them rent me a cabin instead at five dollars a night—which they swore was the full rate—but I gave in on the eating. We were still talking in that disjointed way people do on these occasions when Paul came in.

I would not have recognized him if I'd met him on the street, but I liked him at first sight; a big, dark, solemn kid with a handsome profile he had never discovered and probably never would.

After Mama made the introductions she started worrying about dinner and wondering when Peter would get home. Paul reassured her by saying he'd driven past Peter walking with a gang of kids as he'd come out from town. He said he'd offered his brother a lift but had been turned down.

Something about the way he said it gave me the willies. I remembered what Ernie had said about Peter being younger than Paul, and somehow Paul gave the same impression. He was wearing a college sweater and had the half cocky, half unsure mannerisms of a boy trying to be a man, yet he seemed to be talking about someone much younger.

After a while we heard the screen door slam and light, quick steps coming in. When I saw him I knew I had been expecting it all along. It was Peter, and he was perhaps eight years old. Not just another Italian-looking kid; but Peter, with his sharp chin and black eyes. He didn't seem to recall me at all, and Mama bragged about how not many women could bear healthy sons at fifty like she had. I went to bed early that night.

Naturally I had been keyed up all evening waiting to hear something that would show they knew about me; but when I fell asleep I was thinking about Peter, and I hadn't been thinking about anything else for a long time.

The next day was Saturday, and since Paul had the day off from his summer job he offered to drive me around town. He had a '54 Chevy he had pretty much rebuilt himself, and he was very proud of it.

After we had seen all the usual things, which didn't take long in Cassonsville, I asked him to take me to the island in the river where we had played as boys. We had to walk about a mile because the road doesn't come close to the river at that point, but there was a path the kids had made. Grasshoppers fled in waves before us through the dry grass.

When we got to the water Paul said, "That's funny, there's usually a little boat here the kids use to get out to the island."

I was looking at the island, and I saw the skiff tied to a bush at the edge of the water. It looked like the same one we had used when I was a kid myself, and who knows, maybe it was. The island itself interested me more. It was a good deal closer to shore—in fact, the Kanakessee was a good deal narrower—than I had remembered, but I had expected that since everything in Cassonsville was smaller, including the town itself.

What surprised me was that the island was bigger, if anything. There was a high point, almost a hill, in the center that sloped down and then up to a bluff on the upstream end, and trailed a long piece of wasteland downstream. Altogether it must have covered four or five acres.

In a few minutes we saw a boy on the island, and Paul yelled across the water for him to row the boat over to us. He did, and Paul rowed the three of us back. I remember I was afraid the little skiff would founder under the load; the silent water was no more than an inch from pouring over the sides, despite the boy's bailing with a rusty can to lighten the boat of its bilge.

On the island we found three more boys, including Peter. There were some wooden swords, made by nailing a short slat crosswise to a longer, thrust into the ground; but none of the boys were holding them. Seeing Peter there, just as he used to be when I was a kid myself, made me search the faces of the other boys to see if I could find someone else I had known among them. I couldn't; they were just ordinary kids. What I am trying to say is that I felt too tall out here to be a real person, and out of place in the only place where I really wanted to be. Maybe it was because the boys were sulky, angry at having their game interrupted and afraid of being laughed at. Maybe it was because every tree and rock and bush and berry tangle was familiar and unaltered—but unremembered before I saw it.

From the bank the island had seemed nearer, though larger, than I recalled. Now, somehow, there was much more water between it and the shore. The illusion was so odd that I tapped Paul on the shoulder and said, "I'll bet you can't throw a rock from here to the other side."

He grinned at me and said, "What'll you bet?"

Peter said, "He can't do it. Nobody can." It was the first time any of the boys had spoken above a mumble.

I had been planning to pay for Paul's gasoline anyway, so I said that if he did it I'd get his tank filled at the first station we came to on the way home.

The stone arced out and out until it seemed more like an arrow than a pebble, and at last dropped into the water with a splash. As nearly as I could judge it was still about thirty feet from the bank.

"There," Paul said, "I told you I could do it."

"I thought it dropped short," I said.

"The sun must have been in your eyes." Paul sounded positive. "It dropped four foot up the bank." Picking up another rock, he tossed it confidently from one hand to the other. "If you want me to, I'll do it over."

For a second I couldn't believe my ears. Paul hadn't struck me as someone who would try to collect a bet he hadn't won. I looked at the four boys. Usually there's nothing that will fire up a boy like a bet or the offer of a prize, but these still resented our intrusion too much to talk. All of them were looking at Paul, however, with the deep contempt a normal kid feels for a welcher.

I said, "O.K., you won," to Paul and got a boy to come with us in the skiff so he could row it back.

When we reached the car, Paul mentioned that there was a baseball game that afternoon, Class "A" ball, at the county seat; so we drove over and watched the game. That is, I sat and stared at the field, but when it was over I couldn't have told you whether the final score was nothing to nothing or twenty to five. On the way home I bought Paul's gas.

It was suppertime when we got back, and after supper Paul and Papa Palmieri and I sat out on the porch and drank cans of beer. We talked baseball for a little while, then Paul left. I told Papa a few stories about Paul hanging around with us older kids when he was small, then about me fighting with Peter over the frog, and waited for him to correct me.

He sat without speaking for a long time. Finally I said, "What's the matter?"

He re-lit his cigar and said, "You know all about it." It wasn't a question.

I told him I didn't really know anything about it, but that up to that minute I was beginning to think I was losing my mind.

He said, "You want to hear?" His voice was completely mechanical except for the trace of Italian accent. I said I did.

"Mama and me came here from Chicago when Maria was just a little baby, you know?"

I told him I had heard something about it.

"I have a good job, that's why we come to this town. Foreman at the brick works."

I said I knew that too. He had held that job while I was a kid in Cassonsville.

"We rented a little white house down on Front Street, and unpacked our stuff. Even bought some new. Everybody knew I had a good job; my credit was good. We'd been in the town couple months, I guess, when I came home from work one night and find Mama and the baby with this strange boy. Mama's holding little Maria in her lap and saying, 'Look there, Maria, that's-a your big brother.' I think maybe

Mama's gone crazy, or playing a joke on me, or something. That night the kids eat with us like there was nothing strange at all."

"What did you do?" I asked him.

"I didn't do nothing. Nine times outa ten that's the best thing you can do. I wait and keep my eyes open. Night time comes and the boy goes to a little room upstairs we weren't going to use and goes to sleep. He's got an army cot there, clothes in the closet, school books, everything. Mama says we ought to get him a real bed soon when she sees me looking in there."

"Was Mama the only one . . . ?"

Papa lit a fresh cigar and I realized that it was growing dark and that both of us had been pitching our voices lower than usual.

"Everybody," Papa said. "The next day after work I go to the nuns at the school. I think I'll tell them what he looks like; maybe they know who he is."

"What did they say?" I asked him.

"They say, 'Oh, you're Peter Palmieri's papa, he's such a nice boy,' soon's I tell them who I am. Everybody's like that." He was silent for a long time, then he added, "When *my* Papa writes next from the old country he says, 'How's my little Peter?'"

"That was all there was to it?"

The old man nodded. "He stays with us, and he's a good boy—better than Paul or Maria. But he never grows up. First he's Maria's big brother. Then he's her twin brother. Then little brother. Now he's Paul's little brother. Pretty soon he'll be too young to belong to Mama and me and then he'll leave, I think. You're the only one besides me who ever noticed. You played with them when you're a kid, huh?"

I told him, "Yes."

We sat on the porch for a half hour or so longer, but neither of us wanted to talk any more. When I got up to leave Papa said, "One thing. Three times I get holy water from the priest an' pour it on him while he sleeps. Nothing happens, no blisters, no screaming, nothing."

The next day was Sunday. I put on my best clothes, a clean sport shirt and good slacks, and hitched a ride to town with a truck driver who'd stopped for an early coffee at the café. I knew the nuns at Immaculate Conception would all go to the first couple of masses at the church, but since I had wanted to get away from the motel before the Palmieris grabbed me to go with them I had to leave early. I spent three hours loafing about the town—everything was closed—then went to the little convent and rang the bell.

A young nun I had never seen before answered and took me to see

the Mother Superior, and it turned out to be Sister Leona, who had
taught the third grade. She hadn't changed much; nuns don't, it's the
covered hair and never wearing makeup, I think. Anyway, as soon as I
saw her I remembered her as though I had just left her class, but I
don't think she placed me, even though I told her who I was. When I
was through explaining I asked her to let me see the records on Peter
Palmieri, and she wouldn't. I'd wanted to see if they could possibly
have a whole file drawer of cards and reports going back twenty years
or more on one boy, but though I pleaded and yelled and finally threatened she kept saying that each student's records were confidential and
could be shown only with the parent's permission.

Then I changed my tactics. I remembered perfectly well that when
we were in the fourth grade a class picture had been taken. I could
even recall the day, how hot it was, and how the photographer had
ducked in and out of his cloth, looking like a bent-over nun when he
was aiming the camera. I asked Sister Leona if I could look at that. She
hesitated a minute and then agreed and had the young sister bring a
big album that she told me had all the class pictures since the school
was founded. I asked for the fourth grade of nineteen forty-four and
after some shuffling she found it.

We were ranged in alternate columns of boys and girls, just as I had
remembered. Each boy had a girl on either side of him but another boy
in front and in back. Peter, I was certain, had stood directly behind me
one step higher on the school steps, and though I couldn't think of
their names I recalled the faces of the girls to my right and left perfectly.

The picture was a little dim and faded now, and having seen the
school building on my way to the convent I was surprised at how much
newer it had looked then. I found the spot where I had stood, second
row from the back and about three spaces over from our teacher Sister
Therese, but my face wasn't there. Between the two girls, tiny in the
photograph, was the sharp, dark face of Peter Palmieri. No one stood
behind him, and the boy in front was Ernie Cotha. I ran my eyes over
the list of names at the bottom of the picture and his name was there,
but mine was not.

I don't know what I said to Sister Leona or how I got out of the convent. I only remember walking very fast through the almost empty
Sunday-morning streets until the sign in front of the newspaper office
caught my eye. The sun was reflected from the gilded lettering and the
plate glass window in a blinding glare, but I could see dimly the figures
of two men moving about inside. I kicked the door until one of them

opened it and let me into the ink-scented room. I didn't recognize either of them, yet the expectancy of the silent, oiled presses in back was as familiar as anything in Cassonsville, unchanged since I had come in with my father to buy the ad to sell our place.

I was too tired to fence with them. Something had been taken out of me in the convent and I could feel my empty belly with a little sour coffee in it. I said, "Listen to me please, sir. There was a boy named Pete Palmer; he was born in this town. He stayed behind when the prisoners were exchanged at Panmunjom and went to Red China and worked in a textile mill there. They sent him to prison when he came back. He'd changed his name after he left here, but that wouldn't make any difference; there'll be a lot about him because he was a local boy. Can I look in your files under August and September of 1959? Please?"

They looked at each other and then at me. One was an old man with badly fitting false teeth and a green eyeshade like a movie newspaperman; the other was fat and tough looking with dull, stupid eyes. Finally the old man said, "There wasn't no Cassonsville boy stayed with the Communists. I'da remembered a thing like that."

I said, "Can I look, please?"

He shrugged his shoulders. "It's fifty cents an hour to use them files, and you can't tear out nothing or take nothing out with you, understand?"

I gave him two quarters and he led me back to the morgue. There was nothing, nothing at all. There was nothing for 1953 when the exchange had taken place either. I tried to look up my birth announcement then, but there were no files before 1945; the old man out front said they'd been "burnt up when the old shop burned."

I went outside then and stood in the sun awhile. Then I went back to the motel and got my bag and went out to the island. There were no kids this time; it was very lonely and very peaceful. I poked around a bit and found this cave on the south side, then lay down on the grass and smoked my last two cigarettes and listened to the river and looked up at the sky. Before I knew it, it had started to get dark and I knew I'd better begin the trip home. When it was too dark to see the bank across the river I went into this cave to sleep.

I think I had really known from the first that I was never going to leave the island again. The next morning I untied the skiff and let it drift away on the current, though I knew the boys would find it hung up on some snag and bring it back.

How do I live? People bring me things, and I do a good deal of fishing—even through the ice in winter. Then there are blackberries and walnuts here on the island. I think a lot, and if you do that right it's better than the things people who come to see me sometimes tell me they couldn't do without.

You'd be surprised at how many do come to talk to me. One or two almost every week. They bring me fishhooks and sometimes a blanket or a sack of potatoes and some of them tell me they wish to God they were me.

The boys still come, of course. I wasn't counting them when I said one or two people. Papa was wrong. Peter still has the same last name as always and I guess now he always will, but the boys don't call him by it much.

HALLOWEEN

MANY MANSIONS

Old Woman: So you are the new woman from the Motherworld. Well, come in and sit down. I saw you coming up the road on your machine.

Oh yes, Todd and I, we've always been friendly with you people, though there are some here still that remember the War. This was a rich district, you know, before; for a few, that's hard to forget.

Well, it's all behind us now, and it wasn't us anyway. Just my father and Todd's—and your grandmother, I suppose. Even if you were carried in a bottle, you must have had a grandmother, and she would have fought against us. Still, it's good of you now to send people to help us rebuild here, though as you can see it hasn't done much good.

I didn't mean this place was here before the War—not much that you'll see was. Todd built this thirty years ago; he was younger then—couldn't do it now. You know, you are such a pretty thing—can't I get you a cup? Well, we call it tea, but your people don't. The woman who was here before you, she always said how much better the real tea was, but she never gave us any.

I tasted it once, but I didn't like it. I was brought up on our own brewing, you see. I'll pour you a glass of our wine if you won't take tea; this cake has got a trifle dry.

Oh, I can imagine well enough what it's been like. Going around from one to another saying, "Have you seen her? Do you know what happened to her?" and getting hostile looks and not much else. It's because of the War, you know. That's what my mother always said. People here weren't like that before the War. Now—well, they know that you're supposed to help them, to make up for it; and you're not doing it now, are you? Just going about looking for your friend.

I doubt you'll ever see her again. She's been taken. I don't suppose you know about that—the old houses? She didn't either when she came; we had to tell her about it. I would have thought they'd teach you—put it in a little book to give out or something. Did you get one of those?

Never mind—I've seen them. Saw hers, for all of that. She was such a pretty thing, just like you.

I don't mind telling you—it's the old houses, the ones built before the War. Todd's family had one down at Breaker, and my own family, we had one here. I hear yours are different—all shiny metal and shaped like eggs, or else like nails stood on end. Ours weren't like that; not in the old days, and no more now. More like this one you're sitting in: wood, or what looked like it. But for all that you beat us, our fathers and grandfathers—and our mothers and grandmothers too, for our women weren't what you think, you don't really know about it—they had more power over machines than you do. They didn't use them to make more machines, though; just put them in their houses to help out. They were friendly to their homes, you see, and thought their homes should be friendly to them.

Some say the brains of people were used to make the houses think. Taken out of the heads and put in jars in secret rooms, with wires running all over to work little fusion motors. Others say that the heads are still there, and the bodies too, to take care of the brains; but the houses don't know it anymore, or don't care. They say that if you were to go inside, and open the door of the right room, you'd see someone still lying on a bed that was turning to dust, while the eyes watched you from every picture.

Yes, they're still here—some of them. Your girls burned most—I've never understood why. Beautiful things they were, so my mother used to tell me. Ours was white, and four stories high. They kept themselves up, you understand, the same as a woman. If there were people's brains in them (and I've never been sure that was true) then they must have been women's brains mostly. They kept themselves up. There were roses climbing up them, the same as a woman will wear a flower in her hair; and ours pinned wisteria to her like a corsage. The roofs were tight and good all the time, and if a window broke it mended itself with nobody troubling. It's not like that now, from what I hear.

I've never seen one myself, not to speak of. Todd has, or says he has. He'll tell you about it, if you like, when he comes in. But I'm not thinking, am I? Here you've sat all this time with your glass empty.

It's no trouble—it's our courtesy, you see, to host strangers. I know you don't do it, but this is my house. Now, don't you get angry; I'm a headstrong old lady, and I'm used to having my own way.

Don't you use that word anymore? It just means *woman* now. Drink this and I'll cut you some more cake.

None at all? I won't force it on you. Yes, people see them—they're

still here, some of them, and so why not? Take our land; it ran back as
far as you could go if you walked all day—clear to the river. The south
property line was at the edge of town, and the north way up in the
mountains. That was in the old days. Most of it was plowed and culti-
vated then, and what woodlands there was were cleared out. Then the
War came. Half the autochthons were killed, like most of us; those that
were left were happy enough to run off into the fens, or lie around the
towns waiting for somebody to rob. We would have civilized them if
you'd given us another century.

But you wanted to know about the houses. Pull the curtain there to
one side, will you? It's starting to get dark, and I always worry when
Todd's not home. No, dear, I'm not hinting for you to go—that machine of yours has a light on the front, don't it? And a girl—woman—
like you, that's not afraid of anything, wouldn't be afraid of riding
home in the dark, I would think. Besides, I'd feel better if you'd stay;
you're a comfort to me.

Well, the War came, and most of the houses were told to hide themselves. Your people bombed them while we were still fighting, you
know, and burned them after we gave up. So they hid, as well as they
could.

Oh, yes, they can move around. It must have been so nice for the
people before the War—they could have their homes down by the river
in summer, and wherever the firewood was in winter—no, they didn't
need it for heat, I said they had fusion motors, didn't I? Still, they liked
wood fires.

So the houses hid, as I said. Hid for years while your girl soldiers
went over the country and your ornithopters flapped around all day. In
the deepest parts of the woods, most of them, and down in the crevasses
where the sunlight never comes. They grew mosses on their roofs then,
and that must have saved quite a few. Some went into the tarns, they
say, and stood for years on the bottoms—Saint Syncletica's church is
under Lake Kell yet, and the people hear the bells ringing when
they're out on the water in storms.

If you're fond of fishing, it's a good lake, but there's no roads to it—
you'd have to walk. Your patrols used the roads mostly, so we let a lot
of them grow up in trees again. The houses make false ones though,
slipping through the thickets. That's what the men say. Todd will be
hunting in deep timber, where there shouldn't be any road and there's
no place to go if there were, and come on one twice or three times the
size of this room and the porch together, just going nowhere, winding
down through the brakes. Some say you can follow those roads forever

and never come to anything; but my Todd says that one time he walked one till it was near dark, and then he saw a house at the end of it, a tall, proud house, with a light in the gable window. My own home, that was, is what I think. My father used to tell how when he'd go out riding and not come back till midnight or later, there'd be a light burning for him in the highest window. It's still waiting for him, I suppose.

Does anyone live in them? Well, some say one thing, some another. I told you I've never seen one myself, so how would I know? You'll meet people who say they've seen faces staring out through the windows—who knows if they're telling the truth? Maybe it was just shadows they saw on the walls in there. Maybe it wasn't.

Oh, a lot of people go looking for them. There's money inside, of course. Wealth, I should say, because the money's worth nothing now. Still, the people who had those big houses had jewels, and platinum flatware—there was a fad for that then, so I've heard; and who could be trusted better to take care of it than their own homes? The ones that say they go hunting for people tell stories about little boys finding a spoon gleaming in the ferns, and seeing something else, a creamer or something, farther on. Following the trail, you know, picking up the things, until the house nearly has them. Then (this is the way the story always goes) they get frightened and drop everything and run away. I don't believe a word of it. I've told Todd, if he should ever find any platinumware in the woods, or gold, or those cat's-eye carbuncles they talk about, to turn around right then and bring it home. But he's never brought back anything like that.

Don't go yet—you're company for me. I don't get much, out here away from everybody. I'll tell you about Lily—have you heard of her? It might have some bearing on the woman who was here before you.

I don't know how you feel about morality—with your people it's so hard to tell. Todd says we ought to forgive women like her, but then men always do. She was pretty enough—beautiful, you might say—and it's hard for a woman alone to make a living. Maybe I ought not to blame her too much; she gave good value, I suppose, for what she received. A pretty face, men like that, not round like yours, but a long oval shape. Waist no bigger than this, and one of those full chests—at least, after she had begun doing what she did regular, and was getting enough to eat and all the drink she wanted. Skin like cream—I always had to hold back my hand to keep from running my fingers over it.

As well as you know me by now, you know I wouldn't have her in my house. But it was an act of charity, I thought, to talk to her sometimes. She must have been lonely for woman-company. I used to go into town every so often then, and if I met her and there wasn't anybody else about, I'd pass the time. That was a mistake, because when I'd done it once or twice she came out to visit me. See the two chairs out there? Through the window? Well, I kept her sitting there on the porch for over a hour, and never did ask her in or give her a bite to eat. When she went home she knew, believe me. She knew what I thought, and how far she could go. Coming to ask if she could help with the canning, like a neighbor!

Here's what she told me, though. I don't imagine you know where the Settles' farm is? Anyway, up past it is where Dode Beckette lives— just a little shack set back in the trees. She was going up there one spring evening. He had sent for her, I suppose, or maybe she was just looking for trade; when a man has a woman alone knock at his door . . . a woman like that—I don't intend you, dear—why, nature is liable to take its course, isn't it? She was carrying a load, if you know what I mean; she told me so herself. The air was chill, possibly, and it's likely someone had left a bottle with her the night before. Still, I don't think she was seeing things. She was accustomed to it, and that makes all the difference. Just enough to make her hum to herself, I would say. I used to hear her singing on the various roads round and about in just that way; it's always those that have the least to make music about that sing, I always say.

First thing you know she went around a bend, and there was the house. It wasn't the Settles', or Dode's shack—a big place. Like a palace, she said, but I would think that was stretching it a bit. More like the hotel, I should think. Not kept up, the paint peeling here and there, and the railing of the veranda broke; some of them have got a little careless, I think, hiding so long. Hunted things grow strange sometimes, though I don't suppose you've noticed.

There was a light, she said. Not high like the one Todd saw, but on the first floor where the big front room would be. Yellow at first, she told me, but it got a rosy cast when she came closer; she thought someone had put a red shawl over it. There was music too. Happy dancing music, the kind men like. She knew what sort of house it was then, and so did I. She told me she wanted to walk up on that porch right then and never come out; but when she had the chance she was afraid.

She's gone now, all right, but not because she found her house again. She's dead.

I'm sorry, though there's others I would miss more. They found her in a ditch over on the other side of Pierced Rock. Some man didn't want to pay, very likely; her neck was broken.

Here comes Todd now. Hark to his step?

Old Man: Got company, do we? I think I know who you are—the new young woman sent out from town. What is it they call it, the Reconstruction Office? Well, I hope Nor has entertained you. We ain't much for society out here, but we try to treat our company right, and don't think we're high enough to look down on a visitor just because there wasn't no father in her making. Nor fetched you a piece of cake, I see, and I'll pour something for us all a trifle stouter than that wine you've been drinking. Keep the stabbers off.

Tingles your nose, don't it? Sweet on the tongue, though.

That's only this old house a-creaking. Old houses do, you know, particularly by night, and this one was carpentered by Nor's dad just after the War. It's the cooling off when the sun sets. Drink up—it won't hurt you.

No, I can't say I felt a thing. Know what it is, though—Nor filling you with tales of the walking houses hereabouts.

It's true enough, ma'am, though we don't often mention them to your women. I've seen them myself—Nor will have told you, no doubt. There's those that think them so frightful—say that anybody setting foot in one just vanishes away, or gets ate, or whatever. Well now, it's true enough they're seldom seen again; but seldom's not never, now is it? I'll tell you a tale of my own. We had a man around here called Pim Pyntey; a drinking man in his way, as a good many of us are. Everybody said no good would come to him, though drunk or sober he was about as friendly a soul as I've known, and always willing to pitch in and help a neighbor if it was only a matter of working—didn't have any money, you know; that kind never does. Still, I've gone fishing with him often, though I wouldn't hunt with him—always afraid he'd burn one of these here legs of mine off by accident. I'm 'tached to both of them, as they say.

Anyhow, Pim, he started seeing them. I'd run into him down at the Center, and he'd tell me about them. Followin' him—that was what he always claimed. "They're after me, Todd, I don't know why it should be, but they are. They're followin' me." You've got drink, I know, where you come from, ma'am; but not like here. The Firstcomers didn't feel it was up to what they were accustomed to—said the yeasts were different or some such; at least, that's what I've heard. They put other things in them to raise it up, and we use them yet. There's—oh, maybe twenty or thirty different herbs and roots and whatnot we favor, and a little whitey-greeny worm we get out of the mud around aruum trees that's particularly good if there's a den in the roots, and then a fungus that grows in the mountain caves and has a picture like an autochthon's hand in the middle sometimes and smells like haying. Those are poison when they're old, but if you get a young one and cut it up and soak it in salt water for a week before you drop it in the crock, it'll give you a drink that makes you feel—well, I don't know how to put it. Like you're young and going to live forever. Like nothing bad ever happened to you, and you're likely to meet your mother and dad and everybody you ever liked that's dead now just around the next turn in the road.

What I'm trying to tell you is that Pim, when his head was full—which it was most of the time—was not entirely like anybody you're likely to have known before. Now you may say, as a lot did, that it was the drinking that made him see the houses; but suppose it worked the other way, and it was the drinking that made them see him?

Be that as it may, when he was going across the Nepo pass he saw one up on a high rock. At least, that's what he said. Maybe it's true; it was snowing, according to what he told me, and a house would figure—as I see it—that it would be hard for any ornithopter to see through the falling flakes, and the buildup on the roof would be no different from what it would see on the stones of the Nepo. Angled stone, you see, looking a lot like angled roofs, with the snow on both.

There were buildings up there a long time ago—I don't know of anybody who'll say how long. Buildings and walls that run along the crests of the mountains for as far as a man can see to either side (all tumble-down now, some of that stone will run like sand if you rub it between your fingers), and closed-in places that don't look like they ever had roofs or floors; and doorways, or what look like them, in front of the mouths of caves. People go up there on picnics in the summer, and go back into those caves carrying torches now. You can see the smoke marks on the ceilings. But there's whippers farther back—you know about those, I expect, because they bother your flying machines after dark; and in the winter there's other animals that come into the caves to get out of the cold, so the picnickers find bones and broken skulls in places that were clean the year before. Some say the autochthons cut the stone and built the buildings and the walls; some say they only killed the ones who did.

I can't believe it matters much. The builders are gone now, whether they came from off-world and tried to stay here, like us, or were earlier people of this world, or the autochthons—in happier days, as you might say. We're dying out too, now—I mean, the old settler families. You'll be persuading your own people to come here to live soon, just to fill the place up. Yes you will. Then we'll see what happens.

What Pim saw was a house. Three stories and a big attic. Lights in all the windows, he said, but only just dim. For some reason—I would guess it was the drink—he didn't feel like he could turn around and go back; he had to go forward. He'd been to Chackerville, you see, and was coming home across the pass. A man with that much in him will get to where he can't help but sleep sometimes, and he'd been worried about that, because of the snow, before he saw the house. Well, that was one worry less, was how he put it. Seeing it woke him right up. I guess I never will forget how he told me about all the time he spent climbing up to the saddle, him keeping open his eyes all the time against the snow, afraid of losing sight of the house up there because he thought it might jump down on him. It wouldn't do such a thing, you know. They can't jump. They'd crack something if they tried. Still, it was strange for him; and as he said himself, it's a wonder he went on.

If you had been there, you'd know how it is—a hollow, like, between the two mountains, with the ground falling away to front and back. The old road, built I guess by the same ones that built the buildings there, went right through the middle of it; and when the Firstcomers started to travel in this part of the world, they laid a new road over the old one. That new one's wearing away now, and you can see the bones of the old through it. Anyway, that was where Pim was walking, on those big lava blocks. One up, one down, one sidewise—that's the way the slant of them always seems to me to run. There's them that will tell you every seventh one is cracked, but I won't vouch for that.

They were icy that night, so Pim said, and he had to pick his way along; but every so often he'd look up and see the house perched there on the outcrop. It reminded him, he said, of what the Bible tells about the man that built his house on rock; and he kept thinking that he could go into it and be home already. There was a fire there—he knew that because of the smoke-smell from the chimney—and he would sit down and put his feet up on the fender and take a pull or two at his bottle and finally have a nap.

In the end he didn't do it, of course, or he wouldn't have been in the Center telling it to me. But he said he always felt like there was some part of him that had. That he split into two, some way, coming through the pass, and the other half was in that house still—wherever it was, for it ain't up there now or more people would have told about seeing it—doing he didn't know what.

But the funny thing was what happened when he went past. He could hear it groan. The snow was flying right into his face, he said, but he knew it wasn't just the wind; the house was sorry he hadn't stopped. All the way down, until the pass was out of sight, he watched the lights in the windows blink out one by one.

Sure you won't have another? The evening chill is coming now, and that machine of yours don't keep the air off you, or so it looks to me. Still, you know best, and if you must go, you must; sorry Nor and me couldn't be of more help.

I've got her—set easy, Nor.

Ma'am, you've got to be careful of your footing in here. These floorboards are uneven, and a lot of our furniture has those little spindly legs on it, just like that table. They can be tricksy, as you found out.

There's no good ending to that story of Pim's—no more than I told already. He dropped out of sight a while afterward, but he'd done that before. Old Wolter, down to the Center, says he looked out one night, and there was another house setting beside his, and in at the window of it he could see Pim laying there with someone else beside him; he said he couldn't be certain if either of them was dead or not. But Wolter ain't to be believed, if you know what I mean.

I didn't feel no shifting, ma'am. I oughtn't to have given you what I did out of my flask. You're not used to it, and it's not for the ladies anyhow. I helped build this place, though, and it's solid as a rock.

Not that way, ma'am. The door's over—

Sure, I see your gun, and I know what it will do, too. I think you ought to put it away, ma'am. I don't believe you're feeling quite yourself, and you might harm Nor with that thing. You wouldn't want to do that. Still, I don't think you ought to open that door.

There! No, I won't give it back; it's safer, I think, with me. I doubt that you'll remember; and if you was to, you couldn't find us.

I didn't want you to see her—that's all. You'd have been happier, I think, without it—and it would've saved you that yell. Nor's grandmother's sister, she was. Still is, I guess. Great-aunt Enid. She talks to us still—there's mouths, you see, in various places; would you credit she remembers people that was born before the first transporter left? That far back. Didn't you ever wonder how different it was—

Old Woman: Well, Todd, that's the last of her—at least, for now. Hear that machine kick gravel. She expected you'd try to stop her

when she ran for it, and she'll be disappointed you didn't, once she gets
away down the road. Hope she don't run that thing into a tree.

We'll move on now, Enid.

You're right, she's not ready yet; but someday—I suppose it might be
possible. Look at that other one. Someday this one will be ready to seek
her peace. Come into a woman. I've said it before and I'll say it again—
that's why we're all so comfortable here: we've been here before. Feel
the motion of her, Todd. How easy she goes!

AGAINST THE LAFAYETTE ESCADRILLE

I have built a perfect replica of a Fokker triplane, except for the flammable dope. It is five meters, seventy-seven centimeters long and has a wing span of seven meters, nineteen centimeters, just like the original. The engine is an authentic copy of an Oberursel UR II. I have a lathe and a milling machine and I made most of the parts for the engine myself, but some had to be farmed out to a company in Cleveland, and most of the electrical parts were done in Louisville, Kentucky.

In the beginning I had hoped to get an original engine, and I wrote my first letters to Germany with that in mind, but it just wasn't possible; there are only a very few left, and as nearly as I could find out none in private hands. The Oberursel Worke is no longer in existence. I was able to secure plans though, through the cooperation of some German hobbyists. I redrew them myself translating the German when they had to be sent to Cleveland. A man from the newspaper came to take pictures when the Fokker was nearly ready to fly, and I estimated then that I had put more than three thousand hours into building it. I did all the airframe and the fabric work myself, and carved the propeller.

Throughout the project I have tried to keep everything as realistic as possible, and I even have two 7.92 mm Maxim "Spandau" machineguns mounted just ahead of the cockpit. They are not loaded of course, but they are coupled to the engine with the Fokker Zentralsteuerung interrupter gear.

The question of dope came up because of a man in Oregon I used to correspond with who flies a Nieuport Scout. The authentic dope, as you're probably aware, was extremely flammable. He wanted to know if I'd used it, and when I told him I had not he became critical. As I said then, I love the Fokker too much to want to see it burn authentically, and if Antony Fokker and Reinhold Platz had had fireproof dope they would have used it. This didn't satisfy the Oregon man and he finally became so abusive I stopped replying to his letters. I still believe what I did was correct, and if I had it to do over my decision would be the same.

I have had a trailer specially built to move the Fokker, and I traded my car in on a truck to tow it and carry parts and extra gear, but mostly I leave it at a small field near here where I have rented hangar space, and move it as little as possible on the roads. When I do because of the wide load I have to drive very slowly and only use certain roads. People always stop to look when we pass, and sometimes I can hear them on their front porches calling to others inside to come and see. I think the three wings of the Fokker interest them particularly, and once in a rare while a veteran of the war will see it—almost always a man who smokes a pipe and has a cane. If I can hear what they say it is often pretty foolish, but a light comes into their eyes that I enjoy.

Mostly the Fokker is just in its hangar out at the field and you wouldn't know me from anyone else as I drive out to fly. There is a black cross painted on the door of my truck, but it wouldn't mean anything to you. I suppose it wouldn't have meant anything even if you had seen me on my way out the day I saw the balloon.

It was one of the earliest days of spring, with a very fresh, really indescribable feeling in the air. Three days before I had gone up for the first time that year, coming after work and flying in weather that was a little too bad with not quite enough light left; winter flying, really. Now it was Saturday and everything was changed. I remember how my scarf streamed out while I was just standing on the field talking to the mechanic.

The wind was good, coming right down the length of the field to me, getting under the Fokker's wings and lifting it like a kite before we had gone a hundred feet. I did a slow turn then, getting a good look at the field with all the new, green grass starting to show, and adjusting my goggles.

Have you ever looked from an open cockpit to see the wing struts trembling and the ground swinging far below? There is nothing like it. I pulled back on the stick and gave it more throttle and rose and rose until I was looking down on the backs of all the birds and I could not be certain which of the tiny roofs I saw was the house where I live or the factory where I work. Then I forgot looking down, and looked up and out, always remembering to look over my shoulder especially, and to watch the sun where the S.E. 5a's of the Royal Flying Corps love to hang like dragonflies, invisible against the glare.

Then I looked away and I saw it, almost on the horizon, an orange dot. I did not, of course, know then what it was; but I waved to the other members of the Jagstaffel I command and turned toward it, the Fokker thrilling to the challenge. It was moving with the wind, which meant almost directly away from me, but that only gave the Fokker a tailwind, and we came at it—rising all the time.

It was not really orange-red as I had first thought. Rather it was a thousand colors and shades, with reds and yellows and white predominating. I climbed toward it steeply with the stick drawn far back, almost at a stall. Because of that I failed, at first, to see the basket hanging from it. Then I leveled out and circled it at a distance. That was when I realized it was a balloon. After a moment I saw, too, that it was of very old-fashioned design with a wicker basket for the passengers and that someone was in it. At the moment the profusion of colors interested me more, and I went slowly spiraling in until I could see them better, the Easter egg blues and the blacks as well as the reds and whites and yellows.

It wasn't until I looked at the girl that I understood. She was the passenger, a very beautiful girl, and she wore crinolines and had her hair in long chestnut curls that hung down over her bare shoulders. She waved to me, and then I understood.

The ladies of Richmond had sewn it for the Confederate army, making it from their silk dresses. I remembered reading about it. The girl in the basket blew me a kiss and I waved to her, trying to convey with my wave that none of the men of my command would ever be allowed to harm her; that we had at first thought that her craft might be a French or Italian observation balloon, but that for the future she need fear no gun in the service of the Kaiser's Flugzeugmeisterei.

I circled her for some time then, she turning slowly in the basket to follow the motion of my plane, and we talked as well as we could with gestures and smiles. At last when my fuel was running low I signaled her that I must leave. She took, from a container hidden by the rim of the basket, a badly shaped, corked brown bottle. I circled even closer, in a tight bank, until I could see the yellow, crumbling label. It was one of the very early soft drinks, an original bottle. While I watched she drew the cork, drank some, and held it out symbolically to me.

Then I had to go. I made it back to the field, but I landed dead stick with my last drop of fuel exhausted when I was half a kilometer away. Naturally I had the Fokker refueled at once and went up again, but I could not find her balloon.

I have never been able to find it again, although I go up almost every day when the weather makes it possible. There is nothing but an empty sky and a few jets. Sometimes, to tell the truth, I have wondered if things would not have been different if, in finishing the Fokker, I had used the original, flammable dope. She was so authentic. Sometimes toward evening I think I see her in the distance, above the clouds, and I follow as fast as I can across the silent vault with the Fokker trembling around me and the throttle all the way out; but it is only the sun.

THANKSGIVING

THREE MILLION
SQUARE MILES

"Hey," Richard Marquer said to his wife Betty one August afternoon. "Hey, ninety percent of the United States is uninhabited." They were reading the Sunday paper.

"That's right," Betty said, "it's parking lots."

"No, really. It says so right here: 'At least ninety percent of the land area of the United States is employed neither in agriculture nor as sites for roads and buildings.'"

"I didn't know Texas was that big."

"Listen, this is serious. Where the hell is it all?"

"Dick, you don't really believe that junk."

"It says so."

"It says the department store is selling percale sheets twenty percent under cost too."

Richard put down his part of the paper and went to the bookcase. After five minutes work with pencil and paper he said, "Bet?"

"What?"

"I've been making some calculations. According to the almanac—"

"That's an old one. Nineteen sixty-eight."

"It still ought to be pretty accurate, and it says there are—get this—two hundred and ninety-six million eight hundred and thirty-six thousand harvested acres in the United States. Now there's six hundred and forty acres in a square mile, so that means about four hundred and sixty-three thousand harvested square miles. Only the gross area of the United States is three *million* six hundred and twenty-eight thousand one hundred and fifty square miles."

"So it isn't ninety percent. You just proved it yourself."

"I'm not arguing about the exact figure, but look at the size of the thing. Say that half as much is taken up for buildings and backyards as for all the farms. That still leaves over three million square miles unaccounted for. More than three quarters of the country."

"Richard?"

"Yes?"

"Richard, do you really think that's really there? That everybody wouldn't go out and grab it?"

"The facts—"

"Dick, those are talking facts—they're not real. It's like what you were telling me when we bought the car, about the miles on the little thing—"

"Odometer."

"You remember? You said they didn't mean anything. It said thirteen thousand but you said it might be fifteen or twenty thousand really. Anything. Or like when they raised the city income tax. They said it was inflation, but if it was inflation everybody's pay would go up too so the city'd get more—only they took another half percent anyway, remember? You could prove they didn't need it, but it didn't mean anything."

"But it has to be somewhere."

"You really think it's out there? With deer on it, and bears? Dick, it's silly."

"Three *million* square miles."

"When we drove to Baltimore last summer to see my mother, did you see any of it?"

Richard shook his head.

"When you flew to Cleveland for the company—"

"It was so foggy. Everything was socked in, and you couldn't see anything but haze."

"From factories! See?" Betty went back to her paper.

That night *The Wizard of Oz* was shown on television for the two hundredth time. Judy Garland sang "Over the Rainbow."

Richard took to going on drives. He drove, sometimes for two or three or four hours, before coming home from work. He drove weekends, and once when Betty spent a weekend with her mother he drove from six a.m. Saturday until twelve p.m. Sunday and put sixteen hundred miles on the car. He knew all the best ways into and out of the city, and the best places for food and coffee. Once he was the first person to report an accident to the state highway patrol; once he helped college girls change a tire.

At a roadside zoo he made friends with three deer in a pen—a buck with fine antlers nuzzled his hand for popcorn, and Richard said softly, "I bet if they'd let you out you'd find some of them." Later he asked the operator of the zoo if any animals ever escaped.

"Don't worry about that." (He was a desiccated man of fifty who wore checked sports shirts.) "We keep everything secure here. Look at it from my angle—those animals are valuable to me. You think I'd let them get out where they could hurt people?"

Richard said, "I'm not trying to accuse you of anything. I just wondered if any of them ever got loose."

"Not long as I've had the place, and I been here eight years."

Later Richard asked the boy who pitched hay into the deer's pen, and he said, "Last year. The little buck. I guess the big one was giving him a rough time, and he jumped the fence."

"What happened to him?"

"He got out on the highway and got hit by a car."

Richard began measuring the farm woodlots he passed, and the little acres of waste ground. He carried a hundred-foot tape in the car and picked up hitchhikers—mostly college boys with beaded headbands and fringed buckskin shirts—who would help him, holding one end of the tape while Richard trotted past five or six trees to put the other at the margin of a county road.

He stopped more and more often to examine the bodies of dead animals. Betty asked for a trial separation, and he agreed.

He bought four new tires and had his wheel bearings repacked.

At a roadhouse he paid a three-dollar cover and seventy-five cents for beer to watch a dark-haired, dark-eyed girl with a feather in her hair being undressed by a trained raccoon. The girl was called Princess Running Bare, and after Richard had given the waitress five dollars more she sat at his table and sipped coffee royal for half an hour. "All us Indians are alcoholics," Princess Running Bare said, and she said she was half French Canadian and half Cree, and had been born in a Montreal slum. Richard tried to call Betty's mother's from a telephone booth next to the bar, but no one answered. He left the roadhouse and drove all night.

Outside a steel-making town he took the wrong lane of a three-pronged freeway fork and found himself rushing, with a hundred other cars, in a direction in which he had no wish to go. He pulled off at a service park and asked the attendant.

"Lots of them does that," the attendant said, pulling at the bill of his green cap. "You want to go—" and he waved in the direction from which Richard had come.

"Yes," Richard said. He named the Interstate he wished to use, which was not the one he was on. "Southeast." For some reason he added, "I want to go home." It was about nine o'clock.

"Yeah," the attendant said. He looked around conspiratorially. "Tell you what. Out that way 'bout three-quarters of a mile is the eastbound lanes." He waved an arm toward the back of the service park, where uneven, down-sloping ground was thick with dead grass. "Know what I mean? See, this here is four lanes goin' west and over there is where they come back. Now if you keep going the way you are it's seventeen miles until you can get off and cross over. But sometimes people just jump their tires over that little curb at the back of the station and drive across."

"I see," Richard said.

"Only when you come in you come into the fast lane, naturally. Course it's against the law."

"I'll be careful."

"And if I was you I'd walk out a little way first to make sure it isn't too swampy. Usually dry enough, but you wouldn't want to get stuck."

It felt soft under his feet, but not dangerously so. The eastbound lanes, presumably a thousand yards or so ahead, were not visible, and as he walked the gentle slope buried the westbound lanes behind him, and at last even the red roof of the service park. The distant noises of traffic mingled with the sound of the wind. "Here," he said to himself. "Here."

His shoes crushed the soft tunnels of moles. He looked up and saw a bird that might have been a hawk circling. An old, rusted hubcap lying on its face held a cup of water, and mosquito larvae, and he thought of it springing from the wheel of its car and rolling, rolling all this distance across the empty ground. It seemed a long way.

At the top of the next rise he could see the eastbound lanes, and that the rest of the ground was dry enough to drive over. He turned and went back, but found he had somehow lost his way, and that he was a quarter mile at least from the service park where he had left his car. He began walking back to it along the shoulder of the Interstate, but the traffic passing only a few feet to his right at ninety miles an hour frightened him. He moved away from it, and the ground became really swampy, the mud sticking to his shoes and insects buzzing up with each step he took; so that he went back to the shoulder of the highway, still afraid.

CHRISTMAS EVE

THE WAR
BENEATH THE TREE

"It's Christmas Eve, Commander Robin," the Spaceman said. "You'd better go to bed, or Santa won't come."

Robin's mother said, "That's right, Robin. Time to say good night."

The little boy in blue pajamas nodded, but made no move to rise.

"Kiss me," said Bear. Bear walked his funny, waddly walk around the tree and threw his arms about Robin. "We have to go to bed. I'll come too." It was what he said every night.

Robin's mother shook her head in amused despair. "Listen to them," she said. "Look at him, Bertha. He's like a little prince surrounded by his court. How is he going to feel when he's grown and can't have transistorized sycophants to spoil him all the time?"

Bertha the robot maid nodded her own almost human head as she put the poker back in its stand. "That's right, Ms. Jackson. That's right for sure."

The Dancing Doll took Robin by the hand, making an *arabesque penché* of it. Now Robin rose. His guardsmen formed up and presented arms.

"On the other hand," Robin's mother said, "they're children only such a short time."

Bertha nodded again. "They're only young once, Ms. Jackson. That's for sure. All right if I tell these little cute toys to help me straighten up after he's asleep?"

The Captain of the Guardsmen saluted with his silver saber, the Largest Guardsman beat the tattoo on his drum, and the rest of the guardsmen formed a double file.

"He sleeps with Bear," Robin's mother said.

"I can spare Bear. There's plenty of others."

The Spaceman touched the buckle of his antigravity belt and soared to a height of four feet like a graceful, broad-shouldered balloon. With the Dancing Doll on his left and Bear on his right, Robin toddled off behind the guardsmen. Robin's mother ground out her last cigarette of the evening, winked at Bertha, and said, "I suppose I'd better turn in too. You needn't help me undress, just pick up my things in the morning."

"Yes'um. Too bad Mr. Jackson ain't here, it bein' Christmas Eve and you expectin' an' all."

"He'll be back from Brazil in a week—I've told you already. And Bertha, your speech habits are getting worse and worse. Are you sure you wouldn't rather be a French maid for a while?"

"Maize none, Ms. Jackson. I have too much trouble talkin' to the men that comes to the door when I'm French."

"When Mr. Jackson gets his next promotion, we're going to have a chauffeur," Robin's mother said. "He's going to be Italian, and he's going to *stay* Italian."

Bertha watched her waddle out of the room. "All right, you lazy toys! You empty them ashtrays into the fire an' get everythin' put away. I'm goin' to turn myself off, but the next time I come on, this room better be straight or there's goin' to be some broken toys around here."

She watched long enough to see the Gingham Dog dump the largest ashtray on the crackling logs, the Spaceman float up to straighten the magazines on the coffee table, and the Dancing Doll begin to sweep the hearth. "Put yourselfs in your box," she told the guardsmen, and turned off.

In the smallest bedroom, Bear lay in Robin's arm. "Be quiet," said Robin.

"I *am* quiet," said Bear.

"Every time I am almost gone to sleep, you squiggle."

"I don't," said Bear.

"You do."

"Sometimes you have trouble going to sleep too, Robin," said Bear.

"I'm having trouble *tonight*," Robin countered meaningfully.

Bear slipped from under his arm. "I want to see if it's snowing again." He climbed from the bed to an open drawer, and from the open drawer to the top of the dresser. It was snowing.

Robin said, "Bear, you have a circuit loose." It was what his mother sometimes said to Bertha.

Bear did not reply.

"Oh, Bear," Robin said sleepily, a moment later. "I know why you're antsy. It's your birthday tomorrow, and you think I didn't get you anything."

"Did you?" Bear asked.

"I will," Robin said. "Mother will take me to the store." In half a minute his breathing became the regular, heavy sighing of a sleeping child.

Bear sat on the edge of the dresser and looked at him. Then he said under his breath, "I can sing Christmas carols." It had been the first thing he had ever said to Robin, one year ago. He spread his arms. *All is calm. All is bright.* It made him think of the lights on the tree and the bright fire in the living room. The Spaceman was there, but because he was the only toy who could fly, none of the others liked the Spaceman much. The Dancing Doll was there too. The Dancing Doll was clever, but, well . . . He could not think of the word.

He jumped down into the drawer on top of a pile of Robin's undershirts, then out of the drawer, softly to the dark, carpeted floor.

"Limited," he said to himself. "The Dancing Doll is limited." He thought again of the fire, then of the old toys, the Blocks Robin had had before he and the Dancing Doll and the rest had come—the Wooden Man who rode a yellow bicycle, the Singing Top.

In the living room, the Dancing Doll was positioning the guardsmen, while the Spaceman stood on the mantle and supervised. "We can get three or four behind the bookcase," he called.

"Where they won't be able to see a thing," Bear growled.

The Dancing Doll pirouetted and dropped a sparkling curtsy. "We were afraid you wouldn't come," she said.

"Put one behind each leg of the coffee table," Bear told her. "I had to wait until he was asleep. Now listen to me, all of you. When I call, '*Charge!*' we must all run at them together. That's very important. If we can, we'll have a practice beforehand."

The Largest Guardsman said, "I'll beat my drum."

"You'll beat the enemy, or you'll go into the fire with the rest of us," Bear said.

Robin was sliding on the ice. His feet went out from under him and right up into the air so he fell down with a tremendous BUMP that shook him all over. He lifted his head, and he was not on the frozen pond in the park at all. He was in his own bed, with the moon shining in at the window, and it was Christmas Eve . . . no, Christmas Night now . . . and Santa was coming, maybe had already come. Robin listened for reindeer on the roof and did not hear reindeer steps. Then he listened for Santa eating the cookies his mother had left on the stone shelf by the fireplace. There was no munching or crunching. Then he threw back the covers and slipped down over the edge of his bed until his feet touched the floor. The good smells of tree and fire had come into his room. He followed them out of it ever so quietly, into the hall.

Santa was in the living room, bent over beside the tree! Robin's eyes opened until they were as big and as round as his pajama buttons. Then Santa straightened up, and he was not Santa at all, but Robin's mother in a new red bathrobe. Robin's mother was nearly as fat as Santa, and Robin had to put his fingers in his mouth to keep from laughing at the way she puffed, and pushed at her knees with her hands until she stood straight.

But Santa had come! There were toys—new toys!—everywhere under the tree.

Robin's mother went to the cookies on the stone shelf and ate half of one. Then she drank half the glass of milk. Then she turned to go back into her bedroom, and Robin retreated into the darkness of his own room until she was past. When he peeked cautiously around the door frame again, the toys—the new toys—were beginning to move.

They shifted and shook themselves and looked about. Perhaps it was because it was Christmas Eve. Perhaps it was only because the light of the fire had activated their circuits. But a Clown brushed himself off and stretched, and a Raggedy Girl smoothed her raggedy apron (with the heart embroidered on it), and a Monkey gave a big jump and chinned himself on the next-to-lowest limb of the Christmas tree. Robin saw them. And Bear, behind the hassock of Robin's father's chair, saw them too. Cowboys and Native Americans were lifting the lid of a box, and a Knight opened a cardboard door (made to look like wood) in the side of another box (made to look like stone), letting a Dragon peer over his shoulder.

"Charge!" Bear called. "Charge!" He came around the side of the hassock on all fours like a real bear, running stiffly but very fast, and he hit the Clown at his wide waistline and knocked him down, then picked him up and threw him halfway to the fire.

The Spaceman had swooped down on the Monkey; they wrestled, teetering, on top of a polystyrene tricycle.

The Dancing Doll had charged fastest of all, faster even than Bear himself, in a breathtaking series of *jetés*, but the Raggedy Girl had lifted her feet from the floor, and now she was running with her toward the fire. As Bear struck the Clown a second time, he saw two Native Americans carrying a guardsman—the Captain of the Guardsmen—toward the fire too. The Captain's saber had gone through one of the Native Americans and it must have disabled some circuit because the

Native American walked badly; but in a moment more the Captain was burning, his red uniform burning, his hands thrown up like flames themselves, his black eyes glazing and cracking, bright metal running from him like sweat to harden among the ashes under the logs.

The Clown tried to wrestle with Bear, but Bear threw him down. The Dragon's teeth were sunk in Bear's left heel, but he kicked himself free. The Calico Cat was burning, burning. The Gingham Dog tried to pull her out, but the Monkey pushed him in. For a moment, Bear thought of the cellar stairs and the deep, dark cellar, where there were boxes and bundles and a hundred forgotten corners. If he ran and hid, the new toys might never find him, might never even try to find him. Years from now Robin would discover him, covered with dust.

The Dancing Doll's scream was high and sweet, and Bear turned to face the Knight's upraised sword.

When Robin's mother got up on Christmas Morning, Robin was awake already, sitting under the tree with the Cowboys, watching the Native Americans do their rain dance. The Monkey was perched on his shoulder, the Raggedy Girl (programmed, the store had assured Robin's mother, to begin Robin's sex education) in his lap, and the Knight and the Dragon were at his feet. "Do you like the toys Santa brought you, Robin?" Robin's mother asked.

"One of the Native Amer'cans doesn't work."

"Never mind, dear, we'll take him back. Robin, I've got something important to tell you."

Bertha the robot maid came in with Corn Flakes and milk and vitamins, and café au lait for Robin's mother. "Where is those old toys?" she asked. "They done a picky-poor job of cleanin' up this room."

"Robin, your toys are just toys, of course—"

Robin nodded absently. A Red Calf was coming out of the chute, with a Cowboy on a Roping Horse after him.

"Where *is* those old toys, Ms. Jackson?" Bertha asked again.

"They're programmed to self-destruct, I understand," Robin's mother said. "But, Robin, you know how the new toys all came, the Knight and Dragon and all your Cowboys, almost by magic? Well, the same thing can happen with people."

Robin looked at her with frightened eyes.

"The same wonderful thing is going to happen here, in our home."

LA BEFANA

When Zozz, home from the pit, had licked his fur clean, he howled before John Bannano's door. John's wife, Teresa, opened it and let him in. She was a thin, stooped woman of thirty or thirty-five, her black hair shot with gray; she did not smile, but he felt somehow that she was glad to see him. She said, "He's not home yet. If you want to come in we've got a fire."

Zozz said, "I'll wait for him," and, six-legging politely across the threshold, sat down over the stone Bananas had rolled in for him when they were new friends. Maria and Mark, playing some sort of game with beer-bottle caps on squares scratched on the floor dirt said, "Hi, Uncle Zozz," and Zozz said, "Hi," in return. Bananas' old mother, whom Zozz had brought here from the pads in his rusty powerwagon the day before, looked at him with piercing eyes, then fled into the other room. He could hear Teresa relax, the wheezing outpuffed breath.

He said, half humorously, "I think she thinks I bumped her on purpose yesterday."

"She's not used to you yet."

"I know," Zozz said.

"I told her, Mother Bannano, it's their world, and they're not used to *you*."

"Sure," Zozz said. A gust of wind outside brought the cold in to replace the odor of the gog-hutch on the other side of the left wall.

"I tell you it's hell to have your husband's mother with you in a place as small as this."

"Sure," Zozz said again.

Maria announced, "Daddy's home!" The door rattled open and Bananas came in looking tired and cheerful. Bananas worked in the slaughtering market, and though his cheeks were blue with cold, the cuffs of his trousers were red with blood. He kissed Teresa and tousled the hair of both children, and said, "Hi, Zozzy."

Zozz said, "Hi. How does it roll?" And moved over so Bananas could warm his back. Someone groaned, and Bananas asked a little anxiously, "What's that?"

Teresa said, "Next door."

"Huh?"

"Next door. Some woman."

"Oh. I thought it might be Mom."

"She's fine."

"Where is she?"

"In back."

Bananas frowned. "There's no fire in there; she'll freeze to death."

"I didn't tell her to go back there. She can wrap a blanket around her."

Zozz said, "It's me—I bother her." He got up. Bananas said, "Sit down."

"I can go. I just came to say hi."

"Sit down." Bananas turned to his wife. "Honey, you shouldn't leave her in there alone. See if you can't get her to come out."

"Johnny—"

"Teresa, dammit!"

"Okay, Johnny."

Bananas took off his coat and sat down in front of the fire. Maria and Mark had gone back to their game. In a voice too low to attract their attention Bananas said, "Nice thing, huh?"

Zozz said, "I think your mother makes her nervous."

Bananas said, "Sure."

Zozz said, "This isn't an easy world."

"You mean for us. No it ain't, but you don't see me moving."

Zozz said, "That's good. I mean, here you've got a job anyway. There's work."

"That's right."

Unexpectedly Maria said: "We get enough to eat here, and me and Mark can find wood for the fire. Where we used to be there wasn't anything to eat."

Bananas said, "You remember, honey?"

"A little."

Zozz said, "People are poor here."

Bananas was taking off his shoes, scraping the street mud from them and tossing it into the fire. He said, "If you mean us, us people are poor everyplace." He jerked his head in the direction of the back room. "You ought to hear her tell about our world."

"Your mother?"

Bananas nodded. Maria said, "Daddy, how did Grandmother come here?"

"Same way we did."

Mark said, "You mean she signed a thing?"

"A labor contract? No, she's too old. She bought a ticket—you know, like you would buy something in a store."

Maria said, "That's what I mean."

"Shut up and play. Don't bother us."

Zozz said, "How'd things go at work?"

"So-so." Bananas looked toward the back room again. "She came into some money, but that's her business—I didn't want to talk to the kids about it."

"Sure."

"She says she spent every dollar to get here—you know, they haven't used dollars even on Earth for fifty, sixty years, but she still says it, how do you like that?" He laughed, and Zozz laughed too. "I asked how she was going to get back, and she said she's not going back, she's going to die right here with us. What could I say?"

"I don't know." Zozz waited for Bananas to say something, and when he did not he added, "I mean, she's your mother."

"Yeah."

Through the thin wall they heard the sick woman groan again, and someone moving about. Zozz said, "I guess it's been a long time since you saw her last."

"Yeah—twenty-two years Newtonian. Listen, Zozzy . . ."

"Uh-huh."

"You know something? I wish I had never set eyes on her again."

Zozz said nothing, rubbing his hands, hands, hands.

"That sounds lousy I guess."

"I know what you mean."

"She could have lived good for the rest of her life on what that ticket cost her." Bananas was silent for a moment. "She used to be a big, fat woman when I was a kid, you know? A great big woman with a loud voice. Look at her now—dried up and bent over; it's like she wasn't my mother at all. You know the only thing that's the same about her? That black dress. That's the only thing I recognize, the only thing that hasn't changed. She could be a stranger—she tells stories about me I don't remember at all."

Maria said, "She told us a story today."

Mark added: "Before you came home. About this witch."

Maria said: "That brings the presents to children. Her name is La Befana the Christmas Witch."

Zozz drew his lips back from his double canines and jiggled his head. "I like stories."

"She says it's almost Christmas, and on Christmas three wise men went looking for the Baby, and they stopped at the old witch's door, and they asked which way it was and she told them and they said come with us."

The door to the other room opened, and Teresa and Bananas' mother came out. Bananas' mother was holding a teakettle; she edged around Zozz to put it on the hook and swing it out over the fire.

"And she was sweeping and she wouldn't come."

Mark said: "She said she'd come when she was finished. She was a real old, real ugly woman. Watch, I'll show you how she walked." He jumped up and began to hobble around the room.

Bananas looked at his wife and indicated the wall. "What's this?"

"In there?"

"The charity place—they said she could stay there. She couldn't stay in the house because all the rooms are full of men."

Maria was saying, "So when she was all done she went looking for Him only she couldn't find Him and she never did."

"She's sick?"

"She's knocked up, Johnny, that's all. Don't worry about her. She's got some guy in there with her."

Mark asked, "Do you know about the baby Jesus, Uncle Zozz?"

Zozz groped for words.

"Giovanni, my son . . ."

"Yes, Mama."

"Your friend . . . Do they have the faith, Giovanni?"

Apropos of nothing, Teresa said, "They're Jews, next door."

Zozz told Mark, "You see, the baby Jesus has never come to my world."

Maria said: "And so she goes all over everyplace looking for him with her presents, and she leaves some with every kid she finds, but she says it's not because she thinks they might be him like some people think, but just a substitute. She can't never die. She has to do it forever, doesn't she, Grandma?"

The bent old woman said, "Not forever, dearest; only until tomorrow night."

NEW YEAR'S EVE

MELTING

I am the sound a balloon makes falling into the sky;
the sweat of a lump of ice in a summer river.

It was the best cocktail party in the world. It took place in someone's
(never mind whose) penthouse apartment; and it spilled over into the
garden outside, among the fountains and marble ruins, and into the
belly of the airship moored to the building, and the ship spilled over
into the city, taking off from time to time to cruise the canyons of
clotheslines and neon signs, or rise to the limbus of the moon. Many
were drinking, and certain of the fountains ran with wine; many were
smoking hashish—its sweet fumes swirled into men's pockets and up
women's skirts until everyone was a trifle dazed with them and a little
careless. A few were smoking opium.

John Edward was drinking, but he was fairly certain he had been
smoking hashish an hour before, and he might have been smoking
opium, but it was the best cocktail party in the world, a party at which
he knew everyone and no one.

The man on his left was British, and had a clipped mustache and the
thin, muscled look John Edward associated with Bagnold and the Long
Range Desert Group. The man across from him was Tibetan or perhaps Nepalese, and wore a scarlet robe. The girl beside him (who stood
up often, sometimes bringing other people drinks, sometimes drinking
herself, sometimes only to wave at the airship as it circled overhead
while partygoers threw confetti from its balconies) was tall and auburn-
haired, and wore a white gown slit at one side from hem to armpit. The
girl to John Edward's right was blond, and beautiful, and had a cage
of singing birds, living but too small to be alive, in her hair.

"This is a good party," John Edward said to the man on his left.

"Smashing. You know why, I take it?"

John Edward shook his head, but before the Englishman could tell
him, a being from the Farther Stars who resembled not so much a man

as a man's statue—with some of the characteristics of a washing machine—interrupted them to ask for a light. The Tibetan leaned forward, kindling a blue flame in the palm of his hand; and the man from the Farther Stars walked away puffing gentle puffs, his cycle on Delicate Things.

The girl with the birdcage in her hair said: "Some of these people are from the past. Mankind's mastery of the laws of Time makes it possible to ask the people of the past to parties. It makes for a good crowd."

The auburn-haired girl, she of the slit dress, said: "Then that man at the piano who looks like Napoleon must *be* Napoleon."

"No, that's his brother Joseph; I don't think Napoleon's here right now."

The Tibetan (leaning forward, so that his robe opened to show a hairless chest puckered with old scars) said: "It is the use of temporal arresters—such is my own opinion—which have rendered delectable these celebrations." He was talking half to the auburn-haired girl, half to the birdcage girl, totally to John Edward. "So. One pays one's fee. One receives a machine so subtle that it is in a card contained. One attends. When wishes, one absents. That, too, is good. One returns at the time of absenting."

"Damned good," the Englishman put in, "for sweating up conversational crushers. You've all the time in the world. If you've got the card."

"I don't," John Edward said.

"Didn't think you had, really."

The birdcage woman, who no longer had a birdcage in her hair, but wore instead chaste coiled braids, said: "The card lets you sparkle as a wit—be Queen of Diamonds. And it's a Chance card, because when you leave, you Go to Jail out there." She drew John Edward's hands to her until they were cupping her breasts. "Do you like my Community Chest?"

"Very much," John Edward said. The auburn-haired girl stood up and waved her glass, shouting, "Everybody's under temporal arrest!" No one paid any attention.

"High cost for cardholders," the Tibetan continued. "Oh, high cost. Others selected for interesting people, as I. Or look nice." He made a little bow toward the (ex)birdcage woman.

Who said to John Edward: "Would you in the dark?"

"Yes, but it's better with a nightlight."

"Or candle," the Tibetan.

The auburn-haired girl: "Or with a bar sign outside. I was born under Aquarius, but conceived over the sign of the Pig and Whistle." John Edward watched her hair to see if it had changed, but it had not.

"Under a blanket at noon," the Englishman said. "Had a Belgian girl up to my room at Shepheard's like that once. I was on Allenby's staff then . . ."

"Many are *tulpas*," remarked the man from the Farther Stars, who was passing by once again, and seemed to remember with gratitude the light the Tibetan had given him. "At least ten percent." (His voice was water dashing against stone.)

"But would you in the dark?" the braided-haired blond woman continued to John Edward. "If I asked you."

He nodded.

"A Belgian girl," the Englishman continued. "Refugee. Didn't know if the Boche would ever be out of Belgium—none of us did then—and would do anything. The colonel one night and the sergeant the next. She's saving you, m'boy. Going to save your bacon—save your sausage. Ha ha!" He hit John Edward on the shoulder.

"What's a *tulpa*?" the auburn-haired girl asked the Tibetan.

"For a little while," the blond woman said. Her hair was straight now, the style John Edward liked best, but it seemed a trifle too young for her. "Not anything that would disgust you, darling."

He stared at her, uncomprehending.

"Ten years. Ten little years, darling. That's nothing. With all they can do now—and I have money, darling—it's less than nothing. In the dark, sweetheart, promise."

The Englishman said: "He's a *tulpa*, old girl. Why bother. A nice chap, but a *tulpa*. I knew at once. Look at those shoulders. See how regular his features are? Handsome devil, eh? Not greasy at least, like so many of them."

"What's a *tulpa*?" the auburn-haired girl asked John Edward.

"I don't know." John Edward turned to the Englishman. "What do you mean, when you say she's saving me?"

"For her old age, you idiot. You flick off the lights and she flicks out for a quarter century or so. Then when no lover will have her, back she comes. One doesn't know in the dark, eh? Not unless the gal's been gone a devil of a long time."

"Please," the blond woman said to the Englishman. "You didn't have to."

"The chap's a *tulpa*, I tell you. If that's what you want, you can get an adept to stir one up for you anytime."

"But don't you understand? I knew him when I was young."

"Certain lamas," the Tibetan was telling the auburn-haired girl, "learn *siddhis* to flesh images from mind-stuff. Much same as ghosts, but never lived. Has been stolen and perverted in West, as all things."

"Can't understand how the blasted Chinese could conquer your country if you could do that," the Englishman said. "Inexhaustible armies."

The man from the Farther Stars, who was leaning over the auburn-haired girl's shoulder now (and peeking down her dress, John Edward thought), moved his head rhythmically from side to side. "Sunspots," he said. "Sunspots destroy *tulpas*."

John Edward said, "But *between—*"

The man from the Farther Stars continued to shake his head. "Always sunspots on the sun, sun-where."

The auburn-haired girl stood up, ducking from under his white marble chin. "I'm going to be sick," she said. "Take me to a lavatory."

She was looking at John Edward, and he stood too, and took her hand, saying, "This way." He had not the least idea where he was, and discovered that the end table beyond the sofa was a rosebush. They were in the garden. *Sober up,* he thought, trying to give himself orders. *Sober up, sober up, straighten out. Find a restroom.*

The auburn-haired girl said, "At least we're away from those terrible people."

"Aren't you really sick?"

"Oh, yes I'm sick. Oh, Lord, am I." She was clinging to his arm. "And drunk. Am I drunk. Are they staring at me? I can't even tell."

The ramp of the airship was in front of them. There would be bathrooms on that; there would have to be.

"The last time my hair went in the toilet. Will you hold it up for me? You can lie down with me afterwards. I want to lie down afterwards; I want to go to bed."

Somewhere a cock crowed.

It could not be heard, of course. It was a hundred miles away, out in the country. But it crowed, and the sun came up, and people went out like candles in the wind.

From the top of the ramp he looked back and saw them go, their glasses crashing to the flagstoned paths and brick-paved patios, their cigarettes dropping like poisoned fireflies.

"I loved you," the girl said. "Or at least I liked you. You'll be gone in a moment and I can't even ask you to kiss me, because I'm going to be sick."

"We're still here," John Edward told her, "both of us." And she was gone.

He walked down the ramp and into his apartment, stamping out every cigarette he saw. Sunshine was making hard shadows on the walls, and the airship vanished like mist. "Mr. Richbastard," he said to himself. "I wonder how much all those *tulpas* cost me."

The garden vanished, and the walls of the apartment rushed in, growing dirty as they came. He sat up. His head was splitting, and he thought that he was going to be sick to his stomach. The book was still propped open on his dresser where he had left it. His eyes were too gummy to read the print, but he remembered it: "Repeat, 'I am the sound of an owl's wings, the heartbeat of a banyan tree.'" He closed the book, and noticed that the hair on the back of his hand was gray; tried to remember how old he really was, then made himself stop.

In the next apartment the washing machine said: "Sun-where, sun-where, sun-where," then "sunspots destroy *tulpas*," as it switched to Rinse.

"By the Lord Harry," John Edward said, "in a day or so—when I'm feeling better—I'm going to do that again." Then he vanished. I was tired of him, anyhow. (I'm getting tired of all of you.)